I was a madman no longer.

I was, once again, a prince. Once again, I was bound by all the dragging obligations and careful courtesies that being a prince entailed.

But still I dared to look at the American again. She gazed at me as if all that she was, all that she had been, or ever would be, was mine. It stunned me how powerfully I wanted to take what she offered. I longed, if not for the refuge of madness, at least for the mask. For the comfort of shadows.

Or I had until that moment.

Until the redheaded American with the wide, honest eyes.

And so in a moment of purest insanity, I held out my hand. I knew she would trust her hand to me, without hesitation. With no coyness.

And she did.

CHRISTINE RIMMER

the Man Behind the Mask

Silhouette Books

Published by Silhouette Books

America's Publisher of Contemporary Romance

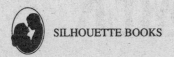 SILHOUETTE BOOKS

THE MAN BEHIND THE MASK

ISBN 0-373-21817-6

Copyright © 2004 by Christine Rimmer

For my guys: Steve, Matt and Jess.

Chapter 1

For me, it was love at first sight.

Okay, okay. Nobody believes in love at first sight anymore. It's like disco. Or the dickey. Went out decades ago, isn't coming back, no matter how many brave fools try to resurrect it.

And, you may ask, how would I, Dulcinea Samples, a semi dewy-eyed young thing of twenty-four, even know about a dickey?

My mom used to wear them. She's wearing one, in fact, in the family portrait that sits on our mantel back home in Bakersfield. The outline of it is just visible beneath her V-neck sweater.

My mom's a true romantic. She's always claimed she fell in love with Dad at first sight.

As I said, like the dickey. People don't *do* that anymore.

But my mom did. And there's more. Witness my name. How many people get named after the purer-than-pure alter ego of the barmaid whore heroine in *Man of La Mancha?* With a last name like Samples? Hel-lo?

Just call me Dulcie. Please.

And back to my mom. Yeah. Romantic. Capital R. And I know some of it rubbed off on me, though I swear I always tried my best to keep my romantic impulses strictly under control. They're about as useful as a dickey if you're a single girl living in East Hollywood. Not to mention a lot more dangerous. Get too romantic in East Hollywood—really, in any part of L.A.—and there's no telling what could happen to you. Did you see *Mulholland Drive?* Enough said.

And maybe that was part of it—why I fell in love with this certain guy at first sight. Because that first sight didn't happen in L.A., where I understood the hazards and would have had my guard up. Not in L.A. but in a ballroom in a palace in a tiny island country called Gullandria.

He was a prince—did I mention that?

And not just as in "a prince of a guy." No. I mean a real, bona fide, son-of-a-king type of prince. A Gullandrian prince. That's right, Gullandria. Remember? That island country I mentioned?

Gullandria is ·a story in itself. Picture the Shetland Islands. Get an image of Norway. And then, midway between the two, a little to the north, put a heart-shaped island maybe a hundred and fifty miles across at the widest part—you know, ventricle to ventricle? Lots of dramatic, jewel-blue fjords. Mountains to the north and rolling lowlands in the south. A capital city named Lysgard. "Lys" means light. And the king's palace, which stands on a hilltop just outside the capital? Isenhalla: Icehall. Oh, I love that.

Now, the deal about Gullandria is the people there

never completely gave up their Norse heritage. That would be Norse as in Vikings. Dragon-prowed long-ships; Odin and Thor and the gang? You're following, I hope.

Because I truly am getting to the part about the prince and me.

On the evening in question, there I stood in the afore-mentioned ballroom. I was wearing one of the two dresses I owned that was even marginally suited to such a strictly white-tie event—a midnight-blue strapless an-kle-length A-line Jessica McClintock, a dress I bought in a moment of wild spending abandon. At Nordstrom. Yes, on sale. After-Christmas, if you just have to know. At the time of the purchase, I felt positively giddy about wasting money I didn't really have, a giddiness com-pounded by a burning awareness of my own foolishness. I knew I'd never find a place to actually wear such a dress, proms and senior balls and the like being pretty much a thing of the past for me by then.

But see? Wild spending abandon and utter foolishness are good things—now and then. You might get invited to a palace ball in some fascinating northern island state. I did.

So you understand. The dress was fine. It showed off my best features: breasts. And skimmed forgivingly over my worst: a not-concave stomach and hips I liked to think of as generous on days when I wasn't consumed with body-image issues. I'd been in Gullandria since the day before when the royal jet flew me in from L.A. Picture it. Just the pilot, a flight attendant and me, the passenger-of-honor, on my way to attend the wedding of my best friend, Brit Thorson.

That night I stood a little off to the side in my pretty blue Jessica McClintock, heart beating too fast with nerves and excitement, hoping I wouldn't end up doing something really gauche that would remind everyone of the basic truth that I was, after all, a bright but ordinary girl from Bakersfield who dreamt of someday actually selling one of the novels she'd written; a girl who, until the day before, had never set foot in a royal palace in her life.

I'd had an escort when the evening started, a dapper prince who appeared at the door to my room and brought me to the ballroom. I'd lost track of him early on.

That was okay with me. It wasn't like I even knew the guy. And I wasn't left dangling. Brit kept dropping by to check on me, to whisper funny comments in my ear on the whole Norse-based culture thing—Gullandrians, remember, were Vikings at heart—and to introduce me to a stunning array of friends and relatives whose names I forgot as soon as they were told to me.

Brit was not your average best friend. For starters, she was a princess. A princess born in Gullandria, one of three fraternal-triplet princesses. When Brit was still a baby, her mom the queen left her dad the king, and took the girls to Sacramento, where they grew up blond and beautiful and rich—and about as American as anybody can get.

And beyond the princess angle, Brit was not a person you messed with. She had a high pain threshold and a scary kind of fearlessness. Once, two years before the night in the ballroom, I watched her go after a guy who'd displayed the bad judgment to try to stick up a coffee shop while Brit and I were standing at the register, waiting to pay after a little serious pigging out on chili dogs and fries. The guy ordered us—and everyone else in the place—to hit the floor. We all did as we were told. Except for Brit. She dived for the guy's knees. Took him down, too—though he put a couple of rounds in the ceiling before the cooks lurched to life and gave her a hand.

As I said, fearless. A fearless tall, blond California-girl princess. And my best friend in the world.

About the fifth time she came by, she edged good and close and murmured in my ear, "Note the redhead." I noted. Drop-dead gorgeous, in petal-pink satin—which I would never dare to wear—the redhead whirled by in the arms of some prince or other.

We were up to the ears in princes at that palace. From what I understood, every male noble, or *jarl* as they called themselves, was a prince. And they were all eligible to someday become king.

But I wasn't really thinking about the rules of Gullandrian succession at that moment. Right then, I was wondering why I couldn't be *that* kind of redhead—the kind like the woman waltzing past Brit and me. The sleek kind, you know? The kind with a waterfall of red silk for hair, with porcelain skin, a cameo-perfect face and a Halle Berry body.

"The Lady Kaarin Karlsmon," Brit whispered, as I reminded myself to get a grip and be at peace with being me. "So very well-bred. And nice, I guess—in her own oh-so-aristocratic way. Always laughs at the right places. But just a little too cagey, if you know what I mean."

I gave my friend a look. "So and?" Grinning, blue eyes agleam, Brit wiggled her eyebrows. I leaned a little closer. "Tell."

"Tell what?" asked a male voice behind us.

It was Prince Eric Greyfell, Brit's fiancé. He wrapped his arms loosely around his bride-to-be and nuzzled her hair.

Brit leaned into his embrace with a happy sigh, the

black chiffon overlay of her gown—Vera Wang, no doubt about it—shimmering against the matte black of his tux. "Just girl talk." She turned her head and whispered to him, only a few words. Something that would have been meaningless to me, I'd bet. Something intimate.

I looked at the silver disc that hung from a heavy chain around her neck. It was an intricate design, like a thousand coiling snakes. Fascinating.

But even more interesting to me was the red burst of angry-looking scar tissue about six inches from it, at the soft, incurving spot where Brit's left shoulder met her torso. The fresh scar kept peeking out from beneath the halter top of her fabulous dress. I wondered, as I'd been wondering since I first spotted it, where it had come from.

Some stick-up guy who'd shot my friend instead of the ceiling? I was keeping myself from asking her about it. I wanted details—hey, I'm a writer. I always want details—and I knew I wouldn't get them that night. Brit was in serious mingle mode, dropping by, flitting off. You can bet I planned to pry the whole story out of her if we ever got a little time to ourselves. I had a *lot* of questions to ask her once I got her alone. It had been six months or so since she'd left L.A. We had some catching up to do.

Eric spared a glance for me. "Dulcie, forgive my intrusion."

I smiled. "Nothing to forgive." What can I say about Eric? It's all good. Tall and lean and...intense. Brown hair, grayish green eyes in which you could see compassion and considerable intelligence. This was the second time I'd met him, the first being the day before, when Brit introduced us. I knew right away that he was like Brit. Not to be messed with. But so honorable it made you want to hug him.

Brit eased herself around so she could face him. She gazed up at him and he looked back at her and—whoa. Call it heat, call it lust, call it passion…call it love.

I want that, I thought. *I want what they have….*

Little did I know.

Eric looked at me again. "May I steal her away?"

I had to stifle a dizzy giggle. It made me feel giddy as buying my blue Jessica McClintock, just to be around all that love and passion. "I'd say you already have."

"Don't imagine it was an easy task." He was faking a frown.

"Oh, I don't. Not for a second." I laughed then. And Eric and I shared a moment of perfect understanding. We both knew Brit.

Brit gave my arm a squeeze. "I'll be back."

I grinned and nodded and off they went. I stared after them for a moment or two, no doubt looking wide-eyed and dreamy. Then I caught myself and jerked my gaze up—way up—toward the arching vaulted ceiling. When in doubt, especially at Isenhalla where there's no shortage of awesome things to look at, study the architecture.

The grand ballroom had plenty for a girl from Bakersfield to ogle. For instance: a musician's balcony about thirty feet up, extending the length of the wall opposite the one where I stood. There was an entire orchestra up there, I swear. The sound of their music was achingly beautiful, big enough to fill every last apse of that ballroom, big enough to swell and soar between the thick stone columns that marched along the sides of the room, and farther, into the shadowed spaces on the other side of those columns, and even farther than that— through the arching oak doors, out to the gallery, on past the high leaded windows and into the icy early-December darkness beyond.

Overhead, massive iron chandeliers, blazing bright, hung from thick black chains. On the side walls trefoil stained-glass windows glittered, four-panel lancet windows below, also of stained glass. On one side, the windows held out the night. On the other, they stood between the ballroom and the gallery.

At my end of the rectangular room: a two story-high fireplace. I swear to you, that fireplace was big enough to roast a couple of reindeer and a wild boar or two and still have plenty of room to spare. The fireplace led the eye up again, to arch upon arch, all very Gothic-looking, only somehow more opulent. The sheer complexity of it could make you dizzy.

I stared up at all those interlocking arches until my neck got a slight crick in it. About then, it occurred to me that I'd lurked near that giant fireplace for too long, alternately gazing at the ceiling and into the fire where three whole tree trunks burned. Not that anyone was looking at me, or would even have cared if they were. But still. I had my pride and a firm determination not to sink too deeply into wallflower mode.

I began working my way to the other end of the ballroom, smiling brightly at faces I'd never seen before—and a few I'd been introduced to but whose names were already lost somewhere in the unattended recesses of my mind. As a rule, I'm pretty good with names. But not that night. I guess I was kind of on overload. Mountains of new data coming my way, no time to process.

Eventually I reached the other end of the room and just kept going, beneath the balcony on which the full-size orchestra was now playing something very Strauss. I finally came to a stop about four feet from a wall on which hung a huge, obviously antique tapestry. And I am not kidding when I say huge. The gorgeous thing started just below the balcony above and ended about a foot from the inlaid hardwood floor. It stretched a good ten feet in either direction. I stepped back a little and tried to take it all in.

And I know what you're thinking. There I was, a guest at the ball, surrounded by handsome Nordic types with "prince" in their names, and I was studying the ceiling and gaping at a rug.

What can I say? It's how I am. Two summers before, Brit and I had done Route 66—you know the song right? We did it backward. From San Bernardino all the way to St. Louis. We stopped in a lot of small towns, each complete with its own très atmospheric seedy bar. Brit would be hanging out with the locals in the main room, doing shots and getting hit on. And me? I'm in the back, copying the graffiti off the ladies' room walls. You'd be amazed the bits of life wisdom and philosophy, the stories of love and loss, you can find on the walls of a toilet stall, stuff I knew I'd use later, in some book or other.

Also, in my defense that night in the ballroom, let me say that you would have to see the rug. We are talking intricate. At first glance, it seemed just swirls of muted color. And then there was that moment when it all spun into focus and I saw that it was a huge, gnarled tree with roots running everywhere and some kind of serpent-creature wrapped through those roots, defining the center of a series of circles, one on top of the other. In the branches perched an eagle, with some other smaller bird woven inside the eagle's head. There were elves, dwarves, men or maybe gods armed with shields and swords, a dragon, deer—four bucks, with huge racks—

women in long gowns with twining golden hair, crone-like figures leering with what I felt certain must be evil intent. I saw a squirrel that seemed to zip along the curve of a root and fountains that shimmered, as if truly wet...

I found it enchanting and wondrous and I shamelessly stared.

Someone behind my left shoulder said, "That tapestry is to represent Yggdrasil, what we call the world tree, or the guardian tree." The voice was male—low and with a ring of authority, yet faintly thready, as with age.

I turned to find a gaunt old man with long silver hair and a wispy beard to match. He had one of those faces that are all sharp bone and shadow, as if his flesh had melted away over the years, leaving the vulnerable shape of his skull revealed beneath the papery skin. His silver-gray eyes were sunken way down in their sockets. And they seemed, somehow, to glow there in the pools of darkness surrounding them. Eerie.

But not scary. He looked otherworldly and infinitely wise. As if he could not only read your mind but also accept absolutely anything he found in there, no matter how evil or petty or banal. He also looked vaguely familiar, though I was certain I would have remembered if I'd met him before.

"Yggdrasil," I repeated, enchanted. The *ygg* was pronounced *ig*—short i—and the rest of the vowels were short as well, the same as the way you would say, *Clearasil,* with *ig* substituted for the first syllable. "I've never heard it pronounced before."

"The world tree—some sources say an ash tree, some a yew—links and shelters the nine worlds of Norse cosmology," the old man intoned. He gestured with a graceful, skeletal hand. "Within the roots, you see the three levels of the worlds." He looked at me again, one grizzled brow lifting. "Ah, but you know this, do you not?"

"I have a...general understanding, I guess you could say." Back when I wrote my epic fantasy—no snickering, please. Every budding writer should try her hand at epic fantasy—I did a little studying up on the major myth systems. Including the Norse one.

The old man chuckled then, a dry but friendly sound. "A general understanding is quite enough, for a pretty young American. May I call you Dulcinea? It is a name as sweet as its meaning, a name that suits you well."

Anyone else would have gotten an automatic, *"Please don't."* I really do prefer Dulcie. But somehow, Dulcinea sounded just right when this magical old guy said it. Plus, he'd said I was sweet to match my name. From him, that sounded like high praise. "Thank you. Dulcinea is fine. And you're...?"

"Prince Medwyn Greyfell."

The metaphorical lightbulb went on over my head. No wonder he knew who I was. "You're Eric's father."

"And there you have it." He gave me a small smile. Brit had mentioned him more than once. Besides being Eric's father, Prince Medwyn was also the second most powerful man in Gullandria, the king's top advisor, the one they called the grand counselor.

Prince Medwyn held out that pale, veined hand. I gave him mine. He brought my hand close and brushed his thin, dry lips—so lightly, the whisper of dragonfly wings—against my knuckles.

I realized I adored him. Who wouldn't? "Tell me more."

"Concerning?"

"Oh, anything. The Norse myths. Who wove this tapestry and how old it is..."

"In 1640, it was presented as a gift from the King of Bohemia to King Velief Danelaw, in appreciation of Gullandria's support in convincing the Swedes to withdraw from Bohemian soil. The creator, more likely than not a woman, as women are the weavers in our lands, is not known."

I turned to the tapestry again. "Artist unknown..." A heated flush crept up my cheeks. "I hate that. Someone labored for months, or even years, creating something so beautiful. And in the end, who remembers her name?"

"Alas, Dulcinea. You do speak true."

"It's as if the artist never even existed. It's just not..." Turning, I saw that the place where the old man had stood was empty. I blinked and glanced around. Nothing. He was gone.

It was pretty bizarre, how fast he'd vanished. And right in the middle of my sentence, too. Yet strangely, I felt neither dissed nor deserted. There was something about him. You just knew the everyday rules of conduct didn't apply in his case. Like he was above them, or beyond them...

With a sigh, I turned to the tapestry again. By then, I'd forgotten all about my firm intention to avoid acting the wallflower. I was thinking of Medwyn, getting that hungry feeling I get when I meet someone interesting, hoping I'd see him again, planning to have a list of questions ready next time.

When I went back home to L.A., I wanted to have loads of Gullandrian background material. I tried to do that wherever I went, to take lots of notes, to get my questions about the place answered and to keep a computer journal of my impressions. I planned to write a lot of books in my life. Every location was a potential setting for a novel. Up till then, the farthest I'd been from California was a trip to New York City, in the spring, right after 9/11. I'd seen Ground Zero, walked down Park Avenue, visited SoHo and the Village. I'd come home deeply moved, full to bursting with ideas and possibilities. I hadn't written my New York novel yet. Give me time. Same thing with Gullandria. I would take it all in, and take notes, as well. And someday...

"Dulce?" It was Brit, jerking me out of my authorly delusions of grandeur and back to the here and now. I was still facing the tapestry and away from her, but from the corner of my eye, I caught a glimpse of a black tux: a man, standing beside her. More cheerful greetings, another name for me to instantly forget...

I turned with a big, hello-and-nice-to-meet-you smile.

And there he was.

My prince.

What can I tell you? That the world stopped? That the stars went supernova?

It was nothing like that.

It was everything like that.

"My brother, Prince Valbrand." Brit's voice seemed to come from somewhere down at the other end of a very long tunnel. She was so far away, she almost wasn't there. Not to me.

The music, the glittering lights, the rise and fall of laughter and conversation around us...everything was overshadowed. Eclipsed.

By him.

He filled up the world. He had dark brown hair and eyes to match. A tender mouth—half of one, anyway. He was tall. Lean. Too lean, really, but with strong, wide shoulders.

And all that is...only fact. The full reality was so

much grander, so much more complete. He was the handsomest man I'd ever seen—and the most terrifying.

How can I tell you?

How can I make you see?

Half of his face appeared to have melted. Remember that old Mel Gibson movie, *The Man Without a Face*? That was Valbrand. It happened, I'd been told, in an accident at sea that almost killed him. An accident that included second- and third-degree burns from temple to jaw on the left side—burns never treated, that healed on their own.

Brit *had* prepared me, or at least she'd tried to. We'd had a few minutes alone the day before and she'd told me of his injuries, so I wouldn't make a fool of myself, gaping like an idiot the first time I saw him, so that I wouldn't pile any more hurt on all that had already been done to him.

So much for Brit's thoughtful preparations. I saw him and the world spun away and I flat-out gaped. Rudely. Blatantly.

There was a sudden, welling pressure at the back of my throat. I was so busy staring, I didn't make myself swallow the emotion. My eyes brimmed and two fat tears escaped. They slid over the dam of my lower lids and trailed down my cheeks.

They felt hot. Scalding. Should I have swiped them away? Probably. Tried to hide them? I suppose.

But I didn't. I only tipped my face to him, higher, as if to display both my face—and those tears.

Somewhere, in some part of me, I realized that Brit had to be thinking she couldn't take me anywhere.

But it wasn't something I could control. It was love like a thunderbolt. And it was my heart breaking.

For him.
For what I saw in his lightless eyes.
What he was once. What he had become.
For all that was lost.

Chapter 2

I gazed down at the redheaded American in the blue gown, at the wide eyes that were some gleaming color, green and gold and brown all mixed, at the tears sliding over those soft, smooth cheeks, leaving a glittering trail.

First one and then the other, the tears dropped. They fell to the front of her dress, just below where her fine, full breasts swelled from their prison of fabric. I watched them fall, watched dark blue turn darker: twin small stains. I wanted to lower my head, stick out my tongue and taste them: the salt of her tears.

That was when I looked away—for a second or two only, long enough to collect my suddenly scattered wits, long enough to remind myself that, while a madman might bend close and lick the tearstains from a woman's breast, I must not.

I was a madman no longer. I was, once again, a prince. Once again, I was bound by all the strictures, all the dragging obligations and careful courtesies that being a prince—and the only surviving son of a king—entailed. This servitude to princely sanity was necessary. I had goals. Sworn. Sacred. And murderous. Goals the madman in me was too disorganized to achieve.

I dared to look at the American again. Her expression had not changed. She gazed at me as if all that she was, all she had been or would ever be, was mine. It stunned me how powerfully I wanted to take what she offered—right there. On the polished, inlaid hardwood of the ballroom floor.

I had to look away again. I glanced toward the dancers in the center of the floor. Once I had loved nights like that one, in the ballroom, all the lights blazing, fine music, the laughter of flirtatious women…

And the absolute assurance that I was where I belonged.

But that was before the horror. Before the madness. By that night, the night I met my sister's friend, it was all too difficult, too hurtful—the pity in such large doses, the expressions of shock followed instantly by broad counterfeit smiles.

I longed, if not for the refuge of madness, at least for the mask. For the comfort of shadows.

Or I had, until that moment.

Until the redheaded American with the wide, honest eyes.

I looked at her again and found she had waited for my gaze to find her once more—waited with her head tipped up, the tear-tracks drying on her velvet skin. I did not smile at her. My smile, after all, had become an exercise in the grotesque. Flesh and muscle pulling in the most bizarre ways.

I was thinking, *A few words only: Hello. How are*

you? So pleased to meet my little sister's dearest friend, at last.

A few words, and then farewell. I would turn and walk away.

But no words came.

Instead, in a moment of purest insanity, I held out my hand. I knew she would trust her hand to me, without hesitation. With no coyness.

And she did.

Somewhere a thousand miles away, my brave and cheeky little sister said, ''Well, um, okay. Looks like I can leave you two on your own for a while...''

Neither I nor the woman with her hand in mine answered her. Brit was far away right then. Everything was far away and I was glad it was. Everything but the American, everything but her soft hand in mine, her honest eyes, the truth in her tears, shed for me.

The music right then was slow in rhythm. No longer a waltz, but a foxtrot. An American classic: ''I've Got You Under My Skin.'' Suddenly I was ridiculously smug, as if the orchestra had played this perfect song at my command. I saw I had the excuse a sane man needs to take a woman he's only just met into his arms: a dance.

I guided her to me, put my left arm at the curve of her back, felt the slightly stiff fabric of her dress—and the warm softness waiting beneath it.

Her flesh, I thought and heat shot up my arm to break at my shoulder into arrows of need. The arrows flew on, cutting all through me. My body responded like the starved thing it was.

I knew shame.

Loss of control was a thing I greatly despised since my slow return from the horror and the madness. I might be hideous now. But I was well-behaved. And in perfect control.

I hadn't thought to worry about my penis betraying me. Since the horror, it kept…a low profile. At times I might imagine the joys of bedding a woman, but those thoughts were like faint echoes from a safer, happier time; not real to me anymore, vague bittersweet fantasies that always remained strictly above the neck.

Or they had until that night, at the first in a gala series of balls honoring the imminent union of my sister and my bloodbound lifelong friend—that night, when I made the mistake of pulling the American I'd just met into my arms for a dance. That night, when I saw something I wanted beyond the triumph of my revenge and knew that it was something I would never have.

I longed to yank her closer—and at the same time, to shove her away, turn on my heel and run.

I didn't fear that anyone would see the way my body shamed me. My trousers, like every other man's in the room, were black. Black is effective at masking unwelcome bulges. And while I held the woman in my arms, no one would be glancing there anyway. And even if they had, I would not have cared.

The shame was not that someone might see. The shame was that I had let my guard down so far and so fast that it had happened at all. One would think I would have learned better, after all I'd allowed to be done to me—and more important, to those who followed me— as a result of failing to stay in control and on guard.

I held the American lightly, enough away that I knew she couldn't feel my physical response to her. And I kept my wreck of a face carefully composed.

As I led her across the floor, I saw in her sweet and dreamy expression that she had no clue of my sudden shame. I began to relax. Soon enough, the front of my trousers lay smooth once more.

The song ended. I led her back to the place I had met her, near the World Tree tapestry. My sister, by then, had moved on to other guests, other introductions.

I let go of the American's hand. She stepped back— at the same time as her body seemed to lift and sway toward me, like a flower seeking the sun.

Didn't she realize? What she sought was not in me. No light. No warmth. In me, there was only darkness and a determination to root out and destroy what had so very nearly destroyed me, what had been responsible for the deaths of good men who had trusted me.

I nodded. She bit her soft lower lip and nodded in response, clasping her hands low in front of her, knuckles toward the floor. Demure—and yet so very eager.

Her soft lips parted.

I put up a hand before she could speak.

She closed her mouth, seemed to settle back into herself. She nodded again. Brave. Disappointed.

I turned and left her there.

Neither of us had said a single word.

Chapter 3

Sunday, December 8, 11:02 pm; the king's palace, Gullandria. Snowing.

Before I drew the heavy window curtains and climbed into bed, I stood for a moment at the tall mullioned windows, watching the white flakes coming out of the blackness to hit the diamond-shaped panes.

Things I learned today

Offshore oil drilling: major Gullandrian industry since the 1970s. Country was poor before its discovery; now, prosperous.

kingmaking: the election ceremony in which the jarl elect the next king.

Gullandrian slate: all of Isenhalla's outer walls are faced in this silvery gray and semireflecting stone.

bloodsworn: a vow of

I looked up and groaned, then bent my head again to the mini word processor in my lap....

Trouble concentrating. Keep thinking of last night, of V. Know I shouldn't. Clearly a case of inbred romantic impulses spiraling scarily out of control. Must keep firmly in mind that it was only a dance. One dance. He didn't speak. Neither did I. He shushed me. Now that should tell me something— that he was shushing me when I hadn't said a word.

No sign of him today, or this evening at dinner. I might have asked Brit about him, but, as usual since I arrived here, we hardly had a moment to ourselves.

I can't help believing that he

I looked up again, blinking, shaking my head.

Oh, lovely. Obsessing over Valbrand. Again. Filling up my AlphaSmart with lovesick babble.

A few minutes on the dance floor with Brit's long-lost brother and there I was, a slave to love. I'd stayed awake all night the night before, typing like mad, filling four whole files with V., V., V. Had to dump most of it. Drivel anyway and the Alphie only had so much space. Until I got home to my PC, I'd have no place to download it. And the point was to pack it with facts and observations about Gullandria—not endless yada-yada about a man I hardly knew.

That morning I had made a firm resolution: if I couldn't keep myself from starting in about him, I would at least switch to longhand. Maybe longhand would stop me. I swear, at the rate I was going, if I put it all in longhand, I'd be sure to get writer's cramp, end up with a hand like a twisted claw.

Which would serve me right. I mean, how could I have spent all night pounding the keys on the subject of a guy with whom I had not exchanged one word?

Don't answer that.

And it wasn't like the two of us were on the brink of something grand. I knew very well that the next time I saw him, it was going to be Hello, how are you? and walk on by. He'd as good as told me so—and I know what you're thinking. How could he have *told* me if he didn't even speak?

Well, he didn't need to say it. I saw it in those beautiful haunted eyes of his: There was not, and never would be, an *us*.

And no, it didn't help that I knew those haunted eyes were right. I mean, what were a recently-back-from-the-dead Gullandrian prince and Dulcie Samples, wannabe writer from Bakersfield, gonna have in common anyway? Couldn't be all that much, even if we ever did get around to actually speaking to each other.

It was hopeless. I knew it.

And I didn't care. That's the way it is with love at first sight.

Sitting there, propped against the carved headboard of that antique bed, amid all the lush featherbedding, I let out a long, sad sigh. I was debating with myself. Would I get back on task with my ''what I learned'' list? Or was I on another Valbrand roll? If so, it was time to keep my promise to myself and switch to a pen and a notebook and—

What was that?

A flicker of movement. In my side vision, to my right. I glanced that way.

The doors to a heavy, dark armoire, shut the last time I looked, gaped open. My clothes were moving, a head emerging from between my winter coat and a little black dress.

I shrieked. The AlphaSmart went flying. I hovered on the verge of my first coronary.

About then, I realized that the head was Brit's. "Sheesh," she said. "Calm down. It's only me." She emerged in a crouch and turned to shut the armoire doors.

"Holy freaking kamolie." *Freaking* was not the word I was thinking. It just proves what a model of self-restraint I am that I didn't say that other word. "I coulda died of fright."

"Sorry." She didn't look particularly contrite.

And that bugged me. I adore horror movies, but when it comes to real life—don't scare me, you know? I have three prank-loving brothers and a devilish dad. They know I'm excitable. When I was growing up, they were always popping out of doorways, shouting, "Hah!" They found my squeals of terror hilarious.

Making ungracious grumbling noises, I kicked off the covers, flung my torso over the side of the bed and retrieved my Alphie, after which I dragged myself back up to the mattress and settled against the pillows again. I tapped a few keys. "At least it's not broken." I shot her a thoroughly sour look. "No thanks to you."

She tried flattery. "Hey. Love your pajamas."

I grunted. We both favored cartoon-character PJs. That night, mine were liberally dotted with widely smiling SpongeBobs. "How long have you been hiding in there?"

Brit dropped to a wing chair and raked her hair back out of her eyes. "I wasn't *hiding*. There's a door at the back of it."

I blinked. "Oh, come on…"

She crossed her heart. "Hope to die."

"A door. As in…to a secret passageway?" I was thoroughly intrigued. It's hard to keep pouting when you're intrigued.

She jumped up again and held out her hand. "Come look."

I peered at her sideways, scowling.

"Don't be cranky. I really am sorry I freaked you out."

"I'm not cranky," I insisted. Crankily. "I just don't see why you couldn't come in through the door."

She made an impatient noise in her throat. "Hel-lo, I'm a princess, remember? Around here, I have an image to maintain." She opened her pink robe to display her own cartoon-character pajamas—Wile E. Coyote, as a matter of fact—then lifted a foot with a fluffy pink slipper on it and wiggled it at me. "I prefer not to go running through the halls once I'm dressed for bed."

The reminder of her royal status put me right back into pouting mode. "You always used to say that being a princess didn't mean a thing to you."

We shared a long look. She said, softly, "I'm learning that it means quite a bit. That it's an important part of who I am."

Did those words surprise me? Not really. I could sense big changes in her. A whole lot had happened since she'd boarded the royal jet in L.A., back in June, for her first visit to her father's land. In June, Valbrand had been missing and considered dead for almost a year; King Osrik, the father she now called "Dad" was a stranger to her—and she'd yet to meet the man she now planned to marry.

"Well?" she demanded, after a too-long pause. "D'you want to see the passageway or not?"

I shoved my AlphaSmart off my lap, jumped from the bed and padded to her side. Brit opened the armoire door and slid my clothes out of the way.

The whole back of the armoire was another door—it opened onto a narrow hallway of the same silver-gray slate as the palace facade. An electric lantern—Brit's, no doubt—sat on the passageway floor just beyond the armoire, casting a golden glow, making strange, shimmery light patterns on the glossy stone. I could see straight ahead maybe a hundred feet. Then a dead end, a shadowed blackness to the right. A turn in the passageway, I guessed. "Amazing."

Brit beamed. "Isenhalla is riddled with hidden hallways. They were included in the original construction, back in the mid-sixteenth century, when King Thorlak the Liberator built the current palace on the ruins of an earlier one destroyed by the Danes. It was a dangerous time. Poor King Thorlak. He never knew when he might need to duck inside a curio cabinet and get the hell outta Dodge. And there's more..."

I loved this kind of stuff and Brit knew it. "Tell."

"In the mid-nineteenth century, King Solmund Gudmond took the throne. King Solmund was, shall we say, more than a little bit eccentric—enough so that by the end of his reign he was known as Mad King Solmund. In the final years before his death, he would wash his hands a hundred times a day and wander the great halls at night wearing nothing but a look of total confusion."

"And King Solmund had exactly *what* to do with the passageways?"

"Before he lost his grip on reality, he had them modernized, adding more hidden entrances and exits, improving the internal mechanisms within the secret doors."

"Fascinating," I said, and meant it.

"Yeah. It's become a minor hobby of mine, to hunt down all the secret hallways and follow them wherever they lead." Her face was flushed, excited. I'd never seen her look happier.

Or more at home.

"You love it here." There was a tightness in my chest.

She quirked an eyebrow at me. "Is that an accusation?"

I shook my head. "I guess it just hit me all over again. You're really never coming home."

"This *is* my home." She spoke gently, with only the faintest note of reproach.

I scrunched up my eyes. Hard. No way I was letting the waterworks get started. "I'll miss you, that's all."

Her mouth kind of twisted. She patted my arm. "Don't forget the royal jet. Flies both ways. And the phone. And what about e-mail? You know we'll be in touch."

"I know," I said and gave her a big smile. I didn't want to be a downer, but I was thinking that visits and phone calls and e-mails could never stack up with her living directly across the walkway from me in our charmingly derelict courtyard-style apartment building. In the months she'd been gone, I'd come to realize how much I counted on her friendship.

East Hollywood with no Brit. Could it really be happening?

She grabbed my hand. "I know I've been neglecting you."

Wrong. Yes, I missed her. Yes, I hated that I was going to have to accept that her life was different now and our friendship would change. But I did *not* feel neglected. "Oh, come on. You've knocked yourself out checking on me every chance you get. You've been crazy busy...."

"Still. We've hardly had a moment to ourselves since you got here. I'm fixing that. Now. Let's go to my rooms. We'll talk till our tongues go numb. Do the mutual pedicure thing. You can mess with my hair."

I had a way with hair. Other people's, anyway. Mine was wild and curly and I pretty much left it alone. I fluffed the sides of her blond mop with my fingers. The cut was fine, really. But that didn't mean I wouldn't try to improve on it. "Hmm. Maybe just a trim. Re-emphasize the feathering around your face..."

"Who knows when we'll get the chance again?"

I didn't want to think about that. Hair, I thought. Hair is the question. "Do you have some decent scissors?"

"I'm sure I can dig up a pair."

I bargained shamelessly. "You'll have to tell me all your exploits since June. I get the sense it's been action-packed."

"One death-defying challenge after another." She said it dryly, but something in her voice told me it wasn't a joke. I thought of the scar on her shoulder.

Finally I confessed softly, "As if I'm going to turn you down, whatever we do."

She caught my hand again. "Come *on*."

"Let me grab my robe and slippers."

It was cold in the passageway—all that stone, with no heat source, I guess. I shivered and pulled my robe closer as we hustled along.

Her rooms were in a different wing than mine, on the next floor up. At one point, we emerged onto a landing in a back stairwell. Brit shut the section of wall that had opened for us, leaving the wall looking as if the doorway we'd come through had never been. We climbed the narrow stairs. She opened a door—a real one, with a porcelain knob. On the other side was a main hallway.

She shot glances both ways, then turned a wide grin on me. "Let's go for it."

Giggling, we took off, racing along the thick Turkish runner as fast as our flapping slippers would allow. Around the next corner, with nobody else in sight to witness Her Royal Highness behaving in such an undignified manner, she led me through a door onto another back stairwell. We stood on a landing. She pushed a place on the wall—and yet another door opened up. We went through. She pushed another spot and the section of wall swung silently shut. I stared. The "door" was gone. All I saw was solid wall. It really was amazing.

Brit had already turned and headed off down the gleaming secret passage. I rushed to catch up.

Two more hallways, and she stopped to open another section of wall. She pressed a latch and the wall swung toward us. On the other side, a full-length mirror gleamed. Beyond the hole it left in the wall, I could see a bedroom even bigger and more luxurious than the one assigned to me.

We went through. She pushed a spot on the heavy gold-leafed mirror frame and the mirror swung silently back into place. "Wait here," she commanded, and went out through a set of high, carved double doors.

I stood by the mirror and gaped at her gorgeous room. The heavy velvet drapes were drawn across the windows. Her bed was bigger than mine—could that be possible?—up on a dais; so much carving on the bedposts and finials, you could sit there staring forever, picking out the moons and suns, the longboats and dragons and mermaids with long, twining hair. Her bedding was crimson velvet, the sheets snowy white against the red. I mounted the dais and sat on the bed, pulling a round red velvet pillow into my lap. I was stroking the thick, soft pile when she returned.

"We're alone," she announced. "And look what I found?" She held up a pair of scissors, snicked them open and shut. "Also, my rooms are undisturbed." I must have looked puzzled. She explained, "It's my dad."

I'd met King Osrik just that evening, at dinner. He was tall and lean. Good-looking, for an older guy. Distinguished, I guess you'd say. Dark hair going gray. Dark eyes—Valbrand's eyes. Upon being introduced, I performed the Gullandrian bow Brit had taught me—fisted hand to heart, a dip of the head—and said how thrilled I was to meet His Majesty.

He gave me a regal nod. "It is my hope that you enjoy your brief stay in my daughter's homeland."

End of conversation. My sense was of a man very few people really knew.

The way she spoke of him, with such affection and humor, I guessed that Brit felt she knew him just fine. She went on, "You know I adore him, but he drives me nuts sometimes. He keeps tabs on me. He's actually bugged my rooms more than once. Which means I've learned to seek out and neutralize all electronic surveillance devices on a regular basis. That leaves only my personal maid and cook and the ongoing fiction that the servants don't spy for my father. Them, I give errands. Lots and lots of errands. Tonight is no exception. I've sent them off to do my bidding. No way they'll be back before dawn. And since we came through the secret passageway, the guards at the main door to the suite don't even know you're in here. We have total privacy, a luxury I appreciate a lot more than I used to. It's so rare these days.''

I was stuck on the part about the guards. ''You have guards at your door?''

She nodded. ''All the members of the royal family do.''

''You *need* guards?''

''Let me put it this way. The guards are there because it's palace protocol. Of course, they'll protect me, if a sticky situation arises—which it never has so far. In the meantime, they're in a perfect position to report all my comings and goings to His Royal Majesty—'' she grinned ''—at least when I leave through the main doors.'' I tossed the pillow back into the giant pile at the head of the bed. She added, ''The life of a princess does have its little challenges.''

''No kidding.'' I got up and took the scissors from her. ''Fine-tooth comb?''

She held up her other hand and I saw she had the comb, too. ''Let's go in my dressing room,'' she said. ''It's got better light, a good mirror and a swivel vanity chair.''

As soon as she'd got her hair wet and I had her in the chair, I asked about the scar on her shoulder.

''From a renegade's poisoned arrow,'' she said—renegades being seriously delinquent teenage boys who terrorized the Vildelund, the wild country to the north. She said she'd barely survived. She was delirious, near death for days, while her body fought off the poison.

I snipped away and she sucked a few peanut M&M's—she'd always had a thing for them—and told me all about her quest to find Valbrand.

"They all swore he was dead." She met my eyes in the wide mirror over the marble counter. "But he wasn't dead. I knew it." She put her hand over her heart. "I knew it here." I'd never seen her so intense and passionate—well, except maybe when she looked at Eric. "So, since no one would believe me, I took a guide and flew to the Vildelund to find the mysterious Eric Greyfell, who had gone looking for Valbrand after he disappeared at sea."

"And this was when—that you went to the Vildelund?"

"Didn't I say in my letters?"

I shook my head. They were postcards, actually. There had been three of them. What can you write on a postcard? *Hello, how are you? I'm fine. Wish you were here...*

Brit said, "I went to the Vildelund in early September."

"And at that point you still hadn't met Eric?"

"Nope. He was a hard man to meet. When he returned from his quest to find Valbrand, he came to Isenhalla just long enough to report to my dad that he was certain Valbrand was dead—and then he rushed off to the Vildelund, where he'd been hanging out ever since. I wanted to hear the story of what happened to my brother from Eric himself."

"So you flew there and..."

"The plane crashed."

I stopped snipping to stare. "With you in it?"

"That's right. My guide was killed." Her blue eyes, right then, looked nearly as haunted as Valbrand's. "I was knocked out when we went down. I came to in the wrecked plane. The guide didn't. The crash broke his neck."

I sighed. "Bad, huh?"

"Yeah. Real bad. I crawled from the wreckage to find the renegade waiting. He shot me. Eric found me and took me to the village where his sweet aunt Asta lived. Asta took care of me until I got well. And eventually, I found my brother—right there, in the Vildelund."

"With Eric?"

"That's right. For a long time, Valbrand wasn't…ready yet, I guess you could say, to come back here and deal with everything he's dealing with now. He'd made Eric promise to stay with him in the north until he could bring himself to come home.…"

Our eyes were locked in the mirror.

It was a good opening. The right place to ask a few questions about her brother—and maybe even to tell her the way I felt. But she looked away and the moment got by me.

I finished trimming. I'd taken some off the sides, in layers, to give it more lift. I worked in a little styling gel, then grabbed the blow dryer she'd set on the counter for me.

"I love it," she announced when I turned the dryer off. She fluffed with her fingers and turned her head this way and that. "It always looks fuller when you do it— now for the pedicures." She dragged me into the enormous marble bathroom, where we soaked our feet in the sunken tub and then took turns in a paraffin bath.

She did me, then I did her, long sessions with a pumice stone and deep foot massage. We yakked the whole time. For polish, she had a rack full of Urban Decay, great colors with Goth names: Asphyxia. Freakshow. Gash. I chose Pipe Dream, a nice barely-there shade. Brit went for Toxin, a sort of Easter-egg purple that didn't fit the name at all.

We wandered back to the bedroom, dropped our robes and stretched out on the bed, where we continued to whisper to each other.

Brit said she doubted she'd ever finish any of her novels now. That was how we'd met—a shared interest in writing. She'd started nine or ten books. About halfway through, she'd always get tired of them. She'd start something else or real life would beckon.

She grinned. "There's a lot going on here in Gullandria. No time for scribbling, if you know what I mean."

"Maybe later, huh? It's not like you don't have plenty of years ahead of you to get back to it."

She made a noise of agreement, but her eyes had doubts in them. Whether the doubts were about her ever writing again or the number of years ahead of her, I couldn't have said. I almost asked.

But she'd already begun the story of her adventures in the north. She'd stopped a rape and met a cousin she hadn't even known she had. And she'd lived among the Mystics. Eric's aunt, the one who had nursed her back to health, was a Mystic. The Mystics lived simply, by the old Norse ways. Eric was at home among them; Medwyn had been born a Mystic and Eric's mother had, too.

She pulled a heavy silver chain out from under her pajama top and showed me the disc-shaped serpent pendant I had noticed the night of the ball. "My marriage medallion," she said. "Among the Mystics, for each newborn son, they create a different medallion. This one was made for Eric. He wore it as a child. He gave it to Medwyn when he turned eighteen. And Medwyn gave it to me—as Eric's chosen bride…"

I knew she wasn't telling me everything. There were those moments when she'd get going on some part of the story and, out of nowhere, her voice would trail off. Her eyes would shift away.

I didn't push her. I figured what she didn't say was probably none of my business.

She wanted to know how my writing was going.

I told her I'd finished my fourth novel—a murder mystery with a female bounty hunter heroine. I was already thinking series. "And lately, I've been raking in the rejections."

We both chuckled. It was a private joke with us. The more rejections, the closer to that first sale. She asked about my job in a boiler room, selling office supplies— toner, pens, inkjet paper, you name it—on the phone.

I groaned. "That was so last summer. I'm on to bigger and better things now. A Mexican restaurant on Pico." Actually I wasn't a hundred percent sure the job would be there when I got back. But such is the life of a struggling *artiste.* "Early shift," I added. "Try not to be too jealous."

"I am doing my very best." She was grinning. And then she *wasn't* grinning. "Dulce..." I knew by her sudden change of tone, by the shadows in her eyes, that something bleak was coming. "Last night, at the ball, I noticed you and Valbrand really hit it off."

I made a sound that could have meant anything. "Um?"

"Well, I, um..." She was having real trouble getting around to it. I kept my mouth shut. Though I loved nothing so much as finishing other people's sentences, right then, I made no attempt to fill in the blanks. She tried again. "That's the first time I've seen my brother dance, did you know that?" I shook my head. She looked so sad. "They say he used to love to dance...."

At that moment, I was absolutely certain that she

knew how I felt—and that she was going to warn me off him. It was all there, in her worried blue eyes.

And yes, I'm aware that reading minds is not dependable, that you're just too damn likely to get it all wrong. A girl should have sense enough to go ahead and ask.

But I didn't want to ask. I didn't want to hear her tell me how he was not the man for me.

It wasn't as if I didn't already know.

"I'm so grateful," she said quietly, "that he's back with us. But how can I tell you? Dulce, he's…damaged, you know, by what happened to him? And I don't just mean his poor face. He's never going to be like your average guy."

"What, exactly, happened to him?"

She was frowning. "I told you. A storm at sea. A fire. He was washed overboard.…"

Yes, she had told me.

When Valbrand went missing, Brit's mother had phoned her with the news that the brother she'd never known was lost at sea and presumed dead. Brit had just moved in across the courtyard from me. She came over to my place and we drank strong coffee and talked all night.

It was really hard for her, to think that he was gone. She hated it so much—that she'd lost him when she hadn't even met him yet. There had always been all those family issues that had kept her from ever getting to know him. Since her father and her mother split—when Brit and her sisters were ten months old—there had been zero communication between the two halves of the family. I say two halves because it was some kind of trade-off, I think. Daughters to Ingrid. Sons—Valbrand and Kylan—to King Osrik.

Kylan was dead within a year or two after the split,

killed in a stable fire at the age of five. Which made Valbrand the only son left—and then he was gone, too.

I'd assumed at first that Valbrand must have been on some kind of cruise when he disappeared. That night in my apartment, sipping coffee, trying not to cry, Brit had set me straight.

In Gullandria it was tradition that any young prince who hoped to someday be king must accomplish a Viking Voyage. I instantly pictured wild men in horned helmets burning down picturesque villages and having their way with terrified women.

But I had it all wrong. There was no raping or pillaging involved, just a sea voyage in an authentic reproduction of a Viking longship. It was a symbolic trip, Brit said. A nod to Gullandrian history, to the time when kings went a-Viking and were unlikely to live all that long.

Valbrand had set off from Lysgard Harbor with a trusted crew of thirty. He made it to the Faeroes and set sail for Iceland. They'd heard nothing from him after that, though it was only a matter of days to Iceland and he had agreed to check in with his father when the ship made land there.

The rest we'd learned later, after Eric went looking for him and returned to report that he'd found the few survivors, all of whom told the same story about a storm at sea.

"The bit about the fire is new," I said. "You never mentioned that until the other day."

Brit pursed up her mouth. "It's not a *bit,* Dulce. It's what happened to him."

"It's vague. You know it is. Who started the fire? And what about these survivors? Who were they? Why did Eric have to track them down, if they were part of a trusted crew? I mean, why didn't they come back on their own and report what had happened, if they were so trustworthy?''

She gave me another long look. "Dulce…"

I waited. She didn't say anything else—I mean, beyond my name, in a weary sort of tone. Finally I said, "You're my best friend. I *know* you. And I know when you're not being straight with me."

"I'm being straight."

"Right."

"I *am*." She lifted up, punched her pillow, dropped back down. "There's just…things I can't talk about, that's all."

"Getting that. Loud and clear."

We lay there, on our separate pillows, looking in each other's eyes, both of us frowning. Finally she sighed. "I've said all I can say about what happened to my brother. So will you just please let it go?"

I could see there was no point in keeping at her. She'd made it painfully clear she wouldn't say any more. "Yeah," I whispered. "I'll let it go." For now, anyway, I added silently. I strove for a lighter tone. "Hey."

"What?"

"You said that Valbrand was never going to be your average guy."

"Yeah?" She was looking at me narrow-eyed—probably anticipating the next question she would have to evade.

"So. Was he *ever* your average guy?"

The corner of her mouth twitched. In relief, I was certain. Here was something she could be honest about. "No. No, he wasn't. Once he was…everything this country needs in its next king.''

"And now?"

"Now..." She paused, considering. "Now, I don't think he's really sure *who* he is."

I rolled to my back and stared up at the sculptured ceiling. "Maybe, over time, he'll...get better."

"I have a lot of hope for that. We all do. He's come a long way already. You cannot imagine..."

I guess I couldn't. And by her silence, I knew she wasn't going to tell me. I rolled to my side again and propped up on an elbow. "Look. I think we'd better get it out there, much as it makes me cringe to do it. You're telling me not to get interested in him, right? That there's zero hope for any kind of...future between him and me."

She shut her eyes and let out a groan. "Yes." She looked at me again. "That's what I'm telling you— Oh, Dulce. I'm so—"

I cut her off. "Do not," I instructed, "say you're sorry."

"Okay," she whispered. "I won't."

"And don't look so worried. As of now, there is nothing going on between your brother and me. And nothing *will* be going on—or at least, I'm about ninety percent sure nothing will."

"Only ninety percent?" She looked so irritatingly hopeful. She wanted my guarantee that nothing had, was, or ever would, happen between Valbrand and me.

I couldn't give her that. "See, this is the deal. If your brother would give me half a chance, I would be on it. No hesitation. No looking back. Crazy as it probably sounds to you, considering I've spent a total of ten minutes in his presence, I have that strong a feeling for him. But as of now, things look seriously *un*promising."

She sat up. "What if I were to ask you right out to stay away from him?"

I held my ground. "Sorry. Won't do it. I'm not going to avoid him."

She flopped back down hard on her back and stared ceilingward. "Terrific."

"Hey. Relax. I have the distinct feeling that *he* will be avoiding *me*."

She rolled her head to look at me. "He's right to avoid you. It can't *go* anywhere."

I said, with what I considered admirable tact, "I think we're getting into repetition mode, don't you?"

She rolled to her side and faced me again, reaching to brush my shoulder—a tentative touch, quickly withdrawn. "Bad move on my part, huh? To make such a big deal out of this…"

I caught her hand and only let go after I'd given it a good, firm squeeze. "See, that's where you're wrong. You're my best friend in the whole wide world. You cannot make a bad move when it comes to me."

Her wide mouth quivered. "God, Dulce. I have missed you."

"Double back at ya."

"There's just so much going on…."

"Hey, I'm picking it up."

"So much I really can't talk about."

"You said that before."

"Well, I feel like you're not hearing me."

"I'm hearing. I just don't like it."

"You have to know. Under ordinary circumstances, I'd be thrilled to see you and Valbrand hook up. But things are far from ordinary here. My father has big plans for my brother. Please don't be offended, but they don't include—"

"Brit."

She stifled a yawn. "Um?"

"At this point what His Majesty would think about your brother and me getting together is seriously moot."

"I'm only warning you that the rules are different here, that a king's son is not going to—"

"Got it." I was yawning, too. "We should get some sleep."

She yawned again, this time full out. "You know, you're right." She closed her eyes.

I swear she was deep in dreamland instantly. I could have been, too. But you ought to try sleeping with Brit. Restless is too mild a word. She tossed and turned and groaned and kicked me repeatedly—all while utterly dead to the world.

Eventually, clinging to my pillow at the far edge of the bed, I drifted off, too.

Someone was shaking me. "Go 'way..." I grumbled, batting at the hand that clutched my shoulder.

"Dulce..." Brit's voice.

I opened one eye. "Huh?"

"Gotta go. Back soon." She was already halfway out of the bed.

I sat up, swiping a swatch of tangled curls back from my face, blinking against the bedside light that we'd never bothered to turn off. "What time is it?" The clock beneath the lamp said 3:10. "Ugh." I fell back to the pillows. "You're nuts, you know that?"

"I just...I have to see Eric." Her face was positively glowing. "What can I say? It's love, you know? I didn't want you to wake up and worry when you saw I was gone...."

I grumbled something unintelligible, turned on my side and shut my eyes again. I was asleep so fast, I didn't even hear her leave.

* * *

The hidden door through the mirror in my sister's room began to move. I doused my palm-size flashlight and stepped back into the shadows.

Brit came through, wearing a pink robe and absurd fat pink bedroom slippers. She shut the secret door, turned and saw me there. I was all in black, including the smooth mask of perfectly tanned karavik skin that covered my face.

She gasped, then shone her light hard in my eyes. "Valbrand. What are you doing here?"

"Keeping watch." I had my arm across my eyes, guarding my night vision. "Shine the light away."

She did as I asked, then reached out a tentative hand to me. Trusting her as I did few others, I allowed her to brush the side of the mask, which fit my face like another skin—one both flawless and without expression.

"Is this really necessary?" She meant the mask. In her eyes there was great sadness.

I saw no reason to answer her. "What brings you into the passageway at this early hour?" I knew what, of course. "Eric?"

"I miss him. Love's like that."

"Ah." They were happy, my youngest sister and my bloodbound lifelong friend. This pleased me. Behind the mask, I smiled.

She wrapped her arms around herself, shivering a little at the chill in the passageway, and sent me a look of dawning suspicion. "It's Dulcie, right?"

I did not so much as blink. "I fail to grasp your meaning."

"You're here in the passageway, by the secret entrance to my room, because Dulcie's in there."

I hadn't known. But my foolish heart beat faster to hear it. "Dulcie. Your friend…"

"Yeah, duh. Like you have trouble remembering who she is."

"You are angry with me."

Her eyes grew tender again. "No. Never. I just…I saw the way you looked at her the other night. And the way she looked at you. Valbrand, you do have to ask yourself, *where can it go?*"

Nowhere, I silently replied. It was a truth I fully accepted. "We shared a dance." I sketched the most casual of shrugs. "It means nothing." And it didn't, not in the greater scheme of things. I had felt something powerful when I looked in Dulcie's eyes, and experienced a thoroughly shaming physical response to her. But it was of no consequence, I kept telling myself. And I would hardly have occasion to see her again. I asked my sister gently, "You object to my dancing with your friend?"

"No. No, of course not. It's only…she doesn't have an inkling of what we're up against here. I don't want her involved. I want her to enjoy her visit to Gullandria and I want her to fly home safe and sound the day after the wedding."

"And so she shall. As for tonight…I knew a strange foreboding. It caused a restlessness within me. I looked in on Eric. And then, unbeknownst to him, on our father. I checked on Elli and Hauk." Elli was our sister and Hauk was Elli's husband. "Hauk woke, of course. He saw it was I and rose to speak with me briefly, vowing that all was well with them and their unborn babe. After that, I came here to assure myself that you, like the others, were undisturbed."

"I'm fine. Honestly."

"Good, then."

"Eric's awake?"

I chuckled. "Go to him. Find out for yourself."

She came closer, laid her hand on my arm and brushed a quick kiss against the mask. "Don't hang around in the passageways all night. Please?"

"You mustn't concern yourself with me." I touched the device on my belt. "I'll signal if I require your aide in repulsing intruders."

She made a scoffing sound. "Valbrand, you're a little overboard on this, don't you think? Nothing suspicious has happened in months." Her pretty lips curved down in a scowl. "Not since that SOB Sorenson escaped us." My sister had a special enmity toward the traitor, Jorund Sorenson. Before we found him out, Sorenson had pretended to be her friend in order to get close enough to try to kill her. "There's no reason for you to—"

I put a gloved finger to her chattering mouth. "Go. Remind my friend what a fortunate man he is."

"Will you go back to your rooms? Get some sleep? Nothing's going to happen here, in the palace, in the middle of the night."

I took her by the shoulders and turned her gently toward the waiting corridor. "Go."

She sent me one last fond, exasperated glance over her shoulder before she hurried off down the gleaming stone hallway.

I watched until she'd turned the corner, and then continued watching, until the light from her lantern faded to nothing.

Utter blackness. It was good. Soothing to the formless anxieties I'd been experiencing that night.

I ducked back into the alcove a few feet from the now-invisible entrance to my sister's rooms and, for a while,

I simply stood there, arms crossed over my chest, surrounded by darkness, lulled by the gift of blindness, velvet black all around me...

Yes. I confess. I was thinking of the redhead on the other side of the looking glass. Thinking how simple it would be: to press the spot that would open the wall, to step through the glass.

I pictured her sleeping, wild coils of red hair poured over white pillows. Myself, the handsome prince I once was, bending close for the kiss that would wake her from her dreams...

It was but a fantasy.

In the world of reality, it never could have been—and it would never be.

Once, as a man who dedicated his life to his country and to the sacred duty to someday earn the throne, I could not have allowed myself a dalliance with a commoner from California. Not such a commoner as she, in any case—one with stars in her eyes and true love on her mind.

That would have been wrong. Cruel.

In the months since my return home, I had come to realize that the man I was on leaving had been vain, one who preened in pleasure at his handsome face and lean form, at his very *goodness*. And yet, all vanity aside, I did strive, in those earlier days, to be a better man. If I gave love casually, it was only to women who gave it back in kind.

Now, since the horror, I gave no love of *any* kind.

Everything was changed. Without *and* within.

My father insisted we could simply continue at the point where we had left off, that I should resume pursuing my former goal. That I would still one day be king.

I knew differently. I would never be king. I lived on

for one purpose only. To root out and destroy the threat to my family.

Thus, when it came to the redhead from California, nothing was changed. The reasons might be different, but the truth remained the same: I had nothing to offer her. I might dream of her a little. But in practice, I would leave her—and the emotions she stirred in me—strictly alone.

How long did I stand there, in the dark, thinking of honest eyes and Titian hair, tormenting myself with what I wouldn't do?

Too long.

At last I bestirred myself. My little sister was right. Lurking in the secret passageways was a senseless waste of time, time that would be better spent in slumber. There was no danger here. Only empty shadows and a futile longing for a tender touch I would never know.

I slid my thumb to the switch of my flashlight.

In that fraction of a second before light spilled out in front of me, I saw a glow—another light, moving toward me down the passageway.

Another light, and the sounds of stealthy footfalls approaching.

Chapter 4

In my sleep, I heard the strangest sounds: heavy grunts, the thuds of fists on flesh.

"Wha—?" My eyes popped open.

For about a half a second, I was sure I must be having a really vivid nightmare. But then something fell against the bed.

A man's voice growled low, "I'll cut yer balls off, fitzhead." The bed shook again. There was another volley of thudding blows.

I let out a disgustingly wimpy little yelp. Scooting fast, kicking with my feet, I scuttled to a sitting position—up hard against the headboard. Cowering there, trying to blink the last traces of sleep from my eyes, I had a clear view of what was going on.

Three masked men. Brawling. I blinked some more and shook my head. But blinking didn't help. They were all three still there, below the dais at the foot of the bed, two in ski masks, one in black leather.

One of the ski masks had drawn a gun. The guy in leather threw up a lean leg and kicked. The gun went flying. I watched it come spinning toward me.

Plop. It landed on the bed, a few feet from my Pipe-Dream pink toes. I gaped at it, gulped—then shifted my gaze to the fight again.

The guy in leather was still kicking. Some major kung fu moves, I kid you not. His boot connected with the other guy's head. That guy went down.

But now the second ski mask had his gun out. The one in leather ducked as the gun went off. It made an odd pinging, airy sound. Silencer? I guess.

The shot hit an armoire over in the corner, splitting the gorgeous dark wood. The guy in leather dived for the guy with the gun. The shooter toppled, his second shot going into the ceiling, sending plaster trickling down. The fall broke his grip and the second gun went spinning under a bureau.

Ski mask number one was rallying, crouched now on hands and knees in a corner, shaking his head, moaning a little. I looked at the gun by my feet.

Better get that, I thought.

In the meantime, the one in leather and the second guy were up again and trading blows. The guy in leather delivered a right hook that sent ski mask number two lurching back. He hit the wall and steadied himself, then leapt on the guy in leather, who reeled back and bumped a chair, which hit a side table. A china lamp tottered and hit the rug, not shattering, but cracking neatly in half with a sound like a big eggshell splitting.

I whimpered some more and reached out my foot toward the gun.

The guy in leather slithered free of the one who'd just

jumped him. He landed a punch—a good one, hard in the belly.

"Whoof," said the guy in the ski mask, a sound halfway between a hard grunt and a big dog's low bark. The one in the leather mask hit him again, a lightning fast karate-type chop to the back of the neck.

The guy crumpled to the fabulous antique rug and lay still beside the split-open lamp. Ski mask number two was down for good, it looked like to me.

I had my pink toes curled over the gun. Wincing, sure any second I would shoot myself in the foot, I inched the gun toward me over the crimson velvet. When it was close enough to grab by just reaching down, I got it in my shaking hands and aimed it, my quivering index finger on the trigger.

"Stop," I said in a terrified croak. "Freeze."

As if anybody cared. Ski mask number one was through shaking his head. He lurched upright and launched himself at the one in leather, taking them both to the floor. They rolled, punching at each other, grunting as each blow connected.

"No," I said, in a tiny squeak. "Uh, ooh, ah, ga...." I held the gun out at them with both trembling hands and jerked and twitched in terror and sympathetic pain as each blow landed.

No, I was not particularly helpful.

But think about it.

Whose side should I have been on, anyway? Who should I be shooting? Like I had a clue. Like I had any idea why this was even happening—and then, all of a sudden, before I could even begin to make up my mind what to do next...

It was over.

The guy in leather was still standing, the other two

sprawled at his feet, neither one moving. The expressionless black mask turned my way. "Are you injured?"

I held the quivering gun on him and slowly shook my head.

He extended a hand. "Bring the gun to me." He said each word with great care—as if addressing a total hysteric. And you know what? At that moment, that's pretty much what I was.

"No," I managed to get out in a wimpy little whisper. "I don't think so."

That gave him pause. For about a half a second.

And then he simply ignored me. I braced against the headboard, the gun still pointed—and still quivering—in his general direction. He went about tying up the guys in the ski masks.

He did it with lamp cords. Just ripped them from the wall and the bases of the lamps and crouched over the men he'd beaten, yanking their lax hands together at their backs and whipping the cords around their pressed-together wrists.

It was all very smooth, accomplished in maybe sixty seconds, tops. Once he'd tied them both, he tore off their masks, one and then the other, grabbing each by the hair to get a good look at his face, then letting go with a shove, so their heads thudded hard against the rug.

Did he recognize them? I didn't ask.

As he stood from unmasking the second guy, it came to me very clearly that now he would be dealing with me. I didn't think I wanted that.

"Stop," I croaked. "Stop, or I'll shoot."

He took a step toward me.

"I mean it. I am going to shoot."

Another step.

About then, I realized…

I couldn't do it. I could not pull that trigger. Not for the life of me—and it seemed at the time that the life of me was precisely the issue. He took another step.

The guards!

The words exploded in my brain. Why the hell hadn't I thought of the guards before? Maybe they were too far off—beyond at least two sets of doors, who knew how many hallways between—to have heard the fight. But by golly they were close enough to hear me scream.

I did scream. "Guards! Help!" And then I just shut my eyes, threw back my head and let the pure sound rip.

It was amazing, the earsplitting perfection of that scream. Jamie Lee in *Halloween* could not hold a candle, you hear what I'm saying? I screamed again, piercing as the first time.

I heard doors flung back somewhere in the suite, booted feet pounding my way.

I stopped screaming and opened my eyes.

The man in the leather mask had vanished—escaped, no doubt, through the empty mirror frame into the secret passageway. There were only the split-open lamp and a couple of overturned chairs, the bound, unconscious men on the floor, and me—in my SpongeBob pajamas with a big black gun in my hand.

Chapter 5

The two guards kicked open the bedroom door at almost the precise second that Brit and Eric burst through the mirror frame.

All four had weapons drawn, though Brit wore her Wile E. Coyotes and Eric had on soft drawstring flannel pants, his chest bare. They all froze at the sight of the two men on the floor. They took in the overturned furniture, the broken lamps and shattered knickknacks—and me. On the bed. With the gun.

All four gaped. Seriously. They went slack-jawed at the sight.

Which struck me as hilarious, just hysterically funny. A wild trill of laughter escaped me.

"Dulce?" Brit said my name as if she wasn't really sure it was me sitting there.

And I was instantly appalled at myself. What was I laughing at? This was not funny. Not funny at all. I shut my mouth on a dry sob.

There was an extended moment of bleak silence.

Then Brit tried again. "Dulce." She spoke softly, with great care. "Dulcie, honey…"

My fingers stopped working. The gun slid from my hands. Suddenly I was freezing cold. I drew my legs up, wrapped my arms around my knees and hunched into myself, shivering convulsively.

"Dulce…" I felt the bed shift and looked up with a startled cry. "Hey." Brit was on the bed beside me. "It's just me." She set her gun and her lantern on the nightstand and gave me a questioning smile. When I didn't object to her nearness, she took the gun I'd dropped, flipped a little notch on the handle, and set it on the nightstand, too. Then she held out her arms. "Come on, come here…"

With a small, strangled cry, I grabbed for her. Her arms went around me. I buried my head against her neck, breathing in deeply, instantly reassured by the warm, healthy scent of her skin, by the perfumy smell of the styling gel I'd used on her hair.

"It's okay," she whispered, "you're all right, you're not hurt…"

Slowly I grew calmer. Brit patted my back and made more soothing noises. Meanwhile, Eric ordered the guys in uniforms to guard the men on the floor. He walked around the room, checking things out, dropping to a crouch now and then to peer under the furniture.

When he dropped low near a certain bureau, I pointed a shaking hand. "Gun," I said. "There's a gun under there.…" He reached way in back and found it. Holding it by the trigger guard, he carried it over and set it on the dais at the foot of the bed.

Near the entrance to the passageway, he bent and picked up something else. He sniffed at it—and jerked back at whatever he smelled. Then he mounted the dais and stood beside Brit and me. He held out what he'd found: a folded square of white cloth.

Brit frowned at it. "Chloroform?"

He nodded. They shared a bleak look.

"What?" I demanded. "Someone tell me. What does it mean?"

Brit said, "It looks like an attempted kidnapping."

"A kidnapping…" I turned the ugly word over in my mind—and knew it couldn't have been me they were after. It was Brit's room. Given that she'd brought me here through the secret passageways, how many people could have known I was here—let alone that Brit wasn't? I met her eyes. "Those men came for you."

She pressed her lips together and nodded. "That's how it looks."

"But then…what about the other guy?" I glanced from Brit to Eric and back to Brit. When I got no re-action from either of them, I realized I'd yet to mention the man in the black mask. "There was another guy. He wore a black leather mask. He was the one who fought those two and tied them up. Didn't you see him? In the passageway?"

Brit started to speak, but Eric caught her eye and shook his head. She pressed her lips together and kept silent.

"Okay," I said. "What's going on?"

Nobody answered me. One of the men on the floor let out a low groan. Eric turned to the guards. "Remove these two from Her Highness's rooms. Wait in the main hallway, by the doors to the suite. Hauk Wyborn has been notified. Guard the prisoners well until Hauk re-lieves you or gives you further instructions."

Elli's husband, Hauk, was some kind of high-level

soldier. I wasn't really clear on it. They called him the king's warrior—and wait a minute. Who'd had time to notify Hauk? Come to think of it, how had Brit and Eric known I needed help?

The guards saluted, fists to chests. "As Your Highness commands." They rolled the intruders onto their backs, grabbed them beneath the arms and hauled them out.

When they were gone, Eric turned to me again. "Dulcie, we need you to tell us exactly what happened here."

I pushed my hair out of my eyes. Why wasn't I getting through? "Did you guys see the man in black, or not?"

Eric said, "Just tell us what you know."

Brit stroked my hair, smoothing it over my shoulder. "Please, Dulce. Just…tell it like it happened. Everything you can remember."

"But it seems to me that you two should have seen the—"

"Shh. Listen." She took my face between her hands and made me look at her. "Start from the beginning. Were you asleep when they entered?"

I jerked my chin from her grip. "What is up with you two?"

They shared another speaking look. Then Brit said, so gently, "We're just trying to find out what happened, that's all."

It wasn't all. I might have been traumatized, but I was not yet brain-dead. There *was* something up with them.

But would they tell me what? Looking at their grim mouths and set jaws, I seriously doubted it.

I gave in and did it their way. "Okay. I was sleeping. I didn't see them come in. It was the noise of the fight that woke me up. I thought at first I was having some kind of nightmare.…"

I told the rest as I remembered it. It was pretty disjointed. Really, what did I know? I woke up to find three men fighting at the foot of the bed. One of them beat up the other two, tied them up and ripped off their masks. I added, "I was so freaked at first, I forgot there were guards I could call. But then the guy in the leather mask finished with the other two. I figured I had to be next on his to-do list and I knew I wasn't up for that. About then, I remembered the guards. I threw back my head and screamed. A lot. When I looked again, he was gone. Maybe five seconds later, you and the guards rushed in."

Brit asked, "Did the intruders say anything—to you or to each other?"

"Well, the guy in the leather mask asked me if I was injured. When I shook my head, he told me to give him the gun. That was after he'd won the fight, but before he tied up the other two."

"Concentrate on the other two," Eric said patiently. "Did *they* say anything?"

By then I was wondering if they even believed me about the guy in the leather mask—but they *had* to know there was someone else. It was pretty obvious I hadn't handled the two thugs in ski masks all by my lonesome.

I frowned at Brit and then at Eric. "So okay. You don't care what the guy in the leather mask said?"

Eric let out a long breath. "Certainly we do."

"We care very much," Brit chimed in. "But the truth is…" She shot a pleading glance at Eric. He frowned, but said nothing. So she went on. "The man in the mask is…known to us. He's an ally, you might say."

"So…he was trying to protect me?" They nodded in unison. "But how did he know to—"

Brit cut me off. "Dulce. Can we get back to what happened please? What did the man in the leather mask say?"

"I told you. He asked if I was hurt and said to give him the gun. Which I didn't." I was way proud of that. Hey. My performance had not been stellar, you know? I was clutching at straws.

And I might be useless in a fight, but that didn't mean I was stupid. Slowly I was putting two and two together. The two in the ski masks had to be the bad guys and the other one had come to my rescue. So it was a good thing I hadn't been able to make myself shoot him…right?

Good a guess as any, I thought.

"And the others?" Brit prompted. "Did they speak?"

I tried to remember. "Someone said something when I first woke up, before I sat up and saw what was going on. The voice was…different. Rougher than the voice of the one in leather."

"Not the one in leather, then?" asked Eric.

"I don't think so."

"What did the other man say? What were his words?"

I thought about it a minute, trying to get it right. "'I'll…cut off your balls, fitz-something,' I think."

A wry smile curved Brit's mouth. "Fitzhead?"

I beamed. "That's it. That's what he said." Then I frowned. "What does it mean?"

"Let me put it this way, you don't call a Gullandrian a fitzhead unless you're in a fight or planning on starting one."

"Big-time insult, huh?"

She nodded. "And that's all? All any of them said?"

"Yeah, I think so…" I was feeling sheepish, wishing there was more to tell.

Brit grabbed me close again and hugged me some

more. "I'm so sorry you had to deal with this," she whispered against my hair.

I hugged her back. "I'm okay, really." And then I pulled back so I could look at her. "But *why?*" I demanded. "Why would someone want to kidnap you? For ransom, you think?"

Eric spoke then. "We'll question the intruders as soon as they regain consciousness." It was a brush-off, no matter how gently he said it. "We'll get some answers, never fear." Uh-huh. Answers no one would be sharing with me. He added, "And now, I think it's best if you wait in another room of the suite. There'll be a few more questions for you when Hauk arrives."

Brit grabbed my hand. "Come on, Dulce. Let's see if we can find your robe and slippers in this mess...."

Brit led me down the hall to a small sitting room and waited with me for Hauk to come. It took a while. We sat on a velvet settee and listened to the sounds of booted feet going in and out of the suite. I tried two or three times to talk to her about what had happened back there in her room. But she was evasive. She'd say, "Let's just wait till Hauk comes," or, "Dulce, we don't really know much of anything yet." When I asked her about the man in the leather mask, she only shook her head and said she couldn't say more about him.

Finally, about half an hour after we entered the sitting room, Hauk Wyborn came to talk to me.

He filled the doorway. Literally. Elli's husband was about six-eight. I swear to you, he looked like a Marvel comics superhero come to life. Massively muscular, with shoulder-length blond hair. And when I say muscular, I mean as in Hulk Hogan, as in Schwarzenegger during his bodybuilding days.

Brit left us. I told Hauk what I knew. Gravely he thanked me. "There may be more questions later," he warned. "And may I take this opportunity to tender His Majesty's deepest regrets for what has happened here tonight?"

"Well, sure," I said, feeling there was probably some proper response to that. But not being Gullandrian, I didn't know what it was. "And, uh, thank you for…everything."

He bowed his big blond head. "I am more than gratified to be of service." He looked at me again, piercingly, without the slightest trace of a smile. "And may the wise eye of Odin be upon you."

Was that a good thing, to have the wise eye of Odin "upon you"? I supposed it must be. He didn't say it as if it was a threat or anything. And what should I say now? He just didn't come across as a small-talk kind of guy.

A tap on the door saved me from having to figure out my next conversational gambit. It was Brit, fully dressed in gray slacks, black shoes and a funnel-neck sweater. "Finished?"

Hauk saluted, fist to chest. "Yes, Your Highness. The interview is concluded."

He left us. Once I knew he was out of earshot, I remarked, "He's your sister's husband, and he calls you *Your Highness?*"

She shrugged. "It's a matter of form, that's all."

"But is he always so…"

She knew the word I wanted. "Reserved? Well, sometimes, when Elli's around, he'll lighten up a little."

"Fun guy to have at a party, huh?"

"Hauk's a soldier, through and through. He'd never have become the king's warrior if he weren't. The training is killing. And I mean literally. Men have died trying to prove themselves worthy of the job. And Hauk's not only good at his job, he's...spectacular. A great warrior. The people adore him—and you should see him fight.''

"Uh. No, thanks."

"Come on. I don't mean a *real* fight."

"Oh. There's another kind?"

She nodded. "In the warm months, my father puts on a series of fairs down in the parkland below the palace. At the fairs, Gullandrian men come from all over the country to fight staged battles in the old, wild Viking manner. Hauk inevitably wins the day—and I can see by the look in those big eyes of yours. You've got a thousand questions."

"At least."

"Sorry, but right now I need to get you back to your own rooms."

I was not thrilled to hear that; I had the feeling she was going to drop me off there. After what I'd been through that night I didn't relish the thought of being alone—at least not while it was still dark outside.

However, my friend was not my baby-sitter. "Good idea." I tried valiantly to appear more enthusiastic than I felt.

"I'm afraid we can't go back the way we came. Hauk's men have taken over the secret passageways." She was frowning at my yellow chenille robe, at all the hugely smiling SpongeBobs peeking out from under it. "Do you want to change before we hit the main hallways?"

"Into what? Something of yours?" Brit was about three inches taller than I was—and thinner, too. How much thinner? Hah. Like I'd tell you that. "And really,"

I added, pouring on the perky, "you don't have to go with me. I can find my own way back."

She waved a hand. "I'm not leaving you to stumble around the hallways by yourself."

"Stumble? Who says I would stumble?"

She sighed. "It's a figure of speech."

"Choose another one."

"Oh, stop. You know what I mean. And as far as something for you to wear, I'll just—"

I was shaking my head. "Look. It's so late, it's early. I doubt we'll run into anyone. And who's gonna care what I'm wearing, anyway?"

Well, I was half-right. Nobody seemed to care that I was not properly dressed. But we did run into people. A number of them.

When we left the suite, I expected to see the men the soldiers had dragged out, sitting propped against the wall on the floor, their hands behind them, still tied with lamp cord. I was picturing sullen, threatening glances and muttered Gullandrian obscenities.

But the prisoners were nowhere in sight. There were, however, soldiers all up and down the hallway. We saw a bunch more every time we turned a corner.

And some of the guests were stirring, poking sleep-rumpled heads through slits in doorways, squinting against the light from the ornate wall sconces, asking, "What's going on? Has something happened?"

Brit gave them regal smiles and a few reassuring words and we moved on by. We saw more soldiers, and several housemaids and an old prince who, for some unknown reason, was up and about, all gotten up in a tweed suit, complete with vest curving over his considerable paunch and a weighty veil of gold chains looping extravagantly from his watch pocket.

"Your Highness." He bowed in the Gullandrian way. "Schemes of the Trickster, what goes? All this commotion has ruined my sleep."

Brit told him there was nothing to worry about. "Please, Prince Sigurd. Back to your rooms. All is safe now, I promise you."

Muttering under his breath, the old prince did as she instructed.

Around the next turn, another prince was waiting, this one young and slim, with pale hair combed back from a high forehead. He was also fully dressed, but not in tweeds. Armani, maybe? Or Dolce and Gabbana? He frowned when he saw us coming, then quickly bowed.

"Prince Onund," Brit said when we reached him. "What are you doing up?"

"Your Highness, I heard all the noise. What's afoot?"

"Nothing to worry about," she coolly lied. "As of now, we have everything completely under control."

"Ah," he said, as if she'd actually told him something. "Then I'll return to my chamber."

"Good idea." Brit pulled me on down the hall.

A minute or two later, we reached our destination. She led me inside, helped me out of my robe as if I couldn't manage it myself and tenderly tucked me into bed.

"I'll stay right here," she whispered, standing over me. "Don't worry. I won't leave you."

I did like the sound of that. I wanted her to stay right there beside me until daylight, at least.

But I just couldn't do that to her. She kept biting her lower lip and fidgeting—and as much as she talked about staying, she wasn't showing any signs of making herself comfortable. It was painfully obvious that she longed to get back where the action was. Also, it did occur to me that I was going to have to get past being treated like the shell-shocked victim of some terrible tragedy.

I looked up from my nest of pillows into her distracted face and I groaned. "Oh, puh-lease. I know you have things to do. Get outta here."

To her credit, she actually put up a little resistance. "No, Dulce. I'm going nowhere. You've had a brutal scare, one that wouldn't have happened if I hadn't—"

I sat up, which made her back off a few inches. "It's not your fault. You know it. I know it. And I'm fine. Honestly. We both know damn well I'm in zero danger, now that I'm back in my own room where no one is going to mistake me for you. You don't need to be here holding my hand and you don't *want* to be here holding my hand."

"I never said that."

"Like you *had* to say it. We both know how you are. You want to be with Eric and Hauk Wyborn and whoever else they've called in by now. You want to be on the case, rousting the bad guys."

She looked at me sideways. "Well. If you're certain…"

"What? You're still here?"

She smiled. Fondly. "Thank you."

"Go."

She started backing toward the door. "One more thing…"

"What now?"

"I know this all has to be really confusing to you, but I have to ask you not to talk about what happened tonight, not to mention it to anyone. At least not until we've been able to decide what to do about it."

Did I have questions? Oh yes, I did. It was plain as

her eagerness to go that she knew a lot more than I did and she was not telling me any of it. But I didn't really have the heart to keep her with me another minute—let alone to try to get her to talk to me right then. "My lips are sealed. Good night."

"If you need me—"

"I won't. Get lost."

She vanished into the shadows of the short hallway that led to my door—and I instantly wanted to call her back. I heard the door open and shut behind her and I longed to leap from the bed and chase her down the main hallway until I caught her. I would tell her it was all a big mistake to have let her go. I really needed her with me, after all.

Okay, I'll admit it. I was still pretty shook up, which made it one of those times when my vivid imagination and I did not need to be left alone.

My travel alarm, which I'd set on the ebony-inlaid night stand, said it was 4:35. In California, at 4:35, it would have been maybe two hours till daylight. But not in Gullandria. Winter nights are long there—which meant that dawn wouldn't be coming until almost nine.

Hours and hours to sit in my room in the dark....

Yes, a little sleep would have been nice. But who was I kidding? Sleep was so not an option at that point.

I threw back the covers, ran down the short hall through which Brit had left me, and engaged the privacy lock on the door. Then I flew around the room turning on all the lamps. There were only four, not counting the lamp by the bed. I wished there were a hundred.

I didn't have a multiroom suite the way Brit did, but I did rate a private bath. I went in there and turned on the light and left the door open so I could see the brightness bouncing off the snow-white gold-trimmed tiles.

Better, I thought. Now I won't have to worry about…what?

I couldn't have said. I only knew I wanted lots of light. No shadowed corners, no place for an armed kidnapper in a ski mask with a chloroformed cloth to hide.

Following the incident in my sister's bedroom, I scoured the passageways.

I was seeking any object, any small scrap of paper or cloth, that the intruders—or whoever had given them access to the passageways—might have let drop. I also sought the point where the two traitorous louts had entered.

I found nothing that they might have left behind. But I did find the way they'd come in—through one of the tunnels that ran beneath the hill on which Isenhalla stood. There were four such tunnels leading into the passageways, one for each of the four directions. For as long as I could remember, each of the thick steel doors at the ends of those tunnels had been sealed with a bar and a heavy lock—a lock to which only my father and Hauk had a key.

Someone had cut the lock on the west entry. Knowing Hauk's men would arrive shortly, I removed the mask and became once again the damaged Prince Valbrand. When three soldiers appeared, I gave two of them orders to stand watch, cautioning them not to touch the door, the lock or the walls. I sent the third man back to Hauk, with a message that a technician should be sent to observe, photograph and dust for prints.

I had no idea where Hauk would find that technician. Any crime occurring in Isenhalla or on the palace grounds fell within the jurisdiction of the NIB—the National Investigative Bureau—which is roughly equiva-

lent to the American FBI. But since an incident in the
Helmouth Pass three months before, when Brit and Eric
had been set upon by a team of traitor NIB agents—led
by the man who'd pretended to be Brit's friend, the now-
vanished former Special Agent Jorund Sorenson—we
held the NIB and its people under suspicion. Hauk
would have to find some way other than the Bureau to
test the entrance for prints and to run identity checks on
the two prisoners. I knew he would solve the problem.
Hauk was not only strong, intelligent and resilient. He
was also unfailingly resourceful.

I left the soldiers to guard the west entrance, donned
the mask again and checked the other three entry doors.
All of them appeared undisturbed. By then, there were
soldiers around every corner. And I had yet to find anything that the intruders might carelessly have left behind.

It occurred to me that my usefulness in the hidden
corridors was ended—at least for the time being. So
what now?

Should I return to Brit's rooms, where I was almost
certain to find a strategy session in progress: Brit and
Eric and Hauk, deciding what the next move should be,
debating whether to immediately inform Prince Medwyn
and His Majesty that palace security had been danger-
ously breached—or to wait for a more reasonable hour?

No. I'd leave all that for now, I decided. There would
no doubt be a formal meeting come daylight, in my father's chambers. We'd go over everything in detail.
Time enough to talk strategy then.

I began making my way back to my suite. I knew of
passageways *within* the secret passageways, of hidden
doors from hallway to hallway, entrances and exits that
I would have wagered even my inquisitive little sister

had yet to find. I used what I knew, easily avoiding the soldiers who swarmed everywhere.

And then, when I was nearly there, it came to me that I could not bear to return to my solitary, silent rooms.

Not yet.

I took a different turn, passed through other hidden doors. In no time I stood by the section of wall that could be opened to reveal the armoire entrance to the American's room—and yes. I knew which room was hers.

After the ball, after her tears, after the dance that we shared...

It is not something I can explain. How she looked at me and saw it all. How knowing nothing, she saw everything. How in that look, in that one short dance, she gave me back something I had thought lost forever.

Was it hope?

Perhaps.

Hope destined to remain unfulfilled, but hope, nonetheless.

That night, the night we first met, it became imperative that I discover where she slept. I knew which servants I could trust—the ones who had indulged me as a boy and kept the secrets of my occasional follies as a youth. I asked and it was answered.

Once I knew which room, I knew which hidden entrance would lead me in there.

It was acceptable that I know it, I reasoned at the time. It was acceptable because I would never *use* that information. I would never actually seek the woman out in her room. It was enough, I told myself in those early hours right after the ball, to know where to find her. It was enough just to know where she slept....

Ah, what lies a man will tell himself.

Chapter 6

"So, okay, Dulcie," I said to myself, standing in the middle of the room with all the lights on. "What now?"

When no answer came, I shrugged and went back to bed. I guess I had some idea that I'd be able to sleep, now that there wasn't a single shadow anywhere in the room.

Hah. Not happening.

So I got up again and collected my AlphaSmart from the chair where Brit had put it when she tucked me in. I carried it back to the bed and switched it on.

Monday, December 9, 4:41 a.m.

I looked up. Had I heard something?

No, of course not. Nothing to hear. Except the wind gusting outside, rattling the old windowpanes. Oh, and maybe the hiss of the gas fire in the grate.

Other than those two sounds, everything was quiet. Too quiet, really...

In my bed in the king's palace.
On the wall to the right of my bed there's an armoire. Of dark wood, heavily carved, like most of the furniture in this room. The back of the armoire is a

I couldn't do it. I could not sit there and write about what had happened since my last entry. My enchanting visit to Gullandria had veered off into something pretty darn scary and what I really needed right then was a way *not* to think about it.

I set the AlphaSmart aside and picked up a book.

Half a page later, I was looking up again. At the armoire.

Now, really. How many people knew about the passageways? About the secret armoire entrance to my room? Would any of them be popping in on me soon? Maybe one of Hauk Wyborn's soldiers: "Beg your pardon, miss. We have orders to check all the secret entrances."

Or maybe someone scarier than a soldier. Maybe someone with murder on his mind.

Me and my imagination. We could see it all then.

It would happen when I'd finally dropped off to sleep, probably with my head turned to the side, my hair flowing back on the pillow, exposing a vulnerable section of neck—a section that would, of course, include the jugular.

I was picturing someone with a hunchback and bulging eyes and a wart on his chin. Someone named Igor—though of course, I'd be dead without ever getting his name. He'd have a huge butcher knife—or wait. A meat cleaver. You know the kind. Big enough to hack up an entire side of beef.

He would be so quiet. And the doors of the armoire would never so much as squeak. He'd slide out from between my charcoal-gray wool suit and my calf-length rib knit cardigan and tiptoe across the rug soundlessly, bulging eyes rolling, a little spot of drool gleaming in the corner of his twisted mouth.

Breathing in a thoroughly unattractive adenoidal fashion, he'd stand over me and raise the cleaver. The fat, deadly blade would twinkle in the light....

"Ugh," I said aloud. "Disgusting. I have got to stop this."

It was about then that it occurred to me I ought to have a look in the passageway.

Just to reassure myself, you know? Just to prove to myself that I was being an idiot and I needed to get over it and read or write or even, as inconceivable a concept as it seemed right then, go to sleep.

Yes, yes. I know. It was the kind of thing only too-dumb-to-live screamer-queen heroines in bad slasher movies did, but I was just not going to be able to relax until I opened the door in the back of the armoire and reassured myself that there was no ugly guy with a cleaver drooling on the other side.

And besides. If a murderer *was* there, I preferred to face my death on my feet and wide-awake.

What can I tell you? It made perfect sense at the time.

I threw back the covers—again—and padded to the armoire, where I pulled both doors wide, shoved my clothes to either side and climbed in.

The problem became instantly apparent. I didn't know the place to press—the one that would make the back of the armoire swing open. And it was dark in there, too dark to see much, even with the doors open.

My own clothes didn't help matters. They flopped around on their hangers, getting in the way, trying to smother me. Finally I had to back out and grab an armful of them and toss them on the bed. About then, it came to me that it was going to be dark in the passageway— not to mention cold.

How would I ferret out any would-be attackers without a flashlight? And really, I ought to at least put on my robe and slippers before going in.

So I pulled on my robe and stuck my feet in my slippers. Dressed more warmly, I stood in the center of the room and turned slowly, making a complete circle, asking myself the pertinent question: If I were a flashlight, where would I hide?

The nightstand.

Bingo. There it was in the single drawer. Right next to the *New Revised Standard Edition Bible.*

I giggled.

What can I say? It had been a rough night.

Brit had told me that Gullandrians always claimed they were Lutherans—even though, when the chips were down, it wasn't the good Lord they called on, but the ancient Norse gods. Judging by the Bible in the nightstand, maybe Brit was wrong.

I grabbed the flashlight, thinking that after I got finished proving to myself that Igor didn't lurk beyond the armoire, I was going to get out that Bible and reread the 23rd Psalm. *Fear no evil,* and all that.

I flicked on the light and climbed back into the armoire. With a flashlight, it was a lot easier to see the almost-invisible edge of the panel I had to press....

* * *

I stood, masked, in the darkness behind the wall that led to Dulcie's chamber, thinking that I only wanted...

To be there, for a moment or two, with no more than a wall between me and the woman who had looked and saw...not what I was. Not what I used to be. But some other man.

Some better man who was, somehow, still I.

I knew I was foolish, worse than foolish. An idiot to be there.

I told myself I would turn and make my way back to my own silent rooms. Immediately.

But first...

The wall seemed to beckon me. As if I could press my hand or my cheek to it and feel her on the other side.

Foolish. Idiotic. I would do no such thing....

But then, with the echoes of a former madness stirring beneath my skin, I reached out. Put my hand flat to the cold wall in a spot nowhere near the spot that would cause it to open.

The instant I touched it, the wall began to move.

"Way to go, Samples," I muttered smugly under my breath.

With just the teeniest push at the right place, the armoire opened onto the cold darkness of the passageway. I stuck out my fluffy-slippered foot and stepped through onto the cold stone floor.

I would leave it open, I decided, because I was only going to walk down to where the hallway turned and shine my light into the next corridor. That would be enough for me. I'd have appeased my overactive imagination and could accept the fact that no murderer was waiting there to hack me to bits as soon as I fell asleep.

I started walking—tiptoeing, really—my flashlight beam making the walls gleam in that unusual, shimmery way. I got to the end of the hallway and shone my light down the next one.

Nothing—but silence, dank air, the empty corridor and the strange, gleaming reflection of my flashlight's beam along the walls.

It occurred to me that, just to be sure, I ought to go on to the end of *that* corridor. Down there, halls branched off either way. I could shine my light down both of them, be truly certain there was no one lurking, waiting for the chance to—

"Halt."

The voice was male. It came from behind me.

I halted. So did my heart. Dead in my chest. But I swear to you, I didn't scream, didn't jump up and down, didn't drop my flashlight. Maybe I was becoming accustomed to a state of abject terror.

The voice spoke again. "Return to your rooms."

And that was when I realized I knew the voice, knew the tone of it, kind of mellow and warm—yet with a sort of regal authority. In my mind, I could hear that voice demanding, *Are you injured? Bring the gun to me....*

"Did you not hear me? Return to your rooms."

I gulped, still frozen in midstep. "Uh. Now?"

"Now."

As that one-word command echoed on stone, I spun around and aimed my light back at him.

For a split second I saw him: a tall, black-clad figure, a black mask covering his face. Yes! It *was* my rescuer, the man who had fought the two thugs in Brit's room. He was there—and then gone. As if he had melted backward, right through the wall itself.

My heart was pounding hard and loud and there was

a coppery taste in my mouth. This habit the guy had of appearing and vanishing at will, it did make me wonder…

Was there a problem with my mind?

To put it more specifically, was I losing it? Going out of my head, imagining I saw a black-masked figure who walked through walls and came running to my rescue when things got tough?

That I might have lost my grip on reality made a scary kind of sense. Me. With my inherent, irrepressible romantic tendencies and my rabidly overactive writer's imagination. I'd fallen in love at first sight and nearly been carried off by kidnappers. All in the span of about thirty hours. Maybe all the thrills and chills had driven me over the emotional edge. I wasn't what you'd call levelheaded, not even in the most tranquil of times.

Cautiously I crept back along the corridor until I came to the spot, about six feet from the open entrance to my room, where I'd seen the masked man disappear.

When I got there, I found nothing but silvery black wall. My heart pounded faster. It seemed to be lurching upward with each beat, getting stuck higher and higher in my throat. I swallowed, trying to push it down. It didn't want to go.

My pulse a swift tattoo in my ears, I examined that wall, inching the light over it in ever-widening circles, laying my hand against it, sliding my fingertips along the slick surface, tracing the hairline seams between the slabs of slate, looking for…

There. A slightly raised spot, an almost-invisible seam at either side. I pressed it.

Success! A section of the wall swung soundlessly away from me. I stared into the darkness beyond the opening and sucked in a long, steadying breath.

The likelihood that I was stark-raving bonkers had just diminished. The masked man hadn't vanished. He'd only slipped through yet another secret door.

The beam of my flashlight revealed a corridor that was narrower than the one in which I stood. It went straight for about twelve feet and then came to a dead end. No sign of my black-masked mystery man.

Figuring there was probably another camouflaged door down there at the other end, I entered the smaller corridor. I went in with my head high, breathing fast, trying to ignore the gruesome mental images of the door I'd just come through sliding shut behind me, locking me into a prison of solid stone.

Twelve feet is only a few steps. I reached the other end, set down the flashlight and used both hands on the wall. I found the raised spot pretty quickly. By then I was getting a sense for where it should be. I pressed and had to grab my light and jump back as the section of wall opened toward me.

Casting a glance over my shoulder to reassure myself that the other doorway remained open, I stepped into the next corridor.

It was as wide as the one where I'd started. I looked back the way I'd come, through the twin openings, at the first corridor.

Imagine that. A hidden link between the secret corridors. There were probably a lot of those. King Thorlak the Liberator had been one crafty dude. He'd built a secret maze in the walls of his palace. And within the maze, a hundred ways to get from point A to point B. Or maybe it was Mad King Solmund who deserved the credit here...

To my left, about six feet away, there was a dead end. I guessed that if I ran seeking fingers over the wall there,

I'd find the spot that would open a door into someone else's room.

Maybe *his* room—the room of my masked rescuer...

But then again, what if the room beyond the wall belonged to some totally oblivious palace guest? Some prince or lady who wouldn't appreciate a complete stranger popping in on them at 5:00 a.m.

I decided I'd better just go to the right. I hurried to the end of the hallway. From there, it went left. I peeked around the corner, pointing my flashlight at the way ahead.

And there he was. My masked rescuer. Just standing there, about eight feet from me.

He brought up a black-gloved hand to shade his eyes from my light. "Turn your lamp away."

I lowered it enough that it wasn't in his eyes. I was afraid to shine it completely away from him. He could disappear on me all over again.

But he didn't. He stood his ground. "I see you refuse to do as you're instructed."

I gulped. "I just wanted to make certain I wasn't hallucinating, that you really do exist."

He turned his head slightly, as if regarding me sideways. I caught the gleam of his eyes through the holes in the mask, which were cut at a catlike slant. "Fear not. I am real."

"That is such a relief." I wasn't scared anymore, which made me giddy. "Listen," I gushed. "I have to tell you. I am so grateful that you were—"

We both heard the noise at the same time: booted feet approaching from somewhere behind him.

The man in black sprang into action, striding toward me, grabbing my arm and leading me back the way I had come. We ducked into the smaller corridor and he shut the opening behind us. It wasn't wide enough in there for us to walk side by side, so I went ahead, checking back more than once to be sure that he followed me.

A few steps and we stood together, in the first corridor, where the back of the armoire gaped open, my clothes hanging in plain sight, the brightly lighted room beyond visible through a gap between a ruffled white shirt and a black velvet vest.

The clothes and the room seemed somehow to be in another world—the *real* world. As if they were just waiting for me to get back in there and shut the back of the armoire behind me, to block off the secret passageways within the walls of Isenhalla, to begin telling myself those passageways didn't exist.

"There." He gestured toward the light. "The way is open. Return to your room."

I put up a hand. "Shh." We both listened. After a few seconds, I said, "I don't hear them anymore."

"No." He sounded only slightly impatient. "They didn't see us—and if they had, they wouldn't know where to look for us now."

"Who are they?" I don't know why I expected him to know.

"Palace guards," he said, proving out my expectation. "Or perhaps Hauk Wyborn's men, His Majesty's berserkers."

I wasn't sure I'd heard right. "Berserkers?"

"The berserkers are an elite squad of highly trained soldiers sworn to perform any challenging task His Majesty might assign them. Hauk, as the king's warrior, commands them."

I peered at him more closely. There was something familiar about him, I just wasn't quite sure what...

He must have thought I looked scared, because he

added, "You have nothing to fear from the guards—or Hauk's men—I promise you. They only seek to learn what they can about the ones who broke in on you tonight. However, it could be…awkward, were they to find you where you are most assuredly not supposed to be."

I was still studying him, trying to figure out where and when I'd met him before, minus the mask. "Who are you?" I asked. Hey. When in doubt, be direct. I always was.

He answered my question with one of his own. "How did you know about the door through the armoire?"

I didn't see what it could hurt to answer him. "Brit showed me," I said, then elaborated, "You know, Her Royal Highness? She took me through them, to get to her room. We were in our pajamas and she said it wasn't, you know, appropriate, for her to go wandering the main hallways half-dressed."

"Ah," he said. "Her Royal Highness. Naturally." Before I could ask him what he meant by that, he went on, "Take my advice. Henceforward, stay out of the passageways. After tonight, they'll be guarded. If you're caught wandering here, you'll be treated as an enemy until Hauk's men learn who you are. That could be unpleasant for you."

"I understand. I just…I had to make sure there was no one lurking on the other side of the armoire waiting for me to drop off to sleep before sneaking in and cutting my throat."

He seemed to study me for a minute. Then he said softly, "There is much real horror in this world. Wiser not to manufacture any."

I sighed. "Tell me about it."

I swear he chuckled. "Think on this. You came through the armoire to face your fears. And what have you discovered? That there *is* someone lurking here, but that someone is a man who means you no harm.'' He gestured again toward the brightly lighted room. ''A safe sleep awaits you.''

''Sleep,'' I said, shaking my head. ''Not going to be happening any time soon.''

Did he smile behind his mask? I had the sense that he did. ''You shall be safe.'' His voice carried a teasing note. ''I will watch over you.''

Well, you know what? I kind of liked the sound of that. ''Thank you,'' I said, feeling suddenly shy. ''But that's way too much to ask. I'm sure you've got other things you need to be doing—other women in jeopardy to rescue from would-be kidnappers.''

He said nothing. I saw he was holding one of those miniature flashlights. It was so small I hadn't noticed it at first, since it was turned off. He tucked it into a pocket and then just stood there, watching me.

Since he was staring, I stared back. He wore close-fitting black pants and high black boots. His shirt was of a heavy but supple material, his black vest without buttons, open at the front. And then there were those black gloves on his hands, the black mask obscuring his face. With so much of him covered, the skin that showed looked somehow so…exposed: a small V of hard chest above the top button of his shirt, the strong column of his neck where the shadow of a dark beard had just begun to appear, the back of a lean wrist when he pocketed the flashlight…

His coffee-brown, slightly wavy hair was shoulder-length, tied low at the nape. I wished I could see his eyes better, but most of the light was coming through the open armoire behind him, so the front of him was in shadow. I longed to shine my flashlight directly into his face, but I didn't. There was something…wild about him. Something untamed and mistrustful. If I shone my light straight at him, he just might take off.

I didn't want him to go. Not yet. Not till he'd answered at least a few of my questions.

Who was he? How did he know about the secret passageways? Why had he been there to take on the guys in ski masks? Who could be trying to kidnap my best friend?

I switched off my light and wrapped my arms around myself to keep the chill away, the flashlight poking out at the crook of my elbow. Our stare-down had gone on for too long. I dropped my gaze and looked at my fluffy yellow slippers.

He took a step nearer. "Will you not go then, into the warmth and the light, where a soft bed awaits you—whether you choose to sleep in it or not?"

It happened right then. As he finished that last sentence on a rising inflection. At that exact second, I knew.

Don't ask me how. Certainly not by his voice, which I'd only heard while he was wearing the mask. He hadn't spoken a single word in those few minutes at the ball.

Maybe it was by scent, a primal sort of recognition, below the level of my conscious mind.

However it happened, I knew he was Valbrand.

"Will you go?" he asked again. He said it so tenderly, as if he were telling me something altogether different: *I will love you always* or *Stay, I beg you. Never leave me….*

I answered lightly. "I'll go. In a minute." I waited. I thought he'd argue some more that I had to go immediately. But he said nothing. So I dared to look up.

I was going to say, *Valbrand. I know it's you.*

But the words just…got all tangled in a ball somewhere in my throat. I stared into the shadows, still seeking his eyes, and I...well, I thought twice.

I mean, if he wanted me to know who he was, he wouldn't have been wearing a mask, now, would he?

Yes, I believe in being direct. But right then, I just couldn't do it to him. I thought of his poor, mutilated face. Of how it was probably easier for him to wear a smooth black mask and let people wonder at that, rather than to have to watch them cringe away in pity and disgust at the sight of him.

And also, there was a little bit of pride involved. My pride. I wanted to unmask him. But I wanted him to *want* me to.

Is that just like a woman, or what?

I switched the flashlight to my left hand and held out my right. "I'm Dulcie," I said as if he didn't already know. I felt a stab of disappointment when his fingers closed over mine—that he wore those gloves, that I couldn't feel his skin. But then, instead of shaking my hand, he raised it to the slit in the mask where his mouth was.

I felt smooth leather—and the warmth of his breath.

Did my knees go weak, did my heart go pitter-pat?

Oh, you'd better believe it.

When he lifted his head and released his featherlight hold on my fingers, it took every ounce of self-restraint I possessed not to shove my hand up under his face again and beg, *Please. Do that to me one more time....*

Since by then, I couldn't trust my arms not to reach for him, I wrapped them around me again. "So. As I said, I'm Dulcie. And you are...?"

He did chuckle then. A low, velvety sound that sent warm little shivers quivering across my skin—and yes, it's true. I was a goner. No sense trying to pretend otherwise.

"I am the Dark Raider."

I blinked, then asked, with as much tact as I could muster, "What is a Dark Raider?"

"A phantom. A figure of myth."

"You're saying…you're not real?"

"Oh, I am real enough."

"You just said you were a phantom."

"And so the Dark Raider is."

"But *you*…the man behind the mask…who are you?"

"It matters not."

"Yes, it does. It matters a lot."

He had his head tipped to the side again. "I have a favor I would ask of you."

Crawl through ground glass? Eat Brussels sprouts with an okra chaser? His wish was my command. "What?"

"Tell no one you have seen me."

Oh, great. More secrets to keep. "And I should do this because…?"

"These are troubled times. I can do my work best in secret."

"And that 'work' would be?"

"To…foil evil deeds."

I gulped. "Oh. Right. A superhero kind of thing…" I stared at the shadowed mask that hid his face. And all at once, it occurred to me that he was insane.

Or wait. I'd been worrying earlier that *I* was insane. Maybe I was. Maybe we both were. Now I knew how Lois Lane must have felt the first time Superman popped out of a phone booth. I stared at him, hugging myself. I must have looked stricken because he said, so softly, as if it hurt him deeply to have done it, "I have frightened you."

"Yeah." I hugged myself tighter. "But you know what?" I shivered, drew my shoulders back. "It's been that kind of night."

The thing was, I realized, I didn't care if he was crazy. Or if I was. Or we both were.

I was set on a course. And that course was loving him.

And yeah, duh. From the point of view of most of the civilized world, that was plain crazy anyway. Crazy was kind of the order of the day.

I remembered my various questions. "So. How did you know to be waiting outside Brit's room tonight when the bad guys showed up?"

"I was struck with foreboding."

I was struck with foreboding. If anyone else had said that to me, I would have told them they really needed to look into hiring someone else to write their dialogue. But on Valbrand, aka the Dark Raider, it worked.

I said, "Foreboding that Brit was going to be attacked?"

"No. It was…a more general sense of unease."

"And it led you straight to the wall behind the mirror in Brit's room?"

"Is there some purpose to these questions?"

"Curiosity. I'm a very curious person."

"A curious person who ought to return to her room."

I stayed right where I was. "So how did you know about the secret passageways?"

"I have known of them virtually all of my life."

"You grew up here? In the palace?"

He let a moment elapse before he said, "I fear the time has come that I must go."

"Oh, no. Stay…"

"I must go. As you must return to your room."

"Who could be trying to kidnap Brit?"

"I do not know. Please. Return to your room and remain there. Don't enter the hidden passageways again."

"Wait." I slid in front of the opening to the narrower passageway just before he reached it.

He brought himself up short to keep from plowing into me. "This is lunacy."

"Please…"

"You must return to your room. And I must go." He was so close. I couldn't resist. I reached up a hand. He jerked his head away before I could touch him. "Step aside. I have dallied here for far too long."

"No. That's not true. It hasn't been long enough. Forever wouldn't be long enough.…"

He went utterly still. Then he said, very softly, "You are mad."

I shrugged. "I have to admit, it's a distinct possibility."

Those dark eyes were on me, looking right through me. "Step out of my way." The words came out tight and harsh, as if he spoke them through clenched teeth.

I couldn't bear his anger. "Yes. I will. I promise. Just one thing more…" He shook his head, but I didn't let it stop me. "Tomorrow night—"

"Don't…" It was a plea.

A plea that I ignored. "Midnight. I'll be here."

"It's not safe."

"Then be here, too. You can protect me."

"Dulcie…"

"Oh, I like that. To hear you say my name…"

"You know nothing of me."

"Hey. Hoping to fix that."

"This can go nowhere. You must see that we—"

I put up a hand and stepped out of his way.

For a moment he neither moved nor spoke. Then he said, "I beg you. Tell no one you have seen me here. There will only be trouble if you do."

I thought of Brit's words, not all that long ago: *I have to ask you not to talk about what happened tonight, not to mention it to anyone....*

Everyone around here seemed to have secrets to keep. I personally preferred things a little more up-front. But whatever. I was sure, if I told anyone—like maybe Brit—and it got back to him, I would lose all hope of ever gaining his trust.

"I promise," I said. "I won't say a word." I waited, kind of hoping he'd give me an opening, so I could get him talking again—*anything* to get him to stay just a little bit longer, to be with me a few moments more.

But it wasn't happening. "Good night, Dulcie."

"Don't you mean good morning?"

"Good morning, then." With a quick salute of a black-gloved hand, he strode past me, into the dark corridor.

I pressed my lips together to keep from calling him back. And I didn't let myself turn to watch him go. I knew I'd only be tempted to follow.

Chapter 7

We met—Hauk, Brit, Eric, my father, Medwyn, and I—among the gold-tooled leather volumes and the busts of Odin, Loki and Thor, in my father's private audience chamber.

It was ten in the morning, an hour past sunrise. I stood near one of the tall, diamond-paned windows that afforded a panoramic view of the city of Lysgard and the misty Lysgard Harbor beyond. The sky was ice-blue and clear. Last night's snow had already melted from the shore. Snow never stayed long on our coastlines. The warm waters of the North Atlantic Drift, a continuation of the Gulf Stream, kept our harbors open through the coldest and darkest of the winter months.

Hauk, whom I could see from the corner of my eye, stood to attention before my father's wide desk. He was reporting on the information he had so far extracted from the two would-be kidnappers.

''The intruders claim to be independents. Mercenaries.

They tell similar stories. Each says he was contacted by a stranger who offered twenty thousand krone—half on accepting the job, half on completion—to kidnap Princess Brit from her bed and transport her to a deserted barn thirty kilometers to the northeast, near the village of Rosborn.'' Rosborn was a picturesque hamlet on the Vagdalen River, in a primarily agricultural area.

Eric, standing to Hauk's right, behind the chair where Brit sat, asked, "Did either of the prisoners happen to reveal who cut the west entrance lock for them?"

"They both claim the lock was already cut, the door slightly ajar when they reached it, that they weren't told who would open it for them and they saw no one nearby when they entered."

I turned from the window to face the others fully. "The entrance is hidden from view. How did these men know where to look?"

"They say they were given instructions by the one who hired them."

"And once inside, they made their way through the maze of hallways to Brit's bedchamber by...?"

"Their employer provided a map." Hauk, always prepared, opened the manila envelope he carried and removed a clear zip-style plastic bag. The bag contained a smudged and rumpled square of paper. He passed it to the king, who was seated in his carved, velvet-padded chair behind his inlaid desk. Osrik studied it briefly and then held it out to me. I left my position at the window to take it from him. After a cursory examination, I passed it on to Medwyn, on the far side of Osrik's chair.

Brit spoke. "So how many people even know of the secret passageways—let alone know them well enough to draw an accurate map?"

Medwyn peered at us over the tops of the wire-rim

glasses he used when he read. "Since Isenhalla's construction, each new king has been charged with the sacred duty of maintaining the passageways, of keeping them free of debris, of ensuring that the mechanisms in the hidden doors remain in good working order."

My sister sat back in her chair with a frustrated sigh. "So you're saying the passageways aren't all that secret, after all."

"Interesting you should mention that," said the king, his voice silky with displeasure. "As you yourself have only last night led a foreigner into them." Before Brit could apologize or make some excuse, Osrik said, "Medwyn. You wish to reply to Her Highness's remark?"

"I would think it fair to say the passageways are not general knowledge."

Brit caught our father's eye, as if she feared more criticism should she dare to speak again without permission. He gave her a nod. So she asked, "How many kings have there been since the palace was built?"

"Sixteen," Medwyn replied, "including His Majesty, your father."

"And how many families have held the throne?"

"Ten, I believe."

"Well, that really narrows the field."

Eric cautioned, "We can't assume that the traitor prince we seek is behind what happened this morning. Consider what my father has just told us. It could have been someone who has worked in the passageways, or someone who *knew* someone who worked in the passageways, someone not a prince at all. Perhaps a freeman hungry for the ransom a king's daughter would bring."

Brit groaned. "Fabulous. We're exactly nowhere."

Eric laid a hand on her shoulder. "Curb your impatience, my love. Hauk will see that every lead is followed."

Osrik said, "Medwyn and I have been pondering the lack of effective palace security in the brief hours since we were informed of this incident. We have decided that, at least until the enemies who dog us are brought to light and eliminated, Hauk shall command not only my berserkers, but also the palace guard. Hauk, I charge you to make warriors of the guard, so that we are never again threatened within our own walls."

Hauk performed a military salute: arm extended, palm out. "As my king commands."

I waited until the saluting was through, and then asked Hauk, "Were you able to find a way to test the west entrance for fingerprints?"

"I was." I didn't ask him to explain how. If Hauk said he'd done a thing, it was enough for me. He continued, "No usable prints were found. We have also taken the prints of the attempted kidnappers and will use them to confirm or disprove that they are the independent mercenary soldiers they claim to be. My sources at the National Investigative Bureau—" He stopped in midsentence, apparently having noted my concerned expression. "Prince Valbrand. Please. Be assured. These are men I absolutely trust. No information has been, or will be, given to the agency at large. We have ways to use the Bureau's resources during hours when our presence there will be unremarked. And the men who will aid us in this can do what needs doing and leave no sign they have been there." He waited, at attention, a soldier to the core.

I nodded. "Please, Hauk. Go on."

"The prints of the two prisoners will be checked—

with no one else at the Bureau the wiser—against the database at the NIB and against the various other databases to which the NIB has access. Also, we'll have the prints run through Interpol, which we can use more directly through their National Central Bureau office here.''

I said, ''Your opinion, please. Do you believe the two we just captured are who they say they are?''

''For as much as it's worth, I do.''

I gave him one of my twisted smiles. ''So now we come to the mysterious employer. He wasn't, by any chance, short in stature and powerfully built, with pale blue eyes and a shaved head?''

''We wish,'' muttered Brit.

The man I'd described was NIB Special Agent Jorund Sorenson, Brit's former ''friend.'' We had captured Sorenson that past September, when he attacked Brit and Eric in the Helmouth Pass. Prior to his escaping us, we'd learned from him that he took his orders from someone among the jarl, a prince who hoped to eliminate as many Thorsons as possible—including, ultimately, my father—and claim the throne for himself.

Unfortunately, before we had sufficient opportunity to pry more secrets from him, Sorenson disappeared from Tarngalla, the tower prison where murderers and traitors had been kept since medieval times.

It was no easy feat to escape Tarngalla's high, thick walls. We took that as yet another sign that Sorenson worked for someone who had infiltrated our various law enforcement agencies at a number of levels.

Hauk was shaking his head. ''Both prisoners described a tall, lean fellow as their contact. A man with graying brown hair and dark eyes. In middle age, one said. The other said forty to fifty. We will exhaust every lead until we find this mystery man.''

Brit was still fuming over the traitor NIB agent. "I know Sorenson is in on this somewhere."

"We must make no assumptions," I cautioned.

By then, Eric had the map. He finished looking it over and handed it back to Hauk, who put it away in the folder. "What about the barn where they were supposed to take Brit?"

"It is no longer in use and has fallen into disrepair. It is owned by Prince Finn."

"Cute," said Brit. "They were going to carry me off to my own brother-in-law's barn."

Prince Finn Danelaw was married to our sister Liv and had moved to America with her so that she might earn her law degree and pursue her ambition to enter California politics. They were expecting their first child in March.

Hauk said, "My men have searched the barn. It yielded no clues. We have it under surveillance, on the unlikely chance that our enemies might make the crucial error of stopping there."

"All right, then." I looked at my sister. "I think we must discuss the wisdom of the wedding itself." Brit's hand stole up to clasp Eric's, which still rested on her shoulder. I said, "In light of the fact that an attempt has been made to take you from your bed—here, in the palace, where we'd assumed ourselves safe—is it wise to go on with the festivities right now?"

Eric squeezed Brit's hand. "What will we gain by postponement? Our enemies can come at us at any time, as they have repeatedly proven."

Medwyn, always one to weigh all the options, said, "Postponement *is* something to consider. So many palace guests would then depart. We would be left with a much more, shall we say, *manageable* group.''

"The wedding goes on as planned," my father announced, ending that argument before it could develop further. He looked up at me, his intention set. "Liv and Finn arrive today. And your mother, our queen..."

Once my mother had sworn never to return to the land where her children had been born. That vow was broken now. She had visited briefly a few months ago, for my sake, when she learned that I was alive, after all. Now she was returning yet again, for Brit's wedding.

"I will not disappoint Her Majesty," my father said. Though Osrik never would have confessed it, I knew he still loved my mother, after all the years without her. I didn't understand it. When I thought of the queen, I felt only emptiness. And a faint but bitter memory of myself as a young child, betrayed by she whom I trusted above all.

The king went on. "The wedding will take place in eleven days, as planned. All members of the royal family will stay near the palace and venture out only under guard. Hauk, see to it that the passageways are well-patrolled, especially at points of entry."

"That I will, sire."

The king looked narrowly at Brit. "And now I have a question or two for my daughter."

Brit's mouth formed a bleak line. Eric still held her hand. I watched his fingers tighten again over hers. "Okay, okay," she muttered. "I blew it and I know it. I shouldn't have been sneaking around in the passageways. I shouldn't have taken Dulcie through them. And I shouldn't have left her alone in my room while I, um, visited Eric."

The king cleared his throat. "Daughter, what have you

been whispering to your American friend? Does she know, then, of the attempts on your life and the life of your brother, of the ongoing threat to our family and the throne?''

Brit pulled her hand free of Eric's and sat tall. "I've told her only what we've agreed to tell anyone who asks. That Valbrand barely survived a terrible storm at sea. That I went to the Vildelund seeking Eric and my plane went down *accidentally*. I said nothing of our ambush by Jorund Sorenson and his men in the Helmouth Pass. I said nothing of our suspicions that another high jarl family schemes to eliminate as many Thorsons as possible and lay claim to the throne.''

"Yet you did lead her through the secret passageways.''

A flush flooded up Brit's smooth cheeks. "I can only say in my defense that until a few hours ago, I thought— like everyone else in this room—that the passageways were secure from outside attack. I went through them to avoid walking the main halls in my pajamas. And yes, I knew she'd get a kick out of them. I was proud of the ingenuity of our Gullandrian forebears. I was showing off. So shoot me.''

"It was an error in judgment,'' my father said in an even tone.

"Tell me about it. I hate myself for leading her where she shouldn't have been. And more than that, for leaving her alone in my room to be terrified out of her wits and almost carried away by a couple of thugs who'd come there after *me*. Don't worry. It won't be happening again.''

Osrik said, "My concern is for what has *already* happened. The girl must have a score of questions.''

Brit sat ramrod-straight by then, her mouth drawn

down. "I said, I have told her nothing. And I *will* tell her nothing."

"Yes. And if you tell her nothing, then she might seek the answers elsewhere. From *whom* will she seek them? Possibly, all unknowing, from our enemies. And were they to draw her out, she might reveal what we don't wish them to know."

"What can she reveal? I told you, she doesn't know anything."

My father charged her, "In the history of our land, daughter, no woman before you has sat in private council with her king and his advisors. Do not disappoint us. Do not make yourself proof of the old adage that a woman's tongue cannot be trusted to remain still inside her mouth."

Brit sat utterly unmoving, the flush in her cheeks flaming red now. She was a fighter. We all knew what it cost her not to strike back when so gravely reprimanded. After a furious pause, she said tightly, "I will not disappoint you, Your Majesty."

Osrik looked at me then. "*You* came to the young woman's rescue." It was an accusation.

I schooled my tone to one of light sarcasm. "Your Majesty would prefer that I hadn't?"

"I would *prefer*—" he paused to grant me a truly withering stare "—that you never put yourself at risk. You are back with us at last, back, in a sense, from the dead. Your life is infinitely precious—to us and to this country. It would be a crime were you to lose it fighting two scurvy villains for the sake of a commoner."

It was hard to believe, as I looked at my father then, that there had been a time when we thought as one on virtually every subject. "Your Majesty. I regret that you don't approve of my actions." I had a flashing vision of

Dulcie's sweet face, of her honest hazel eyes that revealed a spirit open, loving and true. My father had it so very wrong. Fighting was what I did best now. If such as she might survive because I gave my sad and twisted life for hers, I would consider it a perfectly acceptable exchange.

My father asked, "And how did it happen that you were there at the precise moment when rescue was called for?"

"It was but an accident of fate."

"By all the scales of the dragon Nidhogg!" my father swore. His eyes gleamed with barely leashed anger—anger born, I knew, of his frustration with me. He started to speak again, but then Medwyn leaned close and whispered a few words in his ear. My father cast a quick glance into the knowing eyes of the lifelong friend to whom he had been bloodbound since childhood—as had Eric and I, after them.

One to lead; one to provide balance, wisdom and the objective view; such was the relationship between a king and his grand counselor.

I was reasonably certain that Medwyn had whispered something exceedingly wise—and all the more so when my father said, "Perhaps this is a subject better addressed at another time." By way of answer, I bowed, fist to chest. He turned again on my sister. "As to your American friend, after the horrendous events of early this morning, it may well be that she has had enough of our fair land. Mayhap she waits only for your suggestion that she board the royal jet and enjoy our hospitality all the way home to California."

At those words, I felt a tightness in my chest, as if a cruel hand had closed tight around my fool's heart. I knew Dulcie's leaving to be the best course of action for all involved. And even should she stay, I had sworn to myself that I would avoid her at all costs from now on.

Yet already, I counted the hours, suffered each minute, till midnight…

My sister stared at our father in obvious dismay. "You want me to send her home? Before the wedding?"

The king's reply was smooth as fresh-churned butter. "I think you must try to convince her that it would be better—safer—for her to go now."

Brit was shaking her head. "I can't do that. She'd be so hurt, Father. She *is* the truest of friends."

Osrik spoke kindly—*too* kindly. "I ask only that you gently persuade her."

"But I…" She fell silent as Eric bent close to whisper advice. When he stood tall again, she said in a tone that was carefully level, "And if I did mention leaving to her—gently, as you said—and she still insisted that she didn't want to go?"

Medwyn whispered to Osrik again. Were the tension in the air not thick enough to cleave with an axe, it might have been humorous: the grand counselor and his son alternately whispering their sage advice into the ears of the king and his daughter.

Finally, the king said, "At this point, we feel it would be unwise to force the issue. If your friend won't be convinced to leave, you will have done what you can and we shall let it go at that. Though, of course, that she is to be told nothing remains of utmost importance."

Brit nodded, one quick downward jerk of her stubborn chin. "I understand. It shall be as you wish, Your Majesty."

"Then you *will* speak with her." It was not a question.

After a moment, Brit surrendered to our father's will. "Yes. I'll speak with her."

* * *

"Linger, please, my son," Osrik said when the audience was concluded. His words had the sound of a request. But I—as everyone else in the room—knew that a king's request and a king's command are separated only by a difference in tone.

In the end, they are the same.

The others filed out. I had retreated again to the window, wishing myself far below—strolling the quaint cobbled streets of Lysgard's Old Town or moored in a small craft bobbing on the harbor. Anywhere but here, with the king my father's dark and disapproving gaze resting heavily upon me.

"Come, my son. Away from the window. My neck aches with turning to look at you."

Then don't turn, I nearly muttered, surly as some ill bred lout. *Don't look at me....*

Since my return from the grave, a troubled delinquent had been born within me. I was twenty-eight years of age and yet, at times, I felt as a youth often does—as I had never felt when in fact I *was* that young—a rebelliousness, a desire not to do even the smallest thing that my father asked of me. Constantly, as I did at that moment, I found myself quelling the newly born adolescent within.

Osrik gestured at a chair a few feet from his desk, the one where Brit had been sitting. "There. Sit down. Let us speak man to man."

I left the window, strode to the chair and dropped into it.

My father said, "Back to my earlier question. How was it you just happened to be in the passageway near your sister's room when the attack occurred?"

I strove to speak calmly, though I felt trapped in this conversation, as I did so often of late when forced to speak privately with my father. "It was pure coincidence. My mind was troubled. I couldn't sleep."

"So you wandered the passageways and *happened* to end up near your sister's chamber at the precise moment when the kidnappers arrived."

"That's correct."

"My son. You *were* observed, at the ball two nights ago, dancing for the first time since your return. It was the red-haired American with whom you danced. Those who saw remarked that you appeared quite taken with her—as she, with you."

"Who, precisely, remarked on this?"

"It is of no consequence." Translation: he was not going to tell me.

"Father, I must ask. Is there a crime in my dancing with my sister's friend?"

"No. Certainly not. I am only reminding you of what you once understood without question. That you must think of who you are at all times. *And* who the young American is."

"I assure you, I do. I shall."

"Then, will you not tell me honestly? Were you near your sister's chamber because you knew her American friend slept within?"

It should have been so simple to tell him the truth straight out: that I hadn't known. Yet I couldn't do it. It was simply too large a betrayal of my rights as a man. "I have already told you why I happened to be there. If you do not believe me, then a thousand reassurances will not suffice."

He was shaking his head. He looked quite weary, suddenly, the lines of age around his mouth and near his eyes more pronounced than before. "Let us…move on, shall we?" For an answer, I shrugged. He said, "When you battled the attackers, you fought masked—as the Dark Raider?"

Instead of answering, I looked away. My father did not approve of my secret identity. He saw it as the sign of a troubled mind, that I would go masked, all in black, posing as a legendary Gullandrian hero—and perhaps he was right. He could not understand the sense of power and purpose the mask afforded me. I did not blame him for this. I didn't understand it myself, not in any logical sense.

My father went on, lest I try to deny it, "In Hauk's report of the incident, taken from his interview with the young American, the woman says a man in a black leather mask fought and subdued the other two.…"

Hauk, Brit, Eric, my father and Medwyn were among the few who knew of my secret identity. Eric had known from the first. I had taken on the Dark Raider's guise in the months immediately after Eric had lured me back from madness and exile to the Vildelund—the wild north country beyond the Black Mountains. In the Vildelund, as the Dark Raider, I had made myself useful, saving more than one innocent from the renegades, rogues and thieves who would have harmed them.

Often, in retrospect, I wished that the secret of the Raider might have been mine alone. Were that so, I would not be sitting in my father's chambers right then, being scolded for saving Dulcie and for capturing two who might lead us, eventually, to the enemies we sought.

"Yes," I said, sounding as weary as my father looked. "I wore the mask."

"My son..." I knew what he would say before he said it. I could see it in his face, in the dark eyes so like my own. "So much can be done, in this modern day and age, to minimize and even eliminate scarring such as yours. If you would only—" I put up a hand and he fell silent, though he was my king and would have had every right to lambaste me for daring to interrupt while he spoke.

"No," I said. I had said it before. Repeatedly.

He leaned across the wide, shining surface of his desk. "Why do you punish yourself?" He should have known I would not answer him. I never had before. "Will you never tell me?" His voice was low by then, full of pain and love. A father's voice. The king, for a moment, had left us alone. "It was not your fault, what happened to your men. There was simply no way that you could have known—"

I cut him off again, heedless of any consequence. "There was a way, had I been more patient, had I chosen those last five men with proper care..."

He spoke so soothingly, "You are much too hard on yourself."

"My men were my responsibility. I let them die."

"No. It was but an evil twist of fate."

"I don't see it that way. I never will."

"But surely you do see that there is no need, any longer, for you to hide behind the Dark Raider's mask."

I didn't see that. Not at all. "Father, we have covered this ground over and over again. Let's leave it alone now. Please."

"I cannot bear to see you like this."

"I am sorry to distress you."

"Then change."

I only looked at him.

He was the first to look away. "I can't understand what has happened to you...." He laid both hands over his heart. "Here?" He stared at me. I stared back. He tried again, placing four fingers against his brow. "And here?"

Still, I said nothing.

"My son, if only you were willing to speak of it, to more deeply examine the horror that has befallen you. There are counselors who might help you to accept the past and move on."

"Please," I said, without inflection. "No."

"If not a counselor, then won't you confide in me? Don't you know there is nothing you cannot say to me?"

I didn't know that, not at all.

What I did know was that he loved me. And I loved him. But he couldn't call back the man I once was. That man was gone. Forever.

"Ah, Valbrand. If you would only..." He didn't finish.

I lifted the eyebrow I had left, waiting.

He waved his hand and sighed. I suppose he could see in my eyes that there was nothing more to say.

Chapter 8

A series of pounding sounds jarred me awake. *Rap-rap-rap*. Pause. *Rap-rap-rap-rap-rap*. Like that. And then again. And again.

For a minute, I just lay there, staring at the molded ceiling, wondering who I was gonna have to kill to get it to stop. Then, in a flash of blinding insight, it came to me.

Someone was knocking at my door.

I glanced at my travel clock. Sheesh. Not even noon yet. I'd had a whopping three hours of sleep.

"Thank you very much," I muttered, shoving tangled hair away from my face. "Whoever the hell you think you are…"

The knocking continued.

I almost yelled, *Come on in, damn it*. But then I remembered I'd locked the door. "Hold on! I'm coming!"

The knocking stopped. It was a lovely moment. Maybe if I just flopped back down and shut my eyes…

Bu-u-ut no. I'd said I was coming. The maid or who-ever it was would probably just start pounding again if I didn't go open up.

Grumbling under my breath, I tossed back the covers and padded to the short hall that led to the door. Slip-pers? A robe? Hey. You come knocking when I'm sleep-ing, you take what you get.

It was Brit. Looking fresh as a spring daisy, in a snug red cashmere sweater and a pair of nifty herringbone slacks. And I would have sworn her shoes were Manolo Blahnik. She was becoming just *so* stylish since she'd decided to marry a prince and settle down at the palace for a life of royal wedded bliss.

And beyond my friend's great look, there was also coffee, carried on a tray by the maid behind her. It smelled fabulous. And there were two plates, too, with silver warming covers over them.

I realized I was starving. "All right," I grumbled. "Since you brought breakfast, I'm going to let you in."

We sat on the antique—heavily tufted, cabriole legs—sofa that waited by the cozy fire. The maid left the tray on the coffee table in front of us and bowed herself out.

There were scrambled eggs, light as air, seasoned with chives and fresh pepper, bacon that was cooked to crisp perfection. Scones, with marmalade—I had two of those. You just can't be too calorie-conscious when there are scones with marmalade.

And the coffee… Be still my beating heart! Rich and dark and wonderful. Real cream to put in it. By the time I was on my second cup, I'd forgotten how irritated I was to have missed my beauty sleep.

"Well," Brit said, on her third cup—taken black as

always. "Looks like you're not letting what happened last night get you down."

I thought of Valbrand—aka the Dark Raider—in the passageway. I thought of how midnight was getting closer with every second that ticked by. He hadn't agreed to meet me. But I knew that he would.

I was in love. It made everything look soft and rosy, as if the world itself gave off a special, happy glow. Nothing could dim that glow. Not even barely escaping being drugged and carried off by two armed goons in ski masks. I had found my love and all the rest was just so much background noise.

Under any other circumstances, I'd have been babbling away to Brit about my meeting with the Dark Raider in the passageway just hours ago. I'd have told her how I knew who he was, even though he didn't know that I knew.

But I'd promised him I'd say nothing. And my dad might have called me his little motormouth, but when I gave my word, I knew how to keep it.

I grinned at Brit. "How could I be cranky with coffee like this?"

"You're really okay?" She was looking very concerned—as if she suspected I was hiding my true emotional state.

And hey. In a sense, I was. "I'm good. But very, very curious…"

Suddenly she was way too interested in her coffee. She sipped, she looked into the cup. "About what?" she asked at last—as if she didn't know.

I looked at her for a minute over the rim of my own cup, then I sipped, swallowed and asked brightly, "So who were the guys in ski masks?"

She set her cup down. Carefully. "We don't know anything yet. The intruders are still...under interrogation."

"Oh, really?" I said, as if that meant anything. Then it occurred to me that it would seem suspicious if I didn't at least mention the man in black. "And what about the other one—the guy in leather? What's the story with him?"

"As I mentioned, he's an ally. Other than that, I don't know much about him."

Yeah right. My best friend was flat-out lying to me. I knew it. I felt reasonably certain *she* knew that I knew it.

And Brit wasn't the only one telling lies. I was, too—by omission and misdirection. I stared at her and she stared back at me. We might as well have been looking at each other through a foot-thick invisible wall. Yeah, we could see each other. But we couldn't get through to make any real contact.

How could this have happened?

From our first meeting, in that day-long Learning Network seminar on Writing the Popular Novel, we had been the sort of friends who could tell each other anything. Even the worst stuff. You know the kind. The petty stuff that makes you ashamed of yourself, the stuff that you know will put you in a bad light. There was no "bad light" between Brit and me. We were real, forever friends and we always told each other the truth.

Until now.

I never should have come here.

The words popped into my head—and I instantly rejected them. Of course I should have come. This was exactly the place I should be right now. My best friend was getting married here.

And I had met Valbrand here—and no, I didn't hold out big hopes for anything remotely resembling a happily ever after for Valbrand and me. Realistically, I knew it just wasn't going to happen.

But in my heart? Hey, what did I care for realistic? I was my mother's daughter, after all. And there were eleven days until the wedding. I wasn't scheduled to leave till the day after. As a born and bred romantic, I couldn't help dreaming that twelve days might be time enough for love to somehow conquer all.

And as for Brit and me, well, yes, our friendship had changed big-time, and not in a good way. We'd probably never be as close as we used to be. But that didn't mean I loved her any less. I wanted to see her married. I wanted to be there when she and Eric said their vows.

Brit said, "Listen, Dulce. I've been thinking—you know, since what happened last night? I've been thinking that maybe you'd be better off—safer—you know, if you just…" The stammered words trailed away into nothing. She gulped. And then she sucked in a big breath and hit me with it. "Maybe after last night, you wish you hadn't come here. Maybe you're hoping I'll let you off the hook about the wedding, so that you can go home."

It took me a minute or two to believe that Brit had just told me she thought I should get lost. I stared at her and she gazed sheepishly back at me. Finally I said, "So what's the deal? You want me gone because I know too much?"

"No." She said it way too fast. "No, of course not. Don't be silly. I was only thinking that maybe you—"

"Don't think it." I had my shoulders back and my

chin up. Defiant. "And my answer is no. I don't want to go home."

She tried once more. "You're sure?"

"Positive. I want to be there. For your wedding." I almost asked, *Don't you* want *me to be there?* But I didn't. I was too afraid she might say no.

"Well," she said, smiling much too brightly. "Well, okay. Then you'll stay."

After Brit left, I showered and got dressed and pulled the heavy curtains back from the east-facing windows. It was sunny out there. Down below, a shimmering white mantle of snow covered the ground and lay in patches on the hedges that rimmed the now-dormant formal gardens.

I looked at my AlphaSmart and shook my head. I didn't dare start writing. Not then. If I did, I'd only end up recording the sad story of how my best friend had just hinted—with all the subtlety of a charging rhino—that I ought to go home without attending her wedding. Once I'd finished with how much that hurt, I'd move on to V., V., V., V.

It wasn't constructive. Right then, I needed answers. I needed to understand the things that were happening around me—and *to* me. My friend wouldn't give me those answers. And I probably wasn't going to be getting any explanations from Valbrand—who wouldn't even admit he was hiding behind the Dark Raider's mask.

So…

Where to go to get my questions answered?

Housed in the main tower, to the right of the grand front entrance, the palace library was available to all the guests.

I sat at one of the long mahogany tables, a stack of books at my elbow and one open in front of me: *Legends of Gullandria* by Narfi Kolskeg.

I checked the index and turned to a certain page where I found a drawing of a figure all in black. The figure was mounted on a black horse and wore a mask—a mask just like Valbrand's. The caption beneath read: *The Dark Raider. He shall appear in times of trouble and strife, his sworn duty to protect the innocent and to seek out and vanquish all men of evil intent and tyrants without honor.*

I thought, Whoa, my darling. That's one big order.

The Dark Raider, I learned, had first appeared in the early sixteenth century. Legend had it he fought at the side of Thorlak the Liberator, that together with fierce bands of loyal patriots, they drove the occupying Danes from Gullandrian soil. Once Thorlak had secured the throne, the Dark Raider was seen no more.

A century and a half later, during a particularly lawless period, the Danelaw kings, who had ruled in peace for four generations, lost the throne to King Svartkel the Ravenous. King Svartkel beheaded anyone who irritated him and taxed anything that moved.

So once again, the Dark Raider came to the people's rescue. He saved travelers from highwaymen, rescued starving farmers from thieves who would have taken what little they had. King Svartkel died mysteriously and the reign of the Freyasdahls began. Things improved. The Raider vanished.

Since then, there had been numerous sightings—usually at night. In poor light. The Dark Raider would emerge from the darkness and rescue those in need, only to vanish as mysteriously as he'd appeared.

"A scholar, I see."

The voice—low, faintly sibilant—came from just behind my right shoulder. I flipped the book shut and glanced back. At the sight of the gaunt old man with the white beard and the knowing eyes, I grinned in delight.

"Medwyn!"

The owly guy behind the desk by the door looked over at me, thin lips drawn down in disapproval. I scrunched up my shoulders and mouthed, "Sorry," at him.

Medwyn came around the end of the table—he had the strangest, fluid kind of walk. It was as if he floated. I mean, I knew he was walking. I could see his long, thin legs, encased in dark wool trousers, taking one step and then another. But his upper body didn't move at all. It just...sailed. Serene. He was like an old, still-graceful swan drifting on the glassy waters of a tranquil pond.

He stood behind the chair across from me and softly inquired, "May I join you?"

I bobbed my head eagerly. "I have so many questions for you," I whispered. "But I suppose you're too busy to hang around here for a while and—"

"Dulcinea." He pulled the chair back and lowered himself into it with an otherworldly sort of grace. "I am pleased to make time—for you."

I swear, if I hadn't already given my heart to Valbrand, I might have considered the idea of loving an older man: this one.

And I may have been a hopeless romantic, but that didn't mean I was an idiot. As much as I longed to, I wasn't going to start asking him about what had *really* happened to Valbrand at sea, or about the fates of the two fellows who'd tried to kidnap Brit and ended up almost taking me. If Brit wouldn't talk to me about those things, I knew the king's right-hand man wouldn't, either. Plus, if the powers that be thought I was snooping where I shouldn't be, I had a sneaking suspicion Brit would be showing up with coffee and scones again— not to *ask* if I wanted to leave, but to tell me the royal jet was waiting at Lysgard airport to carry me back to good old El Lay.

The deal was, I *liked* Medwyn. I found him totally fascinating and I wanted to be his friend—for his own sake and also because it was becoming pretty clear to me that I could use all the friends I could get in Gullandria.

I leaned across the table toward him, doing my best to keep my voice down for the sake of the other people trying to read at the tables nearby. ''I'm a writer, you see.''

''Ah,'' he said, as if he understood everything—which I had the strangest feeling he probably did.

''And I'm doing research for a possible book that would be set in Gullandria.''

''And you need to know…?''

I grabbed the spiral-bound notebook I'd brought from my room and picked up a pencil. ''I need to know *everything* you want to tell me.''

Monday, December 9, 6:30 p.m. Isenhalla, Gullandria. In my room, relaxing on the sofa by the fire.

Ran into Medwyn in the palace library. What a beautiful, wise man. He answered question after question about life here.

After the library, I took the van that leaves twice

daily to go down into Lysgard, where I visited an
apothecary shop and bought

I paused, glanced up, shook my head, and then put
the cursor over the "t" in "bought." Backspacing, I
erased the part about the apothecary shop. I tried again,

My visit to the capital was too short. I'm going
down again, tomorrow, I think.

    While I was out, the maid brought in tea and a
tiered serving plate of those little crustless sandwiches. By the time I got in, the tea was cold and
the sandwiches had dried out. I sipped and nibbled
anyway.

    Learned so much today—from Medwyn.

    bloodbound: a blood oath of loyalty and com-
mitment between equals—thus a two-way oath.

    bloodsworn: a blood oath of loyalty and fealty
made by one of lesser rank to a ruler or a leader.

    fitz: someone who is illegitimate. Big stigma here
in Gullandria, to be a fitz. They put "Fitz" in front
of an illegitimate person's name. As in, FitzWyborn
(Brit's sister Elli's husband, Hauk Wyborn, was
born a fitz. The king declared him legitimate,
though, so he could marry Elli). No way a fitz could
marry a princess. Sad. The good news is that fitzes
are rare in Gullandria. Medwyn said that both men
and women use particular care that no child is con-
ceived out of wedlock. Which means, I'm assuming, they take their contraceptive use seriously.

    kvina soldar: woman warrior. They live in tribes
in the mountains to the north; nomadic; no men
allowed. Hmm. Definitely a story there…

dragon dials: Gullandrian martial arts discipline;
created by a kvina soldar in the seventeenth century.

skald: a poet/minstrel. Skalds are greatly honored
in Gullandria and often perform their epic versions
of the great Norse myths for the king and his court.

I paused again, my fingers on the keyboard. I had
pages and pages of notes in longhand. Medwyn had
stayed with me for two whole hours. He talked in his
low, thready voice about his country—everything from
politics and government to the white wolves and moun-
tain cats that roamed the wilds to the north, the area
known as the Vildelund.

I bent to the keyboard again, but looked up without
typing anything.

The urge to start in about Valbrand was building. I
hadn't written a thing about last night—not a word about
the secret passageways, or all the stuff Brit had told me
that didn't quite add up, or about the Dark Raider and
the brawl in Brit's room, or the moments Valbrand and
I had shared later, alone in the hidden hallway behind
the armoire.

I was resisting putting all that down. I don't really
know why I was fighting it—partly that I had spent all
those hours typing on and on about him night before
last. And what had it got me? Zip.

There are things that need to be written but don't need
to be read. And maybe, when it came to forbidden love,
especially in Gullandria, there were things a girl was
better off keeping strictly to herself.

Across from where I sat, the curtains were drawn over

the windows on either side of the bed. The maid must have done that, when she came in to straighten up—or maybe when she brought the tea.

Something Brit had said came drifting into my mind—how her father actually bugged her room, how the maid and the cook would spy on her and carry tales back to His Majesty.

Yes, it was possible I was becoming paranoid. But think a minute. Why wouldn't I become more wary, after everything that had happened?

I couldn't help realizing that anything I wrote—unless I found a good hiding place for it, or carried it around with me when I left the room—might be read by the stranger who changed my sheets and dropped off the tea tray.

No. Better to keep my lovesick ramblings safe inside my head. I moved the cursor backward in the file to the short section concerning Valbrand, the one I had written last night, right before Brit came through the armoire.

It began, *Trouble concentrating. Keep thinking of last night, of V. Know I shouldn't...*

I put the cursor on the final word of that section and held my finger on the backspace button until all of it was gone.

Tonight at nine was a gala banquet in honor of Brit's mother, Queen Ingrid. For now, I would draw myself a scented bath and soak my cares away. I would spend a couple of hours fixing my face and fooling with my unruly hair—which I didn't really have to do. Another convenient little feature of life at the palace was the hairdresser they provided nightly if you wanted one. She'd come in and give you a blow-dry and an upswept do so you could look your most smashing for the evening to come. I'd used her two nights ago, before the ball. But tonight, I decided, I'd just wear my hair down.

And once I'd finished my face and brushed my hair, I would put on my other evening dress and find my way to what they called the Chamber of the Skalds on the second floor, where the festivities were to occur.

I was figuring Valbrand would have to be there. I mean, it was in honor of his mother, after all. Maybe I'd get fantastically lucky and he'd seek me out and exchange a few words with me.

And if that didn't happen? Well, there would still be midnight. I had no doubt in my mind—or my yearning heart—that I would see him then.

Chapter 9

That evening, before the state dinner in the Chamber of the Skalds, I met with my mother the queen for the second time in over twenty years.

In a brief note delivered to my rooms, she requested a private interview. Reluctant, ambivalent and yet somehow also reconciled to the coming encounter, I went to her suite.

A gray-haired servant answered the door. She was tall and broad-shouldered, with long arms and big hands. I saw her and the memories washed over me....

I used to call her Hildy. She could be strict, but she had loved me. She had fled Gullandria with Ingrid all those years ago. I faintly recalled that, at the time, the loss of Hildy had made my mother's desertion all the more terrible. As if *two* mothers had turned their backs on me. "Hilda. So good to see you once again."

"I am honored that you recall a mere servant such as I." She put her fist to her chest and bent her gray head.

"How could I forget?" Those long arms around me, holding me close, the comforting scent of the lavender soap she used...

Now, she had on her best servant's face. Composed. Reserved. Careful not to presume. Her dark gaze, giving nothing away, took in the web of scarring that marred my own face on the left side from temple to jaw. "You are...well, I hope?"

"My health is excellent."

"I am gratified to hear it. Please. This way..."

In the formal sitting room, Ingrid was waiting—a still-beautiful pale-haired woman in early middle age, with eyes more turquoise than truly blue. She wore a soft dove-gray suit and a cream-colored silk blouse.

When I entered, she sat perched on a Chippendale sofa. At the sight of me, she swept to her feet. I watched her expression. I took a grim satisfaction in anticipating the typical response to my hideousness: a look of horror or outright revulsion quickly masked by a broad fake smile.

But, as in September, my long-lost mother did better than I expected. Only a slight widening of those turquoise eyes gave away her distress at what I had become. She said, in a low, husky voice, "Valbrand. It's so good to see you again."

As I had in September, when she had come expressly to see me after learning that I lived, I waited for the bitterness to well from within, for the anger to rise—that she had deserted me and my long-dead younger brother, that she had chosen to take my sisters and leave Kylan and me behind.

But as in September, there was nothing. No self-righteous fury, no sullen resentment. Only an awareness that she looked so sad. Only the vague memories of her as she had been all those years ago: the center of my world. Then, I had loved her with all the selfish passion that I imagine most young children have for their mothers. To me, the echoes of my childish love still clung to her—like cobwebs, like the fingers of mist that drift up the black rock walls of Drakveden Fjord from the jewel-blue waters below.

I went to her. I took her hand and pressed my ruined mouth to the back of it.

When I would have let go, she held on.

"Please," she said. "Sit with me. Only for a moment or two."

So we sat, side by side, on the sofa. There was a lengthy pause, as she struggled with what she wanted to say, and as I waited, resigned, for her to find the words. Finally, she said, "Last time I...visited, I didn't want to pressure you. It was enough, just to see with my own eyes that you lived. But now...I have so much to tell you, so much I want to know about you, about how you're...managing." She smoothed her pale hair, caught herself doing it and firmly put her hand down, folding it with the other one, in her lap. "And then again, this seems like the wrong time, too. Maybe for now, just that you're here is enough. That I have seen you one more time with my own eyes. That I have heard your voice..." She laughed then, a laugh both husky and musical and her face was very young, suddenly. I saw at that moment what my father loved. "Well," she said. "I guess I haven't heard your voice, have I? You haven't said a word."

"What would you like me to say?"

She tipped her head to the side—and as she did that, I saw myself in her. Shocked at the ultimate proof of our basic connection, I blinked and sat back a little.

"What is it?" Her eyes burned suddenly bright with concern.

"Nothing. It's nothing."

"Valbrand..." She bowed her pale head over her joined hands. "I know there's no way I can ever make it right that I left you, but—"

"It's long ago," I cut in, wishing she would leave it alone. "And best forgotten."

She was shaking her bent head. "Never. Oh, no. Never forgotten. You see, I..." The words trailed off. She gathered herself, tried again. "Your father says you know why I left."

"Yes. I know. He finally told me a few years ago—at Medwyn's urging." My mother had a brother, Brian, whom she adored beyond reason. He was brutally murdered at the gateway to the Black Mountains. My father refused to hunt down the killer and mete out a vicious punishment. And my mother could not forgive him for that.

She said, "Well. At least you know, then. I'm sure it can never seem like enough of a reason that I...did what I did."

She was right. It wasn't reason enough. In the end, the betrayed small boy within me would always believe that *nothing* could have been reason enough.

I found I couldn't resist taunting her a little. "They called him Brian the Blackhearted, that brother of yours. Did you know? He was evil. He left bastards in the bellies of any number of innocent serving maids. He beat a groom nearly to death."

She nodded, her mouth tight enough that I could see the wrinkles of age that would claim those soft lips in the years to come. "I was very young—eighteen when I married your father, only just twenty-four when Brian was killed. Young. And not in the least wise. I knew only that I had lost the brother I loved so much. And that my husband wouldn't hunt down and punish whoever had killed him.''

"So you took your baby girls and went running home to California." Well, well. There *was* some bitterness left, after all, it seemed. "Kylan was only three," I sneered. "He cried endlessly. He looked for you everywhere."

She shut her eyes, breathed deeply—and then, with clear effort, faced me again. "Please…"

I was suddenly merciless. "But what do they matter, the tears of a small boy? He was dead so soon after that, anyway…"

She couldn't keep her hands folded. One flew up, palm out in front of her face, as if to ward off a killing blow. She brought that hand to her throat. Her eyes were bottomless. And all the way down, there was pain.

And right then, as I saw the depth of her pain—right then, with no warning, I was filled with self-loathing.

Who was I, to torment this woman?

I, who had seen twenty-five fine, true men murdered. I, who had been too vain and cocksure to foresee their coming slaughter. I, who had failed as a leader, who had trusted like a blind fool and led those who followed me straight into a death trap.

I had no right, no right at all, to judge my mother for her folly so many years ago.

She said in an anguished whisper, "Oh, Valbrand. I…see so much now. Now that, in so many ways, it's simply too late. But I didn't see then. I didn't…know then. It was as if I was blind. As if I had set myself on a course of pride and absolute loyalty to someone who himself had no idea what loyalty was. I had set my course and I would not sway from it, no matter the cost, no matter the harm I inflicted on my innocent children, or on the husband who loved me—the ones to whom my loyalty *should* have been given.''

She brought her hand down, folded it—this time tightly—with the other. And she looked fiercely at her lap, at her joined hands, as if she didn't dare confess the rest while staring in my ravaged face. ''And the awful thing, the worst thing…''

I waited. I truly didn't need to hear it. Yet after my realization that I had no right to judge her, I could see how much she needed to say it. And I was willing. It was as it should be, that I sit and listen. That I hear her confession.

''The worst thing,'' she said low, ''is that I never stopped believing I was right in what I had done, that ripping our family in two and dragging my baby girls back to where I'd come from, leaving my husband and sons behind, was the best choice, the *only* choice.'' She raised her head then. She met my eyes. ''But then…Elli found her way back to Gullandria. And married Hauk. And Liv met Finn. And Brit came here to visit and refused to leave…'' She canted her chin higher. I saw the glitter of unshed tears. ''Yes. It took that. It took my daughters coming back to Gullandria, finding the lives I tried to steal from them, for me to begin to see how wrong I'd been.'' She sniffed, tossed her head, blinked back those insistent tears. ''To see that both of my sons were lost and the years I might have had with them— with you, with poor little Kylan—were gone forever and I could never get them back.''

I started to speak.

''Wait,'' she said. ''Please.'' I gave her a nod and she continued, ''I can never express how much I have hated myself, how much I have despised myself for what I have done. I don't expect forgiveness, I swear that I don't. I only want, if you will allow it, a chance to come to know you, just a little.''

The truth tried its best to escape my lips: that I sincerely regretted there was no one left to know. I held that truth back, for it came to me that to say it would have been needlessly cruel; she would have only blamed herself when the blame was not hers. Yes, she had wronged me. But those old wrongs had not stolen my sense of self.

I alone was responsible for that.

And didn't we, then, share a certain commonality beyond the bond of blood, this woman my mother and I? We had both done terrible things—I much more so than she. And now we were living with the awful knowledge of our separate failures. Hers, as a mother. Mine, as a leader of men...

I reached out, took her cool hand, twined my fingers with hers. We sat together for several minutes, unspeaking, in the silent room.

It seemed to me that faintly, far away, I heard the death-cries of my men as they were slaughtered before me. I wondered what cries the woman beside me heard. Perhaps only those of a small, lonely boy searching for the lost mother he would never find.

Chapter 10

So there I was, in my second-best evening gown, my hair loose around my shoulders, all ready to head on down to the Chamber of the Skalds.

As if on cue, there was a knock at my door. I answered to find a tall, sandy-haired fellow all dressed up in white tie and tails.

"I am Prince Rogenvald," the fellow announced, "and I have the honor to escort you to the gala this evening." Another great thing about life at the palace. Not only did they provide a hairdresser if I needed one, but they'd send up an escort without my even having to ask.

I grabbed my evening clutch and off we went.

The Chamber of the Skalds…

What can I say? It was like all the other formal rooms in Isenhalla. Dizzying in its splendor, with a high coffered oak ceiling and a single central row of five massive and bejeweled gold chandeliers, each shaped like a crown, each glowing with at least a hundred lights.

There was a stage at one end, with arched white marble pillars in front and a mural on the wall behind depicting a scene from one of the myths. I made out Odin and Thor and Loki, I think. There were other murals, illustrating other myths, along the side walls behind rows of pillars like the ones that framed the stage.

For the banquet, they'd brought in long tables, covered them with snow-white cloths and set them with gold-rimmed china and sparkling cut crystal and baroque-looking gold candelabras dripping with crystal prisms. As Prince Rogenvald and I entered the hall, a string quartet played something classical from a corner of the stage and many of the princes and ladies had already gathered, all in their glittering formal finery.

I had that moment—you know the kind—where I wondered what I could have been thinking, not to have had the palace hairdresser put up my hair, not to have used my short time in Lysgard to max out my Visa card on a new gown. There are just some events, I scolded myself, when your second-best gown doesn't cut it.

But then I saw Medwyn across the room. He looked at me, gave me the faintest nod and a slight smile of welcome.

And it was okay. I could just…be there and enjoy the beauty and the magic of the evening.

Prince Rogenvald led me to a table in the center of the room—several tables away from where the royal family was seated. He took the chair beside me. We quickly found that we had little to talk about. He spent most of the meal whispering to the brunette on his other side.

Across from me was Prince Sigurd, the old fellow Brit

and I had met in the hallway in the early hours of that morning. He gravely introduced himself and explained to me his lineage. He was a Gudmond, he told me. His great-great grandfather, King Solmund, had ruled Gullandria in the mid-nineteenth century. He announced this fact with pride. I noticed he didn't mention that his ancestor had been known as *Mad* King Solmund—the one, as I recalled from what Brit had said, who'd had the secret passageways improved before completely losing his mind.

Also at my table, seated beside me, was a stocky gray-haired maiden lady in a black gown so heavily beaded that she twinkled all over every time she moved. She was a Wyborn. "I am the Lady Marta," she announced. Hauk Wyborn, she informed me, was her nephew—Hauk's father, deceased for several years now, had been Lady Marta's dear older brother. The Wyborns were all so gratified, she told me, at the honor Hauk had brought to their family. It was only fitting that the king had removed the awful stigma of fitz from Hauk's name. "So that he may be a true Wyborn. So that we may claim him as one who belongs to our proud family."

Lady Marta leaned my way, her jet earrings bouncing merrily, and whispered, "You are Princess Brit's American friend, are you not?" I agreed that I was. She said, "And what was all the excitement, so early this morning? Soldiers running up and down the hallways... I heard there was some attack on Princess Brit and that the young American—you, I presume—was involved...."

"Well, um, it's all worked out now..."

Lady Marta got the message. "I take that to mean you've been asked not to speak of it. Never mind, never mind. I wouldn't put my nose in where it's not wanted."

She smiled a beatific kind of smile and seemed really not to mind that I wouldn't tell her anything. "The queen looks marvelous, don't you think? And see how often she turns to speak with the king? We may have a royal reunion on our hands. She never did divorce him, did you know? That was for Valbrand's sake, it is said."

My heart raced at the sound of his name. I asked, "Why for Prince Valbrand's sake?"

"Well, that his chances at the throne not be diminished. We Gullandrians do have our prejudices. And a king should never be the product of a broken home." She clucked her tongue. "All those years apart, yet still husband and wife. Now, wouldn't it be delightful—wouldn't it be exactly as it should be, were the king and Her Majesty to find their way to each other again in more than name only?

"And see there? Princess Liv is looking ripe. How far along is she now, do you know? I believe—" Lady Marta answered her own question "—she is due to deliver in March.

"And Princess Elli. Our Hauk's wife awaits the most blessed of events, as well. I understand her new little one comes into the world in May. Oh, isn't it...romantic?"

"Oh, yes." I nodded, with enthusiasm.

Lady Marta leaned closer. "And what have we at the next table over? See? The Lady Kaarin Karlsmon. The greatest beauty in all our land—next to Her Majesty and Their Royal Highnesses, of course," Marta hastened to correct herself.

"Of course." I nodded some more.

"See her there, in lavender? Don't make it obvious that you're staring, now, sweet girl."

I glanced, oh-so-casually, at the perfect, slim, silky-haired redhead that Brit had pointed out to me the other night at the ball. She looked as stunning in lavender as she had in pink, her magnificent bare shoulders gleaming in the candlelight. She wore her hair smoothed back from the perfect oval of her face, her only jewelry a pair of huge, dangly gold and pearl earrings. If I'd been the least small-minded, I could have loathed her just on principle.

"Is it any wonder that Prince Valbrand loved her?"

My heart stopped and my stomach lurched. "Excuse me?" I said weakly.

"Well, not to gossip…" Marta waved a plump, bejeweled hand. "And I suppose you already know…"

"Know what, exactly?" I asked, with what I thought was admirable nonchalance.

Lady Marta sighed with gusto, causing all that black beading to sparkle madly. "I shouldn't…" I leaned in closer than ever and presented my ear. She whispered into it, "Well, only that, before His Royal Highness— may Odin smile upon him—went missing at sea, we all felt certain that Valbrand and Lady Kaarin would soon be exchanging marriage swords. We all said what a queen she would make. And they did seem so very madly in love."

I had a kind of hollow feeling, just imagining it. The spectacular Lady Kaarin—and Valbrand. Together. In love.

The most awful thing about it, being in love with the man myself, was that it just seemed so exactly right: the handsome prince, the gorgeous lady…

However, I reminded myself, that was then and this was now. So what if Valbrand had loved the most beautiful woman in the land and she had loved him back? I could live with it—as long as I was certain it was done, dead and totally, utterly completely over between them.

Or if it wasn't, well, better to face facts and start getting over him than to keep on deluding myself.

I asked, "So then…what happened?"

Lady Marta waved her twinkling sleeve. "He was gone for so long. We all thought him lost forever. The gossips whispered of a new love in Lady Kaarin's life— not I, of course. I try not to carry tales."

"I know you would never—but who?"

"Why, Prince Onund Havelock—perhaps you've met him?"

I remembered the other prince, the younger one, in the hallway, after the incident in Brit's bedroom. Brit had called him Onund. "I think so. Tall and slim, with pale blond hair?" Marta nodded and nudged me. I followed the direction of her gaze. Prince Onund sat one table over from Lady Kaarin. "Yes," I whispered. "I've met him. Briefly."

Lady Marta was still nodding. "It would be a fine match, Karlsmon and Havelock. Not as good a match as the one with His Royal Highness, yet certainly an excellent one. Did you know that Prince Onund's grandfather had the throne before King Osrik?" I shook my head. Marta explained, "It was a great upset, the kingmaking in which King Osrik took the throne. It was expected that Gunther Havelock, King Njall Havelock's son and Onund's father, would win. But His Majesty claimed the day. And now Prince Gunther lives in seclusion, a bitter and angry old man, so they say."

With all this talk of who was king when, we were straying from what, to me, was the *important* subject. "And you're saying that now Lady Kaarin and Prince Onund are…engaged?"

"Not formally, no."

"But you think they will be?"

Lady Marta smiled knowingly. "Let me say that I wouldn't be the least surprised."

I made myself say it, though I almost choked on the words, "But if she *loves* Prince Valbrand…"

Lady Marta shrugged her wildly glittering shoulders. "My sweet one, there may have been love, at one time, between Prince Valbrand and Lady Kaarin. But in the circles of power marriage is, first and foremost, a bond between families. Love was not the *reason* they would have exchanged vows."

"Well. It should have been."

Lady Marta chuckled. "So charming. So American…"

"But…does she still love him—Prince Valbrand—do you think?"

Lady Marta pursed up her mouth in thought. "Hmm. His Highness is much changed, since his return. And I do not only mean the terrible scars from his unfortunate injury." I nodded some more, trying to look appropriately somber and no more than politely interested. Marta said, "No, I don't think either of them loves the other anymore. And beyond that, the interest in a lifetime alliance seems to have waned. I don't believe there's any possibility of a marriage between them. From what I have heard, that chapter in both of their lives has come to an end."

"Ah." I said mildly. Inside I was all smiles. I mean, I had assumed that was how it must be. But it's always nice when someone else tells you that no, the one you love doesn't love or want to marry somebody else—especially not somebody else who happened to look like Kaarin Karlsmon.

The next course arrived: small, golden brown game birds drizzled with a berry-red sauce, a perfect miniature baked apple tucked up against either tiny wing.

Valbrand entered just as the game birds were served. I tried not to stare, but the sight of him created a definite rising feeling inside of me. With no urging at all, I could have floated right out of my chair and drifted, smiling, dazed and dreamy, in his wake.

Now, wouldn't that be appropriate?

Pausing now and then to greet any princes or ladies who spoke to him, he made his way to the royal table and took the seat that waited for him, next to the king.

Lady Marta clucked her tongue and murmured, more to herself than to me, "May the gods watch over us. Life is often so cruel."

I decided I ought to concentrate on my food. As long as I was looking down at my plate, it was easier to keep from sending longing glances toward the table where the royal family sat.

As we ate, we were entertained by a series of poems written in honor of the queen's visit and performed by one of Gullandria's most skilled and famous skalds.

There were more courses, more haunting music from the string quartet, more verses from yet another skald. Through it all I occasionally tipped my ear toward Lady Marta to hear another tidbit of gossip. But most of the time, I thought about what she had told me earlier and tried not to let my gaze stray where it shouldn't.

Just before dessert was served, the servants made a quick pass of the entire room, topping off every goblet with sweet Gullandrian ale. Once all the goblets were filled, the king stood. We all followed suit. His Majesty picked up his own goblet and we guests did the same.

"These are joyous times," he announced. "Our royal

family grows. Our beloved queen returns. A toast to Her Majesty.'' He and Ingrid shared a glance—a warm one. Maybe more than warm. Maybe Marta knew what she was talking about and Brit's mom and dad would be getting back together after all the years and years apart. ''Beauty. Pride. Dignity. Strength,'' intoned the king. ''She is all these things. And so much more…'' He lifted his goblet even higher. ''Necessity, Fate and Being. May the three Norns of destiny forever light her way. To our queen.''

''To the queen…''

''The queen…''

''To the queen…'' The toast echoed from every pair of lips, until the sound filled the great hall.

We all drank.

Next, the king toasted the miraculous return of his cherished son. After that, he moved on to the coming marriage of Brit and Eric, to the unions of Liv and Finn, and Elli and Hauk. And then to his grandchildren, soon to be born.

After that, Medwyn stood and offered a few toasts of his own. By that time, I had figured out to take tiny sips whenever a new toast was proposed. I looked around at all the flushed, beaming faces and I knew that there were going to be a few serious hangovers in the morning. I was grinning—yeah, okay. I had a little glow on, myself. Enough of a glow that I forgot, for a fraction of a second, to be careful where I let my glance stray.

And it happened. I looked at Valbrand and he looked at me.

And I was lifted up, out of myself. The Chamber of the Skalds and all the happy, toasting Gullandrians in their glittering evening wear was no more. There was Valbrand. And me. And the too-wide space between us, a space neither of us would allow. We looked only at each other and as we looked, I imagined the space that separated us flashing into flame and burning, in an instant, to nothing.

The king took his seat. So did everyone else.

Somehow, just in time, I remembered myself. Though it ripped my heart in two to do it, I tore my gaze away from those dark, hungry eyes. A servant slid something scrumptiously chocolate in front of me. I sighed and picked up my dessert spoon.

"Delicious, isn't it?" asked Lady Marta after I'd dutifully scooped up a bite.

"Absolutely heavenly," I softly replied.

A few minutes later, I dared to check the watch I was carrying in my evening clutch. It was eleven forty-five.

I slid a glance at the royal table.

Valbrand was gone.

I left the banquet first, before my sweet redhead.

When I went, she had her spoon in her hand and her gaze on her dessert plate. They had seated her next to Lady Marta. I imagined by now her ears must be ringing with all the gossip Lady Marta had poured into them. Hauk's aunt was good-hearted, but frequently indiscreet.

I strode swiftly across the wide entrance corridor, on my way to the stairs and my rooms, looking forward to the comfort of the mask—and more than the mask, to the coming meeting in the secret passageway.

And yes. By then, I understood my true intentions. The burning glance that had passed between us in the banquet hall had seared away all my pretenses. Though I knew it was destined to end in mutual heartbreak, I was through telling myself that I would stay away from my sister's enchanting American friend.

"Valbrand," said a breathless feminine voice behind me. I knew the voice. Kaarin. "Valbrand, wait..."

It flashed through my mind to rush on, more swiftly, to pretend I hadn't heard her, that I didn't know she had hailed me. I felt uncomfortable with the idea of stopping to speak with her. Uncomfortable and somehow vaguely embarrassed.

There had never been any spoken promises between us. But there had been...an understanding, I suppose one might say.

And now?

Now, there was nothing between us. Since my return, I'd felt no desire to seek her out. And until that moment in the entrance hall, she had not come looking for me, either. We saw each other only when it happened that we attended the same function. For me, what had been between us simply was no more. I'd assumed it was the same for her.

I stopped abruptly and turned to face her.

She was rushing so fast, violet skirts drawn up, heavy earrings swaying, that she almost ran into me. "Valbrand!" She stopped just in time, drawing back in a rustle of silk, one delicate hand spread over the swell of her breast as she caught her breath.

"Yes?"

She made the mistake then of looking directly into my face. Those Delft-blue eyes widened the tiniest bit. She recovered well, but not quiet well enough. I was, by then, an expert at recognizing revulsion.

She blinked, met my eyes briefly, and then quickly glanced away. It was well done. As if she fought to mask a great yearning. "It's only that...since your miraculous return to us, I hardly see you." She swept her lashes down and gazed up at me, artfully, from under them. "You never look for me...."

I wondered, without much real interest, what sort of game she might be playing. "And you're implying you have wished for that? For me to look for you?"

A couple of the older princes walked by us, their ladies on their arms. They nodded and spoke polite greetings. I replied in kind.

Kaarin snared my arm. "Please. But a moment, just the two of us..." She pulled me under an archway, to a shadowed corner of the entrance hall, and guided me down beside her onto a short marble bench.

I let her do it. She had, after all, once been the woman I planned to wed.

Our affair had been a passionate one. At the time, she had fascinated me. Such a perfect lady on the surface. Such unquenchable hungers once I had her out of her clothes. Now, I admitted to a certain morbid curiosity. What was she leading to?

More than likely, she feared that I still intended to step forward as a candidate in the next kingmaking. Perhaps she'd come to believe I would win. It had always been Kaarin's intention to be queen.

I wanted to tell her frankly, *Don't concern yourself with me. I am certain now that I will never be king.*

But that seemed, somehow, a betrayal of my poor, hopeful father. Before I casually told others that I wouldn't seek the throne, I felt a duty to give my father time to relinquish his lifelong dream of a dynasty of Thorson kings.

"What do you wish of me?" I looked at her, waiting.

She took a long, slightly shaky breath. So fetching. And so flustered—though until then, I had never known Kaarin Karlsmon to be flustered over anything. "I only hoped that…we might have a little time. Together. A moment or two to talk…''

"Why?"

She looked away. Much easier, I thought with considerable cynicism, than looking at me. "The Norns curse you, Valbrand. You are making this so very difficult.…''

I stared at the smooth line of her neck, at her perfect pink ear, the lobe stretched by the weight of her huge earring, at the swirl of sleek red hair pinned at her nape. The very redness of that hair had me thinking of Dulcie, though the color was different: Kaarin's lighter, Dulcie's darker, richer—a mass of wonderful, unruly curls…

As I thought of my adorable redheaded darling, I turned my head away from the woman beside me—and there she was in her simple green dress, crossing the entrance corridor, passing the shadowed spot where I sat with Kaarin.

Her deep red hair like spun fire, curling free around her shoulders, she walked quickly, with purpose, vanishing from my view but a moment after she appeared. I suppressed a smile at the sight.

Ah, Dulcie.

Off to meet her dark rescuer in the secret space behind the wall.

I turned my head to find Kaarin watching me.

"So," she said flatly. "It's *that* way, is it?"

"Kaarin…" I took her hand.

She allowed my touch, but with a show of reluctance, sliding me a fulminating glance, her perfect nostrils flaring as if at some noxious smell. "I cannot believe it," she muttered. "A nobody. A frowsy, ordinary—"

I raised my free hand for quiet and gave her a dark look of warning. "You go too far."

"Oh, do I?" The blue eyes flashed.

"Do not," I warned softly, "say another word against an innocent woman who brings only goodness and light wherever she goes."

She started to speak. I squeezed her hand, grinding the bones just a little. She shut her mouth and drew a calming breath, the fine nostrils flaring again.

When I saw she would obey me, I released my punishing grip on her fingers and said in the gentlest tone I could manage, "What was between the two of us is gone—has been gone for a goodly time, now. I thought you had accepted the way things are, that you were content. I thought you had moved on to another love."

"You assumed how I felt," she accused. "You never asked."

"And why shouldn't I assume? It's been nearly three months since I returned from my…misadventures at sea and my sojourn in the north country. In all that time, we've hardly spoken. And I have heard from more than one source that you and Onund Havelock—"

She shook her head, the large earrings swaying hard. "Gossip," she hissed. "You heard gossip, that's all. Surely you know better than to listen to the tittle-tattle of old wives and ugly spinsters with too much time on their hands."

"All right, then. If you say it's not true about you and Onund—"

"It's not."

"Fair enough. But either way, it doesn't matter."

"Yes, it does. Of course it does."

"No. That's not so. Whatever your relationship with the Havelock prince, the fact remains I had not the slightest sign from you that you might—"

"*You* had no sign from *me?* How can you be so cruel?

See it from my perspective. I was only waiting—for a word, a kind look..."

I wanted, right then, to simply rise and walk away. I was impatient with Kaarin and I knew a great eagerness to be gone, to see Dulcie, to hear her voice, to gaze for a precious too-brief time into eyes that had met mine that first night in the ballroom without flinching at what they saw. Yet it seemed there ought to be a way to finish this properly, to reach the mutual understanding I had thought Kaarin and I had already found.

Gently I reminded her, "Kaarin, it is wisest not to try to resurrect what is dead." As I said those words, I noted their irony in my own case. For I had, in a very real sense, been dead. My current resurrection seemed to me no more than marginally successful.

Kaarin was not playing this for irony. "But... Oh, Valbrand. What if I were to tell you that what we shared is not dead for me?" She met my eyes hopefully. Perhaps even tenderly. She was extremely convincing.

But you must understand. I had known Kaarin since we were children. She had always possessed an uncanny ability to dissemble. During the time we were lovers, when I honestly thought the day would come that she would be my queen, I had alternately disliked the false faces she could assume—and admired them. It is not such a terrible thing for a queen to be skilled at intrigue. And, as I have said before, I was vain. Also, in ways I would have denied adamantly if challenged, I was inexperienced. At that time, I imagined she might inveigle others, but that I could control her, that she would not dare to deceive *me*.

Now, both innocence and vanity had been blasted away. I looked at Kaarin and saw nothing of interest to me.

Her eyes were dewy, as with barely held-back tears. She gazed at me as though her heart would break. "What if I were to tell you that it is my dearest, most passionate dream that we might somehow find again what we lost when you went away?"

"Why then, Kaarin. I would tell you to look for another dream. And I would ask you, as I already have, to let go of the past and get on with your life."

The dewy look vanished as if it had never been. She regarded me through basilisk eyes. "You're through with me. Is that what you're saying?"

"We are through with each other. And I think you know it, too. I don't know what naughty scheme you've concocted, but whatever it is, it isn't going to work on me."

It was then that she pulled back her slim arm and slapped me with the back of her hand, stingingly, across the face—the right side. The unscarred side. I thought as she did it that it was a good choice. There was considerable numbness on the damaged side. Had she slapped me there, it would have hardly hurt at all. I put my hand to the burning spot and without a word, she rose, gathered her skirts in her fists and stalked off.

I was, as you might well imagine, more than a little relieved to see her go.

By then, the guests were beginning to file out in ever-increasing numbers. I waited for a time, alone on the marble bench, longing to be up and gone and on my way to Dulcie, yet having no desire to be seen leaving the shadowed area beneath the archway with the clear, red imprint of Kaarin's slap on my cheek.

To wait was a mistake. When I did emerge from the shadows, my father and the queen were just leaving the Chamber of the Skalds.

Wearing a broad smile of royal good humor, Osrik called, "Valbrand. There you are, my son. Accompany us, if you please."

In my room, every nerve humming with delicious anticipation, I ripped off my dress and pulled on a big cable-knit sweater and a pair of jeans. I stuck my feet in my trusty canvas Keds and tied the laces, fingers shaking. By then, it was two minutes to midnight.

My heart thudding hard, my cheeks hot with hope and eagerness, I grabbed the flashlight from its drawer and went through the armoire, shining my light ahead of me up the cold, gleaming corridor, expecting to find the dark figure in the smooth black mask.

Nothing.

He wasn't there.

Yet, I told myself silently, firmly. He's not here *yet....*

I shut the opening behind me and leaned against the wall that led to my bedroom and waited.

And waited.

And waited some more.

Eventually, instead of merely leaning, I was slumping. I wished I'd thought to bring my watch. But it seemed too absurd, somehow, to go back for it—it wasn't as if I needed it. I had nowhere else I was going that night. And what good would it do me to be able to count every minute he was late?

I listened—for the sound of footsteps in the corridor, increasingly aware that if I heard anything, it would more likely be the king's men than Valbrand, aka the Dark Raider.

The Dark Raider, after all, could move around without making a sound.

And if the king's men did come—as the Dark Raider

had warned they might—I'd be better off if they didn't know I was here. I turned off my flashlight. Safer that way. If the king's men showed up, there'd be no chance they'd see its glow. And I moved to the other wall, the one through which I could enter the shorter corridor. I figured, if the soldiers came, I'd do what Valbrand had done, melt into the wall itself. I felt for the place to press. Found it. Kept my finger on it so that I would be ready if I needed to be.

And yes, I was getting that feeling.

That droopy, disappointed feeling.

The feeling that he wasn't going to come.

I waited some more. I didn't know for sure how much time passed, but I estimated half an hour at least.

I lasted another few minutes and then I couldn't bear not to have my watch to keep me company. By then, I felt I had to have the time in my hands, so I could keep checking. There was no logic to my reasoning. It was all about longing and increasing misery.

I went back through the armoire. My travel clock said it was 12:46.

I knew it then. I accepted it. He was not going to come.

So why did I get my watch from my evening clutch, strap it on my wrist and go back into the hidden corridor?

I'll give you a hint. It's a four-letter word and it starts with L. And please don't start in about how I couldn't possibly love him, that I didn't really know him, that we'd shared four brief encounters: at the ball, in Brit's room, in the passageway and a few hours ago when our eyes met across the crowded banquet hall. And I know what you're thinking: that the time in Brit's room, when he was beating up the bad guys, hardly counted as a meeting. And yeah, okay, maybe the moment at the banquet didn't count, either. After all, it had only been a look.

But I'll say it again. I loved him the moment I saw him. That was just how it was. So there I stood in the dark with my flashlight ready, occasionally flipping it on to check and see how late he was now.

At 1:22, I finally became discouraged enough to start seeing myself as the utter and complete fool I probably was. Really, I should get professional help.

And even if I didn't pay a visit to a shrink, I had to give up rushing to meet a man who'd told me to stay away, a man who'd never said he'd be there, who'd shushed me the first time I met him—a man who, half the time, pretended to be someone else.

In my disappointment, I saw how really pathetic it was: me, in the corridor, waiting for my deeply damaged masked prince.

And waiting...

And waiting...

It had to stop. I had to accept that he just wasn't coming.

I backed around to the wall that led to my room, opened the door in the armoire by feel and went through. I closed everything up and put my flashlight in the drawer and took off my watch. Hurt and angry that he hadn't come—in spite of the fact that he'd never even *said* he would come—I kicked off my Keds and yanked off the rest of my clothes and put on my pajamas. Then I stuck my feet in my comfy fuzzy slippers and went into the bathroom to get rid of the evening's makeup and brush my teeth.

When I came back into the bedroom, the Dark Raider was sitting on the sofa over by the fire.

Chapter 11

It just proves how accustomed I was getting to surprises that I didn't let out so much as a tiny little shriek. And yes, I admit, my heart leapt in joy and all that. But joy wasn't all of it. There was definite irritation. It had been a long night and too much of it had been spent waiting for His Royal Highness to appear.

"Hey, how're you doing?" I sneered. "And in case you didn't notice, you're in my bedroom." I cast a rueful glance down at myself. Somehow, I hadn't pictured myself wearing flannelette pajamas with dancing ladybugs printed on them the first time I got him alone like this.

He looked seriously sexy, I am not kidding, sprawled on the white damask of the Louis XV sofa—all lean, hard limbs, all in black. And the mask…

Well, I was never one for bondage fantasies. But it did remind me of that, you know? Those leather bondage masks you can buy in certain shops on Santa Monica Boulevard—you know the kind of places I mean. Places with names like The Pleasure Chest—though a bondage mask is more of a hood, and the Dark Raider's mask didn't cover the back of his head. There must have been some kind of thin band, at the back, to hold it in place....

And yes. I'd been in a bondage shop. I'm a writer, remember? I considered it my duty to go anywhere I could learn more about the human condition. And that included the interesting and unconventional sexual practices of same. Thus, in my mind, I had an exciting sex life all the time, whether I had a lover or not. And yeah, okay, I confess. It was mostly *not*. As a rule, I was too busy juggling writing and subsistence jobs to have time for a man in my life.

And speaking of men...

Back to the one on the sofa.

He watched me. Steadily. I looked into those shining dark eyes and I wondered how he could kid himself that I didn't know who he was. I would know him anywhere, if I could look in his eyes. If I could get close enough to take a deep breath and suck in the scent of him, I could pick him out blindfolded, in a crowd, with my ears covered so I couldn't hear and my hands tied behind my back.

"Well?" I said, pugnaciously. And when he said nothing, I said, "Well?" again.

"I apologize—" he regally inclined his head "—for coming to you so late."

His apology didn't impress me. I remained in sneering mode. "Hey, don't worry about it. Just show up anytime, just walk right through the wall."

"Dulcie. It couldn't be helped."

"Because?"

"I was...unavoidably detained."

There was a chair that matched the sofa. I flounced over and dropped into it. "Detained by what?"

He looked away. "I cannot say."

"Well, okay. I'll say it for you. Not a *what*, right? Not a *what*, but a *whom*." I shoved off my slippers and drew up my legs, crossing them, grabbing my ankles and tucking them close. "Yeah. That's probably it. A whom. Some damsel in distress, I bet. Someone gorgeous. With well-behaved hair and the proper pedigree—and you know what? Don't tell me. I really *don't* want to know."

"No damsel, Dulcie. No one but you. I promise you."

I made a humphing sound. "And, besides, you didn't have to come here. You never said you would."

"We both knew I would."

There was one of those moments. We looked at each other. And we looked at each other some more. As we shared that endless look, it seemed to me that the air was humming, along with my body, everything just quivering and warm, full of light and excitement.

Finally, I shrugged. "Yeah. We both knew that you would...." My voice was softer, with a kind of pleasant roughness to it, like when a cat purrs.

He leaned forward, canting toward me, losing the sprawl, his eyes sharper now, and probing. "A moment ago..." I leaned toward him, too. "You said someone with the *right pedigree*."

"Yeah, so?"

Another long moment, with us doing the drowning thing in each other's eyes, with everything shimmering and warm and so, so beautiful...

Finally he whispered, "You *know*, don't you?"

My throat clutched. I swallowed. "Um-hm. I know."

"Say it."

"I know you're Valbrand."

"I see."

There was a pause long enough to drive a flock of fat-tailed Gullandrian sheep through. Finally, he said, "Well, then…"

"Yes?"

"There's no reason not to tell you where I've been. It was my father who detained me. He asked that I accompany him and my mother to his private audience room. I suspect he commanded my presence because he knew it would ensure him Her Majesty's company for an hour or two beyond the formal setting of the banquet. We spoke of many things—her shop in Sacramento. She sells antiques, did you know?" I nodded. "And of the girl she cares for, Finn Danelaw's sister, Eveline. The girl, evidently, thrives in America. There was talk of the coming wedding. And of the grandchildren they would soon enjoy. It was…touching, to see them on such cordial terms. I tried to be patient throughout. But my father remarked more than once that I seemed distracted." He looked at me steadily. "And I was. I was longing to be elsewhere.…" He wore his black gloves. Slowly he removed them, pulling each finger loose, then the whole glove, dropping them, one and then the other, on the low table in front of him. He raised his hands to the mask.

"Oh, please," I said, my voice thick with sudden urgency. "Let me…"

He dropped his hands and lowered his head, a sort of bow that was also a nod. I uncurled my legs and stood. He looked up then, and across at me. I'd never seen those dark eyes so soft. I went to him, padding around the coffee table in my bare feet, brushing a hand against his hard thigh so that he would move it enough that I could step between his legs. Happily trapped between his muscular thighs, I cupped the warm mask, and his face beneath it, in my own two hands.

He looked up at me, yearning. Needing...

I can't tell you, I can't find the words for how perfect and right it was, to stand there, cradling Valbrand's hidden face, my palms pressed to the bare, hot skin of his throat, my fingers brushed by his silky hair.

I wanted it loose, his hair. To comb through it with my fingers. I dared to slide my right hand back, around his neck—he didn't stop me—and grasp the band that held his hair. I gave it a pull, dropped it behind him, and his hair fell loose.

And I did what I wanted, combed the ends of it with my fingers. I loved the satin slide of it. The warmth, the living feel of it. Of him—yet not. One of the few parts of a person that can be cut without pain or bleeding. It will only grow back if taken away.

I bent closer. Felt his breath across my cheek. Laid my face against his hair. I breathed deep, taking in the scent of him. It was a green kind of scent, like new grass—new grass and leather and something else, something very male. I lifted up just slightly, enough to press a kiss at the crown of his head, on that vulnerable place where his hair parted.

When I would have moved back, he stopped me, his strong hands at my waist—and that was a new thing, a thing as wonderful and intoxicating as the rest. To feel his hands on me, holding me, through the soft flannel of my pajamas.

I said something meaningless, a hopeful, tender sound.

He turned his masked face into my hair and whispered, "I love your hair. So full and wild. Like a cloud of red silk. It smells like lemons...."

"Valbrand..." I slipped my hand around, found the bands—there were two of them, crisscrossed—that held the mask in place. "I went to the palace library today...."

He pulled away enough to look up at me. "And?"

"I researched you—that is, I researched the Dark Raider. It's a fascinating legend...."

"Yes, it is."

"What gave you the idea—to play the Dark Raider?"

He caught my hands, held them between his, away from the mask. "I do not play. I *am* the Dark Raider, when I put on the mask. I am, as much as any of the others were."

"Others..."

"The Dark Raiders before me."

"But I thought it was only a legend."

"Most legends have their basis in fact. The first Dark Raider, for example..."

I couldn't resist showing off what I'd learned. "The one who fought the Danes at King Thorlak's side?"

"The same. Many of our scholars are certain that he was Ander Thorson, a freeman who rose from obscurity—my ancestor, who became high jarl in a lifetime and grand counselor to King Thorlak, who was the first of the Wyborn kings."

I was enchanted. "The first Dark Raider might have been your ancestor?"

"Yes."

"Wow. But you still haven't said why you decided to, um, resurrect him."

He let go of my hands and sat back to look at me in a measuring way. "And what leads you to believe I *will* tell you?"

"Because you're here. Because you've admitted that

An Important Message from the Editors

Dear Nora Roberts Fan,

Because you've chosen to read one of our wonderful romance novels, we'd like to say "thank you!" And as a special way to thank you, we've selected two books to send you from a series that is similar to the book that you are currently enjoying. Plus, we'll also send an exciting Mystery Gift, absolutely FREE!

Please enjoy them with our compliments.

Pam Powers

Peel off seal and Place inside...

EDITOR'S
FREE GIFT
SEAL
THANK YOU

How to validate your Editor's
FREE GIFT
"Thank You"

1. Peel off gift seal from front cover. Place it in space provided at right. This automatically entitles you to receive 2 FREE BOOKS and a fabulous mystery gift.

2. Send back this card and you'll get 2 brand new novels from Silhouette Romance®, the series that brings you traditional stories of love, marriage and family. These books have a cover price of $3.99 each in the U.S. and $4.50 each in Canada, but they are yours to keep absolutely free.

3. There's no catch. You're under no obligation to buy anything. We charge nothing—ZERO— for your first shipment. And you don't have to make any minimum number of purchases— not even one!

4. The fact is, thousands of readers enjoy receiving their books by mail from the Silhouette Reader Service™. They enjoy the convenience of home delivery...they like getting the best new novels at discount prices BEFORE they're available in stores...and they love their *Heart to Heart* subscriber newsletter featuring author news, horoscopes, recipes, book reviews and much more!

5. We hope that after receiving your free books you'll want to remain a subscriber. But the choice is yours—to continue or cancel, any time at all! So why not take us up on our invitation, with no risk of any kind. You'll be glad you did!

6. And remember...just for validating your Editor's Free Gift Offer, we'll send you THREE gifts, *ABSOLUTELY FREE!*

GET A *Free* MYSTERY GIFT...

THIS SURPRISE MYSTERY GIFT COULD BE YOURS FREE AS A SPECIAL "THANK YOU" FROM THE EDITORS OF SILHOUETTE BOOKS

Visit us online at
www.eHarlequin.com

The Editor's "Thank You" Free Gifts Include:

- Two Silhouette Romance® novels!
- An exciting mystery gift!

PLACE
FREE GIFT
SEAL
HERE

YES! I have placed my Editor's "Thank You" seal in the space provided above. Please send me 2 free books and a fabulous mystery gift. I understand I am under no obligation to purchase any books, as explained on the back and on the opposite page.

310 SDL DZ3T   210 SDL DZ3S

FIRST NAME	LAST NAME

ADDRESS

APT.#	CITY

STATE/PROV.	ZIP/POSTAL CODE

(N-SR-1-04)

Thank You!

The Silhouette Reader Service™—Here's How It Works:

Accepting your 2 free books and mystery gift places you under no obligation to buy anything. You may keep the books and gift and return the shipping statement marked "cancel." If you do not cancel, about a month later we'll send you 4 additional books and bill you just $3.34 each in the U.S., or $3.80 each in Canada, plus 25¢ shipping and handling per book and applicable taxes if any.* That's the complete price and — compared to cover prices of $3.99 in the U.S. and $4.50 in Canada — it's quite a bargain! You may cancel at any time, but if you choose to continue, every month we'll send you 4 more books, which you may either purchase at the discount price or return to us and cancel your subscription.

*Terms and prices subject to change without notice. Sales tax applicable in N.Y. Canadian residents will be charged applicable provincial taxes and GST. Credit or debit balances in a customer's account(s) may be offset by any other outstanding balance owed by or to the customer.

If offer card is missing write to: The Silhouette Reader Service, 3010 Walden Ave., P.O. Box 1867, Buffalo, NY 14240-1867

BUSINESS REPLY MAIL

FIRST-CLASS MAIL   PERMIT NO. 717-003   BUFFALO, NY

POSTAGE WILL BE PAID BY ADDRESSEE

SILHOUETTE READER SERVICE
3010 WALDEN AVE
PO BOX 1867
BUFFALO NY 14240-9952

NO POSTAGE
NECESSARY
IF MAILED
IN THE
UNITED STATES

you're Valbrand. Because you know in your heart I can be trusted. I will never betray any secret you share with me. I will die first.''

He sat forward again and reached up to brush his warm hand from my temple, along my cheek, to my chin. I shivered in delight at that touch. ''How would I know so much about you?'' he asked. ''I have spent no more than a few brief moments in your charming company.''

I beamed. ''Charming. I like that.''

''It is only the truth.''

''And you *do* know,'' I insisted. ''You know that I can be trusted.'' I pulled a wry face. ''Too bad your sister doesn't.''

He touched my lips and made them tingle. ''Try to understand. My sister is counted in the council of the king. That is a rare thing, for a woman. To remain there, she must constantly prove herself. Should my father ever discover that she was indiscreet…'' He let the thought finish itself.

''I understand,'' I said. And I did, I supposed. ''And back to why you—''

He put his finger against my lips again. ''Shh…''

I faked a glare. ''You know, you shushed me that first night, in the ballroom. Before I even said a word.''

He traced my brows and the line of my nose. ''You are a woman who occasionally requires shushing, I'm afraid.''

I stuck out my chin at him. ''Have I just been insulted?''

He caught my hands again, brought them to either side of the mask. I cradled his hidden face and, from behind the slanted eyeholes, he looked at me, a deep look. I could have fallen in, I swear, just dropped right through the center of those midnight eyes. "Will you unmask me, then? Or would you prefer not to confront the horror beneath?"

My heart ached when he said that. It ached for him, for his suffering in the past, and now. For the sad fact that this—his unmasking and my response to what waited beneath—was a test. I knew I would pass it. And I hurt all the more for him, that he feared I might not.

I bent close, pressing my right cheek to the left side of the mask, feeling the warmth of the ruined flesh beneath. "I will tell you my secret," I whispered. He made a low sound, of acknowledgement—or maybe encouragement. I said, "Because I trust you, absolutely..."

He murmured, "More caution is called for, I think."

"That's where you're wrong." I stroked his silky hair, caressed the side of his neck, let my hand stray outward, over his hard, wide shoulder. I kissed his ear. I felt a shiver go through him at the touch of my lips. I shivered myself in pure joy. I spoke low, against his ear. "When I tell you, I don't want you to think I'm asking anything more of you than you want to give. Because I'm not. Do you understand?"

After a moment, he answered. "Yes."

"Then okay. It's only this. That I love you. I loved you the moment I saw you." I pulled back to look in his eyes again. He watched me. I got the sense that he didn't know what to do—get up and get out? Grab me and kiss me and rip off my PJs?

See, I didn't care—what he did, what he said. Yeah, okay, I would have preferred that he didn't jump up and walk out. But it wasn't about what he would do when I told him. It wasn't about him loving me back.

My mom always said that you shouldn't be looking for what you're going to get. You should be asking yourself, *What am I willing to give?* And I already knew that I would give everything. And that no matter what happened, I wouldn't count it a loss.

I had my hands on the mask again. He allowed that. I said, looking straight in his eyes, "I loved you when I first saw you. And when I first saw you, you weren't wearing this mask."

His eyes burned into mine. "Then remove it."

I obeyed—gently, with great care. I eased my fingers under the soft, supple leather and I slid the black mask up and off, dropping it beside him on the sofa.

I cupped that beautiful, horrible face in my two hands again, tipping it up to me. He watched me from those dark, dark eyes. Wary. Shattered. I brought my mouth down and I kissed his mangled cheek. I traced, with my lips, the shape of the scarring, the white ridges like raised veins over the uneven red and purple skin beneath. Lightly, tenderly, I brushed my mouth over every inch, every last crevice and discolored place, from the rough ridge at his jaw, to the pinched, mangled skin of his ruined eyelid and on up to his temple, where the scarring clung to his skull, making the damaged tissue all the more prominent.

When I had kissed all of the left side of his face, I moved my mouth near his ear again and whispered, "I love you."

He was very still, his breathing carefully controlled.

And then, with a suddenness that brought a startled cry from me, he reached up, cupped the back of my neck and dragged my mouth down onto his.

Chapter 12

I grabbed for Dulcie, pulling that tender mouth down to mine. I kissed her hard—as if I would hurt her, punish her, make her wish she had never been so foolish as to unmask such a man as I.

She let me. She helped me, parting those soft lips for the harsh attack of my tongue, spearing her fingers into my hair. I tasted her, devouring.

She never pulled back, never tried to make me soften my attack. And by that very acceptance, she gentled me.

The kiss changed.

Became something tender, something young and questing and tentative. She stood between my spread thighs, bending over me, her hair, wild silk and the scent of lemons, falling against my face, making a curtain to shelter us.

When she pulled back, her full mouth was red and swollen. And she was smiling.

I clasped her waist again in both my hands. She was

soft, fleshier than some. Generous—her body, somehow, a mirror of her spirit.

I wanted to see her breasts, her soft belly, all of her— I, who had thought never again to know sexual pleasure. It was part of my penance, my self-inflicted punishment, for my heinous vanity and blindness. My manhood had died. It lay, between my thighs, a useless dangle of flesh, limp and forever unresponsive, though my body lived on.

Or so I had thought.

Until Dulcie.

I wondered at my willingness to have her—when I could promise her nothing and she was the kind of woman who deserved to have it all. I saw my lust for her as yet more proof of how low I had fallen, that I even considered taking her, a good woman, a woman of pure heart, a woman to whom a husk of a man such as I had no right.

But at that moment, when she looked down at me, her mouth bruised from my hurtful kiss, I knew there was one thing that saved her from me.

I was Gullandrian. And I wasn't prepared.

"Dulcie…" My voice was rough, the edge of need clear in it.

"Um?" She stroked the side of my throat, trailed her hand back, beneath my hair to rub my nape.

I turned my mouth to the pale velvet of her inner arm, a few inches above where her pulse beat at her wrist. I kissed her there, whispered against her skin, "I must go."

She laughed—a low, lovely, delighted laugh. And she kept on caressing me, tracing my ear, touching again the blasted, semi-numb skin of my face, then trailing her hand down, along my neck to the V at the top of my shirt. She traced that, too, her imprudent finger descending to the top button, twisting a curl of hair there briefly, then slowly moving up again. "Why?"

My manhood strained at my breeches. No useless dangle now. "I have no contraceptives, I can't—"

"But you see—" her finger was against my lips "—I do."

My heart slammed hard against my breastbone. And the bulge in my breeches throbbed, without conscience, knowing nothing but need. If I took her, I knew it was going to be awkward. It was going to be fast.

She sweetly explained, "Oh, well, yeah. I guess I'm shameless. I knew I wanted you. And so I figured if I got my chance, I ought to be prepared. So today, I went down into Lysgard and I bought a box of condoms."

I swallowed, hard. "You shouldn't have done that."

"Oh, I think you're wrong. I think I should have. I'm glad I did." She scooted in closer, so her knees pressed the edge of the sofa. And then she slid her hand out, over the curve of my shoulder and down until she captured my hand. "Come. To bed. With me…"

I searched her flushed, enchanting face. "So simply, without a care? You are not a woman to give herself without a care."

"Yes, I am, if it's you I'm giving myself to."

"Dulcie, *I* have nothing to give *you*. No promises to make you. If we are lovers, that's all it will be. A few finite days of kisses and caresses. My sister's wedding. And then, you go."

She sighed. "I understand. I truly do." She brought my hand up, to her mouth, kissed the knuckles, one by one. "I told you, and you *can* believe me. I can love you and be with you and…be glad. For whatever we have, for however long it might last."

I simply was not man enough to continue to refuse her. I wanted her. It was a deep, demanding hunger. And if she would insist on offering herself up to me...

"So be it."

She laughed again—joyous, ardent, eager—and stepping free of my legs, she tugged on my hand. "If our time is short, we shouldn't waste a minute."

I rose and I reached for her.

She came into my arms with a long, sweet sigh, all curves and tender hollows, all woman in the truest sense. I lowered my head and I kissed her, long and with thoroughness. Then I scooped her up against my chest and carried her to the bed.

I set her down among the froth of blankets and kissed her some more—long, sweet, lingering kisses. One and then another and another after that.

She pulled me onto the bed with her and, giggling against my hungry mouth, she pushed me back. On her knees beside me, she announced, "Boots first." And she pulled them off, taking my stockings after that. And after that, the rest of it. Every stitch of clothing I had. She peeled off the pieces and she tossed them away.

I lay quiescent as she undressed me, only moving this way and that at her urging, so that she could get my vest down my arm, or pull loose a sleeve. Such passivity seemed the wisest course, to let her do as she wished with me—for then.

I sensed a swift and, for her, unsatisfactory conclusion. At least, that first time.

She had me naked, manhood jutting, sprawled among the bedclothes, in no time. Her tender task accomplished, she sat back on her haunches and studied her handiwork. "Excellent," she declared. Her tone teased. Her eyes were moss-green, soft and glowing.

I lifted my arm and wrapped my fingers around her wrist. "Come here."

There were no objections, only a yielding sigh. I pulled her toward me. She accommodated, hitching a leg across my hips, straddling me. "Valbrand..." Her sweet face, over mine, that fire-bright cloud of fragrant hair falling forward, brushing my chest...

I reached up, speared my fingers in that red luxuriance. Cupping the curve of her head, I pulled her mouth down to mine.

She opened, sighing. With a greedy tongue, I charted the moist terrain beyond her lips as she pressed her sweetness against me, the cove of her hips at my waist now, her full breasts, soft as down pillows, pushing at my chest.

I put my hands to the slope of her shoulders, clasping. She made a questioning sound as I pushed her up so I could see her above me, hair a wild red nimbus, pale cheeks flushed pink, her mouth swollen from my plundering kisses. She lifted her hips, settling herself more comfortably upon me, the groove of her sex pressing the hard ridge of my member, but still shielded by the nightclothes she wore. She groaned a little—as did I—at that intimate settling, and she looked down at me through lazy, low-lidded eyes. "Um..."

"You are, I think, much too well-covered."

She slid her hips, naughtily, against me, forcing from me a muffled, anguished sound. And she laughed, gesturing wide with both hands. "You don't like my pajamas?"

"I adore them. Yet I adore all the more what is beneath them." I slid one hand down from its place on her shoulder, slowly, to the middle of her chest.

She looked down and sighed. One by one I loosed the

shiny red buttons. Beneath my hand, I felt the radiance of her body's heat and the slight movement of her chest at each breath she took and the beating of her true and tender heart. She watched, mouth slightly parted, cheeks flushed, as if the sight of my hand against those enchantingly foolish pajamas excited her. I knew for a fact that the sight excited me.

When I reached the last button, I eased both hands beneath her downy textured collar, palms sliding along the curves and hollows of the velvet flesh beneath. She gasped, tossing that mass of Titian curls, and a shudder went through her. Her eyelids drooped lower. She whispered my name.

I eased the shirt back. She straightened her arms so I could guide it down. I whisked the thing off and tossed it away.

And she looked down again, at her own lush white breasts, with their vulnerable tracings of delicate blue veins, dusted near her breastbone with tiny freckles, the nipples small and pink and tight with arousal. She looked at me and she crossed her eyes, wide mouth stretching in a silly face. "I'm almost naked. Now how did that happen?"

I smiled, not caring now that my smile was abhorrent, knowing she saw beneath whatever masks I wore. I smiled, and she smiled in answer, her mouth blooming slowly to a bold, naughty grin.

I said, "You are not nearly naked enough."

She looked at me coyly, from under her lashes. "Well, what shall we do about it?"

Holding her shining eyes, I cupped one full breast, letting the impudent nipple slip between my first and second fingers. I rubbed those two fingers together and found much satisfaction, not only in the hot, ripe weight of her breast in my hand and the feel of her nipple trapped by my fingers, but also in her breathy, guttural moan.

"It is so simple," I said.

"Ah," she replied, a sound that might have been agreement—yet perhaps not. Perhaps, in actuality, it was another moan.

I explained, "You will remove what remains."

"Ah," she said again, her full hips dragging on me, forward and then back, the barrier of cloth more enflaming each time she moved. I wondered if I would last, even, until I entered her, or if I would shame myself, spilling my seed like an untried boy, merely from the feel of her rubbing against me.

My manhood throbbed, the skin that encased it now far too tight, the heat of it aching, demanding the one burial for which men have always yearned—the sweet burial in woman that culminates in the only happy death: the little one. I groaned.

She said, "But removing the rest could be a problem, since I'm sitting on you and I can't get my bottoms off while you are so—" she paused to heave a quivering sigh "—very much in the way."

I groaned. Again. "In the way, am I?"

She rubbed some more, back and forth. "You are, you are…"

It was too much. I let go of her breast and gathered her in, all that soft, giving sweetness. Velvet and heat and the smell of citrus and woman, of fresh cream and roses… I buried my face in her hair and breathed deep.

And then I caught her hot mouth and kissed her some more, my two hands, starved for the feel of her, roaming her soft back, counting the tender bumps of her spine.

Then, holding her to me with my left arm, I let my right hand stray....

Around the gentle inward curve of her waist, over her rounded belly to the drawstring waist of her pajamas. I caught the end of the bow at the front. A tug and the bow gave way. I slid my hand inside. She whimpered into my mouth. I took that sweet, surrendering sound inside of me as I explored the tangle of thickly curling silk between her open thighs, sliding my fingers down to cup her mound, lifting.

Her body obeyed my silent command. She raised up enough that I had more playing room.

And play I did, slipping a finger along the slick, wet groove that was already soft and ready for me. Delving in—one finger, then two, aware always of that tender nub, the bud where the petals parted. That, I attended with the heel of my hand.

She was moving now, above me, moaning into my mouth, whimpering a little, breaking our kiss to bury her head in the curve of my shoulder as I guided her onward with my stroking hand.

She gave herself up, riding my hand, madly, then slowly, then madly again. In the end, she cried out, grabbing my wrist, holding it still. I felt the pulsing, the rush of increased wetness, silky and thick as some rare and magical oil. She put her mouth to mine again, and she kissed me deeply, groaning as her climax slowly faded to a tender glow.

In the end, she collapsed on top of me. I wrapped both arms around her and kissed her fragrant hair.

She made a growling sound. ''That was *so* not fair....''

I kissed her soft cheek, guiding a wild coil of hair out

of her eye, the scent of her on my fingers, musky and rich. "You didn't like it?"

She giggled then. "No. I only came to be polite."

I caught her face between my two hands and soundly kissed her nose. "Good of you."

"Yes, I thought so." She pulled back.

I demanded, "Where are you going?"

She was bouncing upward, levering back to her feet and then standing to her height on the mattress, straddling me. She had the waist of the pajamas in each fist, holding them up since I had untied them. From the waist up, she was gloriously naked to my hungry eyes. She looked down between those beautiful, heavy breasts. "Time to get rid of these..." She shoved them down, lifting one foot at the last possible moment, whipping her leg out, then toppling to the side with a cry of mock-dismay.

She fell to the right of me, legs akimbo, yanking the hindering pajamas free and tossing them over the end of the bed to the floor. I turned to my side and canted up over her.

She was grinning—and then everything changed. Her mouth went soft, lips slightly parted. And her eyes spoke of wonder, and sadness as well. "Oh, Valbrand..." She raised a hand and brushed the hair back from the blasted side of my forehead.

I grabbed her hand, kissed it. She looked up at me, trusting. Hopeful. And I wanted to give her everything. To make a hundred impossible promises—and then to set about keeping every one.

In her eyes, I saw what might have been, were I some other man, not my father's son, not sworn to wreak a brutal revenge. I saw years and years of simple pleasures. I saw how life might be a gift and not a curse. I longed for what I saw, for all that would never be.

I guided her captured hand up to my shoulder. She pulled me close and we shared another kiss.

When I lifted my head, I asked, "Where?"

"The drawer. In the nightstand. There." She pointed.

I took out the condoms, peeled the cover from one. But something had happened. Something was lost.

I looked down at myself, limp and useless once more. And I looked at her. "It's no good. I should—"

And then she was the one reaching up, laying a soft finger to my lips. "Shh…"

"Dulcie, it's not—"

"Shh…" She pushed me down and she came up over me, pressing her soft lips first to the hollow of my throat and then down, and down—little, brushing, yearning kisses all along the center of my body. My belly jerked when she kissed me there. She dipped her tongue into the well of my navel.

And down she went, nuzzling, rubbing, finding me, claiming me, taking me, half-hard again already, into the warmth and wet beyond her soft lips, drawing, coaxing, licking…sucking.

Her hair trailed over my belly, a warm foam of wild red strands. I took her head in my hands, groaning, bucking my hips at her, rising once more, high and hard and eager as before.

"I can't…" I growled.

"Oh, yes. You can." She took the condom from my hand and rolled it down over my now-ready manhood. And then she mounted me, rising up, reaching down to position me—and lowering, slowly, a centimeter at a time…

"Sweet," I whispered, "Freyja's eyes, so very

sweet…'' I was groaning, trying to hold still, trying not to go over the edge right away.

When she had all of me, she started to move. "No," I commanded, my voice low, guttural, harsh. "Don't move. Do. Not. Move…"

I grasped the round globes of her bottom, pressing, keeping her from doing anything sudden, anything that would end what had hardly begun. She nuzzled my neck, my throat, the ridge of my jaw. I lifted my head so our lips could meet.

A long, hungry kiss—as I held her below, hard in place against me. It was too much, to say it true, just the feel of her heat and her silky wetness all around me, encompassing the length of me. Right then, I could not have borne movement. The sensations, already, had me right on the brink.

She lifted her mouth from mine, but a fraction. Whispered, "Valbrand," and "Valbrand," again. I surged up and took her mouth once more, kissing my own name from her moving lips.

I was going.…

I couldn't last.

I held on so tight, determined to stay there, seated snug within her as I rolled, taking the top position.

By then it was too late. There was no stopping it.

I gave myself up to it, to the searing rush of climax. She moaned into my mouth, wrapping her legs around me, heels digging in, urging me onward as she met me, thrust for thrust.

The wave of hot sensation washed over me, dragging me under. I froze, head straining back, pulsing into her, feeling how she met me, and went on meeting me. Her body contracted around me, pulsing in response to mine.

We rose, a tandem throb of whitest light, to hit the

peak and hover there as time spun out on twin threads—one agony, one the most exquisite pleasure.

Afterward, she tucked herself close against me. She whispered to me, words of love and tenderness. We drifted on a sea of pillows and featherbedding, sharing lazy caresses and brushing kisses.

The kisses grew longer. Deeper. Wetter. The wonder was beginning all over again....

Chapter 13

It was after five when Valbrand got up to go. I watched him as he pulled on his trousers and his boots. I was feeling lush and lazy, wishing he didn't have to leave, and yet…okay with it. Sated, I guess you might say. Limp and deliciously used up, so thoroughly loved I was willing to let him out of my sight—right then, anyway—without a whisper of complaint.

I had that smug feeling a woman can get, when she knows the guy she wants will be back, when she's certain that what's happened between them has meant something to him, too—whatever might come of what they shared.

"What will you do today?" He was buttoning his shirt.

"Go down into Lysgard, I think." I stretched and yawned, wriggling my toes under the blankets. "I want to visit the Museum of Norse History."

"What time will you go?"

I *did* like the sound of this. "Two?"

"Would you like company—a tour guide, you might say?"

"I would love a tour guide, especially if that tour guide is you."

He paused with his vest in his hand and we shared a tender look. Finally he said, "The main staircase, in the front entrance hall, then?" He pulled on the vest. "I'll have a car waiting outside to take us down to the city."

"I'll be there."

He got the mask from where I'd dropped it on the sofa and he approached the bed. He leaned close. I felt his breath across my cheek, breathed in the scent that was only his, reached up and touched the ruined side of his face, felt the ridges and the hollows, loving them because they were part of him. He said, "Our time together, I think, will be much too short."

My throat got tight. I smiled anyway. "Ten days. And we should make the most of every one."

"Openly, then?"

"Oh, yes. Proudly. Please."

He kissed me. Sweetly. Lightly. And then, with a quick caress of a black leather glove against my cheek, he turned and slipped out through the armoire.

My eyes were drooping shut as I watched him go. With a sigh of contentment, I let sleep carry me away.

In my own large suite of rooms, after I left my sweet redhead, I sat alone, staring into the middle distance. I had somehow managed to promise her that we would be together openly, that there would be no hiding in the shadows when I was with her. It surprised me a little, how willingly I'd agreed to those terms.

That *she* wanted it that way didn't surprise me in the

least. For a woman of Dulcie's integrity and mettle, it was the only way it *could* be.

I wondered at myself. There was no wisdom in embarking on this affair with her—in the shadows or otherwise. But then I thought of her shining eyes, the feel of her mouth under mine, the sound of her voice, so soft in my ear. She had told me she loved me. Repeatedly. And I, who had no right to love...

I believed her.

That was the thing, that I *believed* her. Truth shone in her eyes, spoke through her words, echoed in every beat of her loving heart.

It was that, the very truth in her, that I could not turn away from—not yet. Not until the short time allotted us had passed.

So we would not hide what was between us. We would walk together proudly, in the light. I wasn't much accustomed to the light anymore. But for her, for a short time of joy and laughter in the blasted heath that was my life, I would do it.

Which meant my father would know very soon—if he didn't know already. And *that* meant I must take immediate action with him. Somehow His Majesty must be made to see that what Dulcie and I shared was our concern alone.

At five in the morning, my father wouldn't be up. But I knew Medwyn would. The grand counselor rose every day at four, no matter how late he'd found his bed the night before. He used the early morning hours for prayer and meditation—and to practice the dragon dials.

I picked up the phone and rang the grand counselor's rooms, feeling no more than a slight twinge of guilt for interrupting the old man's time of discipline and contemplation. He answered on the first ring.

"Prince Valbrand," he said, before I spoke.

The palace phone system was antiquated. It included no feature for caller identification. Yet somehow, Medwyn always knew it was I. Some said he had the power of second sight, that he knew the secrets hidden in the hearts of men, that he saw what would be before it came to pass. Did I believe what some said? Yes. I had known Medwyn all of my life and in that time had witnessed proof after proof of his mystical power of knowing. There were times, especially since my return from the dead, when I felt closer, more...at home, you might say, with Medwyn, than with any other living soul.

We dispensed with cordialities. Between us, there was no need for them. I said, "I must speak with my father, in private, this morning. What time would be wisest?"

"You seek a *wise* time to speak with His Majesty?"

Leave it to Medwyn to ferret out the too-meaningful word choice. "Your pardon. *Wisest* was the wrong word. I meant, what time would be most convenient?"

There was a silence. I waited. Finally Medwyn said, "Come to His Majesty's private audience chamber at nine. He'll have had his breakfast. I'll make certain he is not otherwise engaged."

"Valbrand." My father, beaming in welcome, stood from behind his inlaid desk. His eyes had a definite gleam in them. "So good to see you this fine morning." The morning, from what I could see beyond the windows, looked gray and dreary—not *fine* at all. I wondered, briefly, what my father and Her Majesty might have been up to after I left them the night before. "Will you take coffee? Tea?"

"No." I bowed, fist to chest. "Thank you."

Medwyn, who stood as always at the king's elbow,

greeted me. My father turned to him. "I'll call for you as soon as we're finished here."

"As you wish, sire."

"Please," said my father as the doors closed behind his grand counselor, "let's sit together, shall we?" He led me to a corner where a grouping of wing chairs waited. He gestured at one. I sat, and he took the chair across from me. "Now, my son. What is it you have to say to me?"

"I have a request."

"As always, it is our fondest wish that you should have whatever you desire."

"And for that I am grateful."

"Out with it, then."

I waded right in. "Yesterday, we spoke briefly of Dulcie Samples, Brit's American friend...."

Already, his brow was furrowing. "I remember." The corners of his mouth had turned down. "You were not in the least forthcoming when I asked you about that girl."

I restrained myself from remarking that Dulcie was very much more than just *that girl*. Carefully, I told him, "At the time, there was nothing to be forthcoming about."

"And now, in the span of a day, there is?" The words were heavy with angry sarcasm.

I bristled at his tone, but was careful to cover it. "Yes."

"Are you lovers, then?" When I didn't answer, he demanded, "*Are* you?"

"That," I said at last, quietly, "is between Dulcie and me."

"Things change very quickly with you, my son." His

tone was soft now. Too soft. "Yesterday, the woman was hardly known to you. And today, she is your—"

I put up a hand before he said some ugly word that I could not let pass. "Will you listen, please, to what I have to say? Will you let me say it, all the way through?"

For that, I got a long, fuming silence, followed by a single, regal nod and a low "Proceed."

I spoke with care. "She stays but for ten more days. As planned, the day after the wedding, she will be gone. Until then, I will be at her side whenever possible. I find her charming and—" I sought the right word, found none right enough. So I settled on "—good. She is good, in the truest, most uncompromised sense. She does me the honor of wishing to be with me. I find it is an honor I will not refuse."

"An honor," my father repeated, his anger, for the moment at least, replaced by sad disbelief. "I do not understand." He leaned toward me and spoke low, as if he feared some enemy might overhear. "My son, this is not a thing that you would ever do." When would he understand? The *me* he spoke of was no more. He continued, "If you must flaunt a lover for the world to see, choose an appropriate one. The Lady Kaarin would surely welcome your attentions."

"I thought you knew. It is long over between Kaarin and me."

"I didn't know. But in any case, I'm certain, were you to approach her, that she would be more than amenable to a renewal of your suit."

"No," I said again as an unpleasant thought occurred to me. Had my father suggested to Kaarin that *she* approach *me?* It seemed exactly the kind of thing he might do. Should I confront him with the fact that she had done what he bid her? Should I insist he restrain his irksome matchmaking tendencies, at least where I was concerned?

No, I decided. I had a goal in this discussion and I didn't want to give His Majesty any excuse to lead me off in some other direction.

Balls of Balder, when would he see it? I was, quite simply, not the man I had been. I had told him as much time after time. But he inevitably turned a deaf ear.

I said, patiently, "The Lady Kaarin and I are well and completely parted. As to my friendship with Dulcie Samples, I intend to pursue that friendship for the short time that remains before her departure for America. And I want you, please, to accept my choice." I think he meant to speak then. Before he could, I spoke again. "I understand that you have often found it necessary to keep a close watch over the members of your family. And to intervene when you see fit."

He nodded again. "And that is as it should be. A king has a right and a duty to know all, as well as to act on what he knows."

Not this time, I thought. I said, "I ask you, as a son to a father, not to eavesdrop on Dulcie and me. I ask you not to interfere in any way."

"Eavesdrop?" he growled. "I don't believe I care for that word."

"Your pardon, sire. I speak so bluntly because I long to be clearly understood."

He made a gruff sound. "Ah. Clarity. Is that what you call it?"

"Yes, my lord. And I humbly request—"

"Humbly! You? Hah!"

"Please. No surveillance devices in Dulcie's rooms. And no more suggestions—from Brit or anyone else—

that Dulcie cut her visit short and take the royal jet home. Also, no…mysterious occurrences. No accidents befalling her. No sudden illnesses, I beg of you."

"Illnesses? Accidents?" my father blustered. "Of what horrors do you think me capable, my son?"

"Father, these are not accusations. They are merely, as I keep telling you, sincerest requests."

He swept to his feet and paced a strip of parquet floor between one Persian rug and the next. "You *request* that I don't poison her soup? You *beg* me not to push her down a stairwell?"

I sat still and said nothing. Sometimes His Majesty was like a sudden gale at sea. The only sensible response was to pull in the oars, reef the sail and prepare for some rapid tacking until he blew himself out.

He turned on me. "You insult your king. And you do it boldly."

"My lord, it is not my wish to give offense."

"Hah! Humph!"

"I only hoped to make a few things clear between us."

He stomped over to me and dropped back into his chair. "Harumph." He muttered something I didn't catch, some kind of oath, I had no doubt. And then he cast me a measuring sideways glance. "Ten days, you say?"

"Yes, my lord."

"And you have no intention of keeping her longer?"

"I do not, sire."

"And what of the girl? How do you know she doesn't scheme to stay?"

"She is not one to whom the word *scheme* could ever apply."

He made a snorting sound. "You are clearly besotted."

I almost smiled. "That I am, sire. And she will not stay beyond the allotted time. I will see to it."

"You seem sure of yourself in that regard."

"I am. It wouldn't be good for her, to stay here, with me. I can promise her nothing. She has her life to get back to, a future that will be much brighter than any I could offer her."

"Yet if she *wanted* to stay…"

"It matters not. I won't allow it. When the agreed-upon day arrives, I will send her home."

Those dark eyes were sharp and far-seeing as a falcon's. "I have your word, then. In ten days, she goes."

"Yes. I give you my word. Ten days. No more."

He waved a hand. "And, in the meantime…surely, you must realize we cannot be held responsible if by evil chance some accident were to…"

I stopped him with a look. Once he was silent, I said, "Father, she is a true innocent. I could not bear it, were ill to befall her. I would not go on here, in Isenhalla, if Dulcie were to come to harm in this place."

There was a space of time in which the only sounds were the ticking of the antique French clock on one of the mantels and the faint cries of gulls soaring somewhere past the windows. At last, he muttered, "You're saying you would leave us again, that you would…disappear?"

"Yes."

"But surely you—"

"It needn't come to that. If you will but allow me a small speck of life of my own. No spies. No surveillance. No…untoward occurrences."

The silence then seemed to stretch into eternity. And

then, at last, he asked me, "She brings you happiness, then?"

"Yes. More than you can know."

"Happiness, I think, is a rare and precious thing." His eyes were far away. I doubted it was I and my sweet redhead he was thinking of.

"Yes," I said. "Rare and precious. And often brief."

And so he nodded. "As you wish, so shall it be. Have your time with Brit's friend from California. Privately. With no interference from us."

That afternoon, Valbrand was waiting, as he'd promised he would be, at the foot of the sweeping staircase in the main entrance hall. He wore gray t̶r̶o̶u̶s̶e̶r̶s̶ and a ̶t̶h̶o̶s̶e̶ things ̶s̶a̶i̶d̶ it all.

In front, beyond the privacy glass, sat two men: a driver in red-and-black livery, and a big guy in a plain dark suit with long red hair tied back in a low ponytail. His thick neck and linebacker's shoulders spoke of lots of muscles beneath the suit.

I arched an eyebrow at Valbrand. "Don't tell me. One of Hauk's men, right? A berserker, as they call them."

He gave me a nod. "Since the incident the other night, all members of the royal family have agreed to leave the palace only with a well-trained bodyguard in tow."

I guessed that made sense, though after seeing Valbrand fight, I doubted he needed anyone to protect him. I almost said as much, but then decided against it. After all, he'd been the Dark Raider that night. And maybe he wouldn't want me talking of his alter ego with a driver and a bodyguard near—privacy glass aside. I squeezed his hand and looked out the window, watching for the jewel-blue waters of the harbor below that winked at me pipes, possibly even split the stone. I pulled my coat closer and shivered at the cold.

"This way." He put his arm, protectively, at the small of my back and ushered me between the carved stone pillars and down the wide stone steps to a long, black limousine.

The road down to the city was steep and twisting, lined with proud spruce and bare oaks, their naked branches harsh black lace against the lowering sky. The car smelled of fine leather, with the faint perfume of some kind of polish. A good smell, expensive and soothing.

We held hands in the back seat and hardly said a word. We didn't really need ... ...ere gray trousers a... gray cashmere sweater, a thick red wool scarf around his neck. His gorgeous overcoat was cashmere, too. I could see the rich softness of it from twenty feet away.

His eyes met mine and I stopped in midstep. The world did what the world is always doing when you fall in love. It spun to a stop. Everything glowed...

He chuckled and signaled me forward. I remembered the basics—how to breathe, how to walk. I started toward him again. When I got there, he took my arm and off we went.

Outside, the sky was a frothing patchwork of grays, split here and there with brave rays of silvery sun. Each breath came out as a cloud. Melting mounds of snow dotted the wide cobbled turnaround. The four-tiered central fountain, with its crown of spitting dragons surrounding a thunderbolt-wielding statue of Thor, was dry as it had been on the day I arrived. Valbrand told me it was always turned off from mid-November until the first of May. If not, when the water froze, it would break the now and then through the screen of trees as we descended on the winding road.

My joy was so complete that day. It was a glow inside me, shining out, making the world around me shimmer and pulse with glorious warm light.

We went first to the Norse Museum. The bodyguard stayed close, but silent. Now and then, in my pleasured glow at being with Valbrand, I would even forget the guard was there. But then I'd catch his reflection in a display case, or turn to look at the man beside me and see that big red head in the corner of my eye. A shiver would go through me, mostly because I had forgotten about him, I suppose. And maybe a little for the fact that he was needed as a result of the other night—the night when, if not for Valbrand, I would have been carried off to God knows where by a pair of murderous thugs.

I doubted my kidnappers would have been too happy when they discovered they'd taken the wrong woman. In fact, I was reasonably certain they'd have slit my throat as soon as they learned I was worthless to them. If not for Valbrand, I would have been dead.

But Valbrand had saved me. And so, there I was, holding his hand, glowing with joy. With a bodyguard nearby...

We toured the hall of longships. Valbrand explained to me that Gullandrian shipbuilders still crafted the beautiful flexible warships in the old manner, with a hull of overlapping planks and a belly that bulged out on either side of the keel before rising to the gunwales. With such wide, sleek sides, the ship sat high in the water. Add a deep keel and a single woolen sail to harness the wind and you had a shallow-draft ship that was still capable of handling open ocean.

In the hall, the four ships on display were ancient

ones, brought up from silt beds in fjords or excavated from bogs. There was one, an early warship 75 feet long, that had been built around 350 A.D., during the Iron Age, long before the Viking expansion of the seven hundreds to the eleven hundreds. There was no barrier around it, so I dared—knowing I probably shouldn't— to touch it. The wood felt petrified, smooth as polished stone. The only other one like it, Valbrand told me, had been found in Denmark and now was displayed in a German museum.

I stared at the ancient craft and wondered about the ship Valbrand had sailed on his Viking Voyage—the voyage that had almost cost him his life. How large had that ship been? Did it resemble any of the ships in the museum? But when I turned from the smooth, nearly black hull of the 1700-year-old ship and saw the bleak look in his eye, my questions died in my throat.

Maybe we would talk about it, I thought, about what really happened to him—but not now, not in a public place with the king's watchful bodyguard a few yards away.

We went on to other rooms, to admire intricate Viking jewelry of silver, gold and bronze and beautifully made weapons: axes, swords, daggers, spears, bows and round, heavily decorated shields. There were rooms dedicated to everyday life in a Viking village, and rooms filled with artifacts and tools used by Viking craftsmen. By the time we left the museum, I was dizzy with all I had seen, full to bursting with more information than I could possibly digest.

Outside, we discovered that it had started snowing, fat flakes blowing hard on the wicked Gullandrian wind. The snow was already collecting between the stones of the cobbled street. I tipped my head up and a few flakes caught in my eyelashes and melted against my lips.

"I think we should find a warm pub and order two tall glasses of ale," Valbrand suggested. Before I had a chance to agree with him, he added, "Just one moment..." He took a cell phone from his pocket, one apparently set on silent page. He answered it with a curt-sounding, "What is it?" He listened. "Yes," he said finally. "Right away. Yes." When he slipped the phone back in his pocket, I knew by his expression that our afternoon in Lysgard had just come to an abrupt end.

"I regret I must return to the palace immediately," he said.

"Nothing too terrible, I hope..."

He made a vague sound in his throat, took my hand and wrapped it over his arm. "Shall we go?" I nodded. We went down the wide museum steps to the waiting limousine.

I escorted Dulcie to her room and left her with a glow on her cheeks and questions in her eyes.

In my father's private audience room, the others were already gathered: Osrik, Medwyn, Hauk, Eric and Brit. They had found the man who hired the would-be kidnappers.

He was dead.

Hauk reported, "The headless body was discovered early this morning, floating facedown in a half-frozen pond not far from the barn where Princess Brit was to have been taken. Divers a few hours later discovered the head caught in the tangle of rotting rushes at the edge of the pond. Physically, he's a match for the man our two would-be kidnappers claim hired them. No weapon was found, but our guess at this point, judging by the cleanness of the cuts, is that the man was beheaded with some kind of ax—a well-honed one. Rigor had not yet set in. He was killed last night.''

Brit asked, ''There? By the pond?''

Hauk nodded. ''Judging by the vast quantities of blood we found on the southeast bank, yes. We've only an hour ago shown pictures to the two prisoners. They identify him as the man who hired them. And this one actually had a passport in his pocket. German. Another mercenary. More inquiries will be made, of course, to discover if the name on the passport is his real name.''

I said, ''Whether it is or not probably doesn't matter.''

Hauk nodded, ''My thoughts exactly. He's merely another hireling. And now those who paid him have made sure he'll never tell what little he knows.''

Brit raked her yellow hair back from her forehead. ''What about tracks leading to and from the pond?''

''There are many, unfortunately. Farm vehicles and the like. We're taking photos and impressions of all tracks in the area, of course. Also, it's of note that the victim had rope burns at wrist and ankle and raw spots at the corners of his mouth. We're going now by the theory that he was bound and gagged and carried to the pond pursuant to the loss of his head.''

''Boot prints?'' Brit asked hopefully.

''No clear ones. It appears someone took the time to check the ground around the murder site and smear all tracks.'' Brit muttered something distinctly unladylike. Hauk said, ''I regret I don't have something more satisfying to tell you. The local constable has been convinced to let His Majesty's special forces lead the investigation. We're conducting interviews with everyone who lives in the area, on the chance that someone might have seen what happened near that pond last night. If we learn anything from the interviews, or on further exploration of the evidence, I'll report it immediately.''

My father's mouth was a bleak line. "So. We have next to nothing."

I said, "We have the fact that the man was murdered and dumped near the barn where Brit was supposed to be taken. Why not just kill the fellow and dispose of the body somewhere we'd never find him? No, it was a defiant act. And a taunting one. An act that said there will be more attacks on the house of Thor. And soon."

Chapter 14

That night, Wednesday, there was originally supposed to have been a kick-butt bonfire down in the open parkland below the palace gardens. Brit had mentioned it the first day I arrived. I'd been looking forward to it. Nothing like a big, bright, toasty fire on a snowy Gullandrian night—maybe with the prince of my dreams at my side. We might drink mulled cider and cuddle up close....

But then I took a look at the latest edition of the beautifully printed palace-activities program that showed up in my room daily—dropped off by the maid, I imagined, though I'd yet to see who actually left it. The bonfire had been cancelled. Due to inclement weather, the program said.

Yeah, right. By five, the snow flurries had blown themselves out. It was an icy, clear evening with a white crust of snow on the ground. A perfect night for a winter bonfire.

I had it figured that it wasn't about weather at all, but

beefed-up security in the wake of my encounter with the bad guys in ski masks and the threat to the royal family that the incident represented. Now there was to be a buffet down in the main solarium and then a movie in the media room next-door. Not near as exciting as a bonfire—but hey. I would learn to live with it. I had other things to look forward to.

Though I hadn't heard from Valbrand since he'd left me at my door that afternoon, I just knew I'd be seeing him soon. Maybe during the evening's activities. And for certain later, in my room, where we would proceed to do more of the lovely, intimate things we'd done the night before.

Yes, I was disgustingly eager and incredibly sure of myself—at least when it came to that night and the nights to follow until my departure. Love for the incurable romantic can be like that. Slightly delusional. Utterly grand.

The new slate of activities called for semi-formal attire—it said so in small print—and that was great. I'd used up my two formals and wouldn't have to start recycling them until tomorrow night, at least. Tonight, I could break out my fave little black dress—scoop neck, flutter sleeves, handkerchief hem—and fit right in. Oh, and I'd have the hairdresser come by and coax my unruly hair into an elegant French twist.

The buffet was to be laid out at eight. At eight-fifteen, I was sitting on the sofa by the fireplace all ready to go, wondering if I should head on down to the solarium solo or wait a little longer for the evening's escort to appear. Before I could decide, I heard a knock on my door. I grabbed my clutch and smoothed the feathery chiffon of my hem and went to answer.

It was Valbrand. He wore a dazzling dark wool suit

and a midnight-blue tie and he looked at me as if I were the most beautiful woman on earth.

I said, "Oh my, yes. You are such an improvement."

He arched his remaining eyebrow. "An improvement over...?"

"The usual prince they send up."

"There were problems with your escorts?"

"They were very nice men—with whom I had nothing in common and *to* whom I seemed to have nothing to say."

"You?" He was looking distinctly disbelieving. "With nothing to say?"

"Believe it or not, it does happen—though only occasionally."

He didn't reply to that. We lingered in the doorway and gazed at each other for a while, neither of us caring in the least that anyone could walk by and see us just standing there, staring dreamily into each other's eyes.

"Ahem," I said eventually. "Shall we go?" He was shaking his head. I gulped. He grasped the edge of the door and pushed it open all the way, stepping into my tiny entrance cubicle with me. "Oh!" I said breathlessly.

He asked, "What is the good of a buffet supper if it can't wait until we're ready for it?"

I pondered this question. "You know," I said finally, "you might have a point...." Yes, it's true. The quality of my repartee was progressively degenerating. It was all his fault. The heat in those gleaming dark eyes burned away anything resembling clarity of thought. My heart was beating in a slow, deep way. I was hungry. Very hungry. But not for anything you would find on a buffet.

He kicked the door closed behind him.

I looked up into his gorgeous, monstrous face and suggested, "Why don't you get comfortable?"

"An excellent idea."

"Would like some help?"

"Yes, I would." He waited, arms at his sides.

I dropped my clutch to the floor and slid my hands up his chest, slipping them under the lapels of his jacket, then easing it over his shoulders. It slid down his arms and collapsed to the floor with a soft whooshing sound. I started to bend down and get it.

"Leave it."

"It'll be wrinkled."

"Leave it."

I gulped again. "Okay…"

He took my arm and pulled me toward him. "I would like a kiss."

"I aim to please."

"And you do…" His mouth swooped down and covered mine as both of those lean, hard arms went around me.

The kiss was long and hot and wet. His hands strayed right away to my hair. He shoved his fingers in it and pulled out the pins. By the time he lifted his lips from mine, my smooth French twist was once again a wild red mane.

He scooped me up against his chest. I held on tight as he carried me to the bed. He put me down and came down with me, reaching for the drawer in the nightstand.

There was some fumbling to get the condom out of the box and free of its individual wrapper. After that, it was maybe three seconds to getting his trousers undone and the protection in place.

"Hurry…" I was pulling at him. "Oh, please…"

His knowing hand found me under my skirt. I moaned in delight and expectation.

Unfortunately, my pantyhose were in the way. He tore

at them and when he didn't get them out of the way fast enough, I reached down and helped him.

Ever try to rip a pair of panty hose? The things will run if you look at them, but to actually rip a hole in them? Who knew they could be so tough?

But we were determined. We managed to punch a hole at the central seam, each of us sticking a finger in and pulling until the hole widened and finally tore—a ragged gap that started at the waistband in front and went all the way down and up again to the waistband in back.

He nudged my legs apart and knelt between them, looking down into my eyes as he put a warm hand on each of my thighs. I shivered as he pushed the wisps of my hem up and out of his way.

"Oh, come here..." I was reaching for him, taking him by those broad shoulders and pulling him down to me, wrapping my legs tight around him.

He entered me in one smooth thrust. You cannot imagine. I was *so* ready. We rolled, moaning, and I was on top, holding him to me at first, then pushing myself up so I was sitting on him, my legs folded under me, my handkerchief skirt settling like a pool of black cobwebs around my hips, spilling across his trousers, clinging to the wool, catching on the heels of my black evening sandals, ripping a little.

I didn't care about the damage to my dress. I looked down at Valbrand, into his waiting eyes, as he looked up at me.

The feeling was so incredibly right, so purely lustful and open. The way he filled me, stretching me, pushed in tight and high. I had that shivery, delicious sensation—hollowed out and full at the same time. He was thick and hot and I was so wet.

We were, at that moment, unmoving, caught in a

breath-held kind of stillness that crackled with energy and erotic excitement. Already, I could sense my own climax, feel it beginning to build out of the stillness, through the wet and the waiting, catching fire in the look that passed between us, a look that shimmered with heat.

I groaned and threw my head back and raised up to my knees, slowly, so my body caressed him as I slid along his length. He let out a strangled sound, grabbed my hips and brought me—hard and fast—back down to him. I fell forward, landing against his chest, scooting up enough to capture his mouth. With a groan, he pushed my hips down tight onto him again.

We rolled once more, ending on our sides, facing each other, my upper leg thrown across him, all modesty gone, with my dress bunched up around my waist and my pantyhose held together by a few ragged strips down the sides of my thighs. He reached around and unzipped me, pulling the dress halfway down my arms, his hands dragging back to the front of me, cupping my breasts, lifting them out of the lacy cradle of my bra so he could caress them.

He began to move within me, rocking against me, withdrawing almost to the point where I lost him, then sliding back, letting me take him all the way in. I moaned at the lovely agony of it and the rhythm picked up, until we were rocking each other hard and fast.

I felt him hit the peak and that sent me over, too. I cried out. He moaned low in his throat. We held each other tight as the pulsing wonder of our mutual climax began.

When it was over, we both went limp. He was on his left side. I stroked his perfect cheek. He brushed his hand slowly up and down my bare arm. We murmured to each other, meaningless things, little love words you say after you've done something naughty and undignified and utterly right.

In time, we got up and repaired the damage. He tucked in his shirt, zipped up, straightened his tie, collected his jacket and brushed it out. I took a little longer, wriggling into a fresh pair of pantyhose, spending several minutes on makeup repair. I started to try putting my hair back up, but Valbrand came into the bathroom and stood behind me at the mirror.

He gathered up a handful of curls and rubbed them against his mouth. Then he met my eyes in the glass. "Leave it loose."

I wrinkled my nose at him. "It looks so wild...."

He smiled his shattered smile. "Exactly."

So I spent a little time with a brush, smoothing it as best I could. I spritzed on a fresh cloud of scent and off we went.

It was just nine when we got to the solarium, which is another of Isenhalla's endless array of spectacular public rooms, with its coffered gold-leaf ceiling thick with murals depicting various myths and a row of tall Palladian windows looking out on the back gardens. Out there, the lights were on, pushing back the darkness, revealing bare trees and glistening snowy ground and topiary hedges crowned with white.

We filled our plates and turned to choose our seats at one of the thirty or so round tables set with red cloths and gold-trimmed red china. Many of the tables were full, a few already half-cleared after early diners had left.

I felt the prickle of interest in a hundred pairs of eyes as Valbrand and I moved toward an empty, still fully set table. We didn't make it. Brit appeared at my right. She laid her hand on my arm. I looked at her and she smiled brightly—maybe too brightly. There was a kind of stiffness about her, as if she strove to make the best of an iffy situation. It dimmed my joy just a little, to see that brittle look on my best friend's face. I had a moment's— what? Embarrassment, I guess. That sudden feeling of rough nakedness, as if Brit could tell by looking at me exactly what her brother and I had been doing up in my room not half an hour before.

But then she said, "Come on, you two. Sit with us."

"Us" turned out to be the Thorson princesses and their grooms: Brit and Eric, Liv and Finn Danelaw—and Elli and Hauk. Liv and Elli had blond hair and blue eyes, same as Brit. The sisters were fraternal, but still the family resemblance was clear in the three strong chins and the perfectly sculpted noses. Elli and Liv looked happier than I'd ever seen either of them before—that kind of glowing contentment you see in pregnant women who have good men to love them and bright futures ahead. Seeing Elli looking like that didn't surprise me. She'd always been the one who planned to find the right man and settle down. Liv was another story. Of the three sisters, she was the driven, ambitious one. She'd always, to me, had a certain tension about her, a focus so tight it almost came across as anger.

No more. Now Liv was round, relaxed and so pretty. And when she looked at her husband her face would just light up.

I'd never met Finn until that night. He was killer handsome with soft brown eyes and chestnut hair. I liked him immediately. He had a warm, sexy smile and a great sense of humor. Brit had told me that before Liv, he was a real runaround. The greatest lover in all Gullandria, no lie. Not anymore, though. His devotion to Liv—like hers to him—was unmistakable.

As we ate and chatted, I looked around a little. No

sign of the king and queen, or of Medwyn. But Lady Marta Wyborn, in a mad sparkle of peacock-blue beads this time, caught my eye and waved with enthusiasm. Old Prince Sigurd granted me a nod.

Four tables away, and a little to the left, sat the Lady Kaarin in a tight-fitting sleeveless red silk creation with a Mandarin collar and beautiful embroidery—flowers and butterflies and twining vines trailing from her right shoulder diagonally across her perfect, high breasts and down to curl around her wasp-thin waist. Her earrings, large as the ones she'd worn last night, were of garnet and gold. She sat with the slim, oh-so-aristocratic Prince Onund. When I first spotted her, she was whispering something in his ear. I stared longer than I should have, thinking that maybe Lady Marta had been right: the two were an item.

Lady Kaarin glanced up and caught me watching her. She said something else to the prince at her side, then picked up her gold-filigreed red crystal goblet and toasted me with it, a terrible, artificial smile on her stunning face. She really did look amazing—and her outfit matched the table setting, the dress a shade of red identical to the china and the crystal. It was as if the solarium had been decorated just for her.

She looked pointedly beyond me, at Valbrand, something scary in her eyes. Possessiveness, maybe. Or just plain fury. I glanced at Valbrand. He was talking to Liv on his other side and seemed oblivious to Kaarin. When I looked back at her, she was sipping her wine, her gaze on her dinner companion again. She set the goblet by her plate and leaned close to Prince Onund once more.

About then, Brit looked across at me. "Dulce. Come on. Keep me company while I powder my nose."

I had to restrain a grunt of disbelief. Brit was so not

the type to go powder her nose. I don't think she even wore powder. She had that kind of even, creamy skin that looks luminous without it. But I did get the message. She wanted to talk to me. After a quick nod at Valbrand, I got up and trotted obediently after her toward the marble arches that led to the entry hall.

Once we were out of the solarium, she grabbed me by the hand and towed me toward a corner where a couple of wing chairs waited in an alcove framed by two polished oak pillars: a cozy conversation nook, tucked away where we probably wouldn't be overheard.

We each took a chair.

"I have to talk to you...." She leaned toward me, bracing her elbows on her knees. "About you and my brother..."

I heaved a big sigh. "Now, how did I know that was where this was heading?"

"Dulce..." Her voice trailed off. I waited. She was staring down at her designer shoes.

"What?" I demanded. Yeah, all right. I was pretty irritated. She'd already told me, before anything even happened between Valbrand and me, what she thought of the two of us getting together. I didn't especially want to hear a replay.

She straightened and looked at me—a pained kind of look. "Well, I just don't think you know what you're doing. I don't think you realize..." She stalled out again.

I said, flatly, "I am anxiously awaiting the part where you finish a sentence."

Her face was flushed, her eyes too bright. "It's only that...I know you. You're gonna be so hurt and miserable when you go home. And don't kid yourself. You *will* be going home the day after the wedding. That's not going to change. Yes, there are situations where love conquers all. But this isn't one of them.''

"Let me guess. Your father sent you after me, to tell me he wants me to go home now, right?''

She shook her head. ''My dad hasn't said a word about you to me—and I have to tell you, that makes me nervous. It's general knowledge that you and Valbrand went down into Lysgard together today. And then, here you are tonight, so obviously *together*. My father has to be fuming.''

"How can you know that? Maybe His Majesty is more open-minded than you realize. Maybe he's *glad* to see Valbrand happy for a change.''

"God, Dulce. Don't you get it? My father wants one thing more than anything else in this world. For Valbrand to be king after him. And if Valbrand marries a commoner—especially a foreign-born one—that can never happen.''

"Well, relax. We're not getting married.'' As I said the words, I was aware of a distinct sinking feeling.

Okay, so Brit knew me too well. It wasn't going to be any piece of cake to leave Valbrand. But I would do it when the time came—somehow.

Unless...

Well, what if he realized he could no more bear for me to leave him than I could stand the thought of going?

I mean, if that were to happen, would I go anyway?

Not on your life.

And something had just occurred to me. ''Wait a minute. Your father married your mother—and she was American. And he still ended up on the throne.''

Brit just kept shaking her head. ''My mother's a Frey-asdahl. She can trace her line back more than a thousand years. She might be American by birth, but she's high-jarl Gullandrian by descent.''

I fiddled with the wispy hem of my dress, suddenly forlorn and wishing I wasn't. "So you're saying the Bakersfield Samples just don't stack up, huh?''

She put her hand over mine. "Dulce…''

I looked up into her worried eyes—and the hard truth hit me. "You think your father might…do something to me, right? You think he might try to get me out of the way.''

She took her hand away. "No. No, of course not.''

"You answered that way too fast.''

"Damn it, Dulce.'' She flopped angrily back in her chair. "I just want you to be safe, you know? I just worry about you, that's all. I feel responsible. You wouldn't even be here if not for me. You wouldn't be in this mess if I hadn't—''

"Yoo-hoo.'' I waved both hands at her.

She glared. "What?''

"This is not a *mess* I'm in. This is love. And however long it lasts, I'm gonna go for it, straight on. No limit.''

"You are not reassuring me.''

"Too bad—and I have a question.''

She huffed out a big breath and recrossed her legs. "Sure. Whatever.''

"The other night, at the ball, you pointed out Lady Kaarin Karlsmon to me. You were just about to dish me some dirt on her when Eric came up. Remember?''

She muttered something very unprincess-like, then grudgingly admitted, "Yeah. So?''

"What were you going to tell me?''

"Look. At the time, it seemed like just some harmless bit of gossip, you know? Given the situation now…'' Another sentence died unfinished.

"Given the situation now, what?"

"I probably shouldn't have brought it up."

I kept at her. "Was it about her and Valbrand?"

"God," she said.

"Was that an answer?"

"It's just…"

"What?"

"Oh, Dulce. Sometimes I hate all this, you know? Nothing's simple now. I can't be…the friend I used to be. I can't tell you all my secrets anymore. I can't even whisper a little gossip in your ear without it coming back to haunt me."

I dropped the subject of Lady Kaarin—for the moment, anyway—and I took my friend's hand. "This *is* what you want, right?" I gestured at the splendor around us. "This…world. Your place in it…"

"Yes," she said firmly. "It is."

"So don't…regret what you have to do, okay? I hate it, too—that you feel you can't confide in me the way you used to. It does hurt, that you can't let yourself trust me."

"Oh, Dulce…" The pain in her eyes was very real.

I gave her a determined smile. "But I do *get* it, you know? As much as it hurts, I do understand, deep down. You're in a tough position. You *have* to weigh each word."

She was shaking her head again but this time in a musing sort of way. "You know, you do amaze me. You constantly show me why you're the best friend this particular princess ever had."

"Why, thank you, Your Highness." I solemnly performed the Gullandrian bow. "And now—" I let my grin show "—back to Lady Kaarin. What were you going to tell me about her, that night at the ball?"

Brit pulled her hand free of my hold and gave me a sideways look. "Well, what can it hurt to tell you? It *is* public knowledge, after all...."

I leaned a little closer. "Yeah?"

And at last my friend confessed, "They were right next-door to engaged before his disappearance. But it's totally over between them now."

I smiled. "I know."

"Then why'd you ask?"

"Verification, I guess. You should have seen the look she gave me tonight." I shivered at the memory.

"Dulce, Lady Kaarin is the least of your problems."

"Gee, that's nice to know."

"You're just so...innocent. And utterly determined at the same time. It's a scary combination."

"Innocent, huh?" I was thinking of Valbrand and me, going at each other up in my room, a few hours ago.

"We should go back." The words were freighted with weariness. With resignation.

I wished there was something I could say that would cheer her up. But I could no more give her what she wanted from me than she could relinquish her destiny.

Hours later, in my bed, when we were both limp and lazy after lovemaking, I asked Valbrand about Lady Kaarin.

He rolled his head, the perfect side sliding into shadow, showing me the web of scars. "Has she bothered you in any way?"

"Absolutely not." Well, okay. If looks could kill, I'd at least be in intensive care by then. But other than a deadly glance or two, I'd never so much as exchanged hellos with the woman. "I, uh, did hear that the two of you were pretty much engaged before you left for your Viking Voyage.''

"You heard this from whom?"

I decided to leave Brit out of it. "From Lady Marta."

He grunted. "If gossip didn't exist, Lady Marta would find it necessary to invent it."

"But still…it's the truth, right?"

His gaze didn't waver. "Yes. We were lovers once."

"And you were going to marry her?"

"Yes. At the time, I believed she would one day be my queen." He touched my face, traced my eyebrows, smoothed back my hair and caressed the outer curve of my ear. "It's long over, though, between Kaarin and me." A muscle by the melted corner of his mouth twitched in a faint hint of a smile. "So you needn't become enraged or violently jealous."

I leaned forward, kissed him right between the eyes. "I will try my very best to restrain myself from any vicious displays."

"I am gratified to hear it."

I stroked the blasted skin of his cheek. "Valbrand?"

"You have far too many questions in your eyes."

It seemed, somehow, wrong to ask my next question—as if some silent contract between us had defined certain subjects off-limits.

But too bad. My mom always says it never hurts to ask. So what if you get told no? You're in no worse position than if you hadn't asked at all. And there's always the possibility that the answer will be yes.

So I said, "What really happened to you…at sea?"

I don't know what I expected, exactly. Agitation? Anger? That he would throw back the covers, jump from the bed and start yanking on his clothes?

All of the above, I guess.

He surprised me by asking softly, "Didn't Brit tell you?"

I nodded. "But it didn't make sense. And the story kept changing, you know? There was a storm and you were washed overboard. No, there was a storm *and* a fire. Your face was burned. And *then* you were washed overboard...."

His eyes had a gleam in them, as if he was amused. Good, I thought. Amusement is good. Much better than jumping out of bed and stalking from the room. He said, "What don't you believe? That there was a storm? Or that the longship caught fire?"

"It just doesn't add up, that's all. The part about the fire is like an afterthought—tacked on, you know, because you were burned and there had to be some kind of explanation? But Valbrand, if you were burned that way—in a fire at sea—how would your scars be so strictly confined to the left side of your face? I mean, it's almost like a one-sided mask, your scarring, with a distinct line where the damage stops." I traced that line, tenderly. He didn't try to stop me, didn't so much as flinch. He just lay there, watching me, as I lightly touched the side of his face. "Your ear isn't burned at all. The scars stop about a quarter of an inch from your hairline. I mean, usually, when people get so badly burned on the face, their hair catches fire, doesn't it? They end up with a bald, scarred scalp. You've still got all your hair."

His dark eyes gave away nothing. I waited, hoping he'd respond to what I'd said.

When he didn't, I kept after him. "And what about the supposedly trustworthy men who survived the storm but didn't return immediately to Gullandria to report on what had happened? Instead they were all declared missing at sea. Eric had to go and hunt them down to get the story out of them? That's weird, if you ask me.''

His eyes were so soft. ''*Did* I ask you?''

I touched his face again. ''No, you didn't. *I'm* asking *you*. Valbrand, what really happened when you disappeared at sea?''

Chapter 15

Canting onto an elbow above her, I caught a lock of Dulcie's hair between my thumb and forefinger, rubbing it, loving the springiness of it, the living warmth...

"Tell me," she whispered.

I looked down into those wide, honest eyes and found myself thinking, *What's the harm if I only tell her the part of the truth she seeks and no more?*

I could give her the bleak story of what had happened on that island off the coast of Iceland and the series of events leading immediately up to it. I'd leave out any mention of traitors *behind* the traitors who had tortured and killed my men. When I finished, she'd have no information that could prove dangerous to her *or* to the Thorson cause.

However, once she had the story, she would surely think less of me. I didn't want that—then again, truly, that she should think less of me was as it should be.

I caught her hand and kissed the knuckles. "You will not be happy with what you hear."

"I can take it."

I pulled at the blankets a little, smoothing them around her shoulders—reconsidering the wisdom of this.

"Tell me," she said again.

I stared into her eyes, a cowardly ambivalence tugging at me. On further reflection, it was not a story she needed to hear. And it was certain to distress her. I tried to demur. "It is an ugly tale...."

She touched my mouth to silence my excuses. "Just tell it."

And then there was the fact that I wouldn't want the tale bandied about, to possibly get back to His Majesty, who would be far from pleased to hear I had confided in Brit's American friend. "I would require your word first, that you would tell no one what I have to say." Perhaps she'd refuse....

She sighed. Deeply. "There are just too many secrets around here."

"If you don't wish to keep my confidence, there is no harm done. I simply will not tell you. And the more I ponder the idea, the more foolish it seems, in any case, that I should speak of this with you."

She chewed rather mutinously on her pretty lower lip, after which she announced, "Oh, all right. I promise. I'll never tell anyone."

"Are you certain?"

"Yes. I'm certain."

Why was it, with the way she could chatter on and on, that when she promised to keep silent about something, I believed her? By Verdandi, it made no sense.

But whatever the why of it, I *did* trust her absolutely to keep her word to me.

Trapped, I dropped to my back and stared up at the iron fixture suspended from the molded ceiling above. She stirred beside me, nuzzling in closer. I wrapped my arm around her and wondered that I had let myself be led so neatly into revealing the central hideousness of my life—into describing my greatest folly, my blind arrogance and my utter failure as a leader of men.

My belly felt tight and queasy. My heart beat hard and heavy, a rhythm of dread, as if it wanted only to escape my chest—yet knew there was no hope to get away. I'd thought myself accepting of the horror and its consequences. My knotted gut and pounding heart proved otherwise.

I commanded myself to begin.

"You saw the dragon ships yesterday in the museum...." She made a soft noise and nodded her head against my shoulder. "The greatest of those ships could carry seventy men. My ship, the *Mooncutter,* was of average size. It required twenty-eight oarsmen. Add the helmsman and the lookout, I needed thirty men.

"I didn't have them. When I was ready to set out, I was five oarsmen short—and impatient to begin my voyage. To build a trustworthy crew takes time. I should have waited—another year, if necessary. I should have waited and found my men in the proper way, through recommendations of others I knew well, through a process of careful interviews. But as I said, I wanted to be gone. The *Mooncutter* was a beautiful ship, built by the best of our modern-day shipwrights, in clinker design, according to the ancient ways. She was sleek as a snake and as flexible, her single sail of the finest wool, trimmed with leather in the old way, displaying the thunderbolt of the Thorson arms on a background of red. I wanted to be out on the sea in her. I was proud and self-assured.

And I was sloppy..." She stirred. I said, "I sense a question."

"Well, I always wondered..." Her breath was warm against my shoulder.

I pulled her closer and planted a kiss in her fragrant hair. "And what is it you wondered?"

"Why didn't Eric go with you? I mean, he's kind of your right-hand man, isn't he?"

"He is—or, he was. But it isn't done, for the prince who would be king and his prospective grand counselor to make the voyage together. Throughout his reign, a king has his grand counselor to advise him. His Viking Voyage is something he must accomplish first, and on his own." Now, in hindsight, I could see the wisdom in the rule. Had Eric been at my side, things most assuredly would have ended differently. Had he been there to caution me, I might never have made certain terrible choices. And I never would have learned that I was not fit to be king. I added, "And beyond that, a man who sets his sights on the position of grand counselor does not go a-Viking."

"Why not?"

"Tradition." I pulled back enough to look at her, saw the skepticism in her eyes. "What? Tradition isn't enough?"

"Well, there has to be some valid reason for the tradition to get started in the first place, right?"

I settled in close to her again and idly stroked her hair. "I could hazard a guess as to why the tradition began."

"Please do."

"A future king doesn't want competition—and certainly not from his second in command. Were Eric to make a Viking Voyage—with me or otherwise—he would then, as high jarl, be considered eligible in the kingmaking himself. It would…confuse the issue, shall we say?"

"I see." She was twirling her finger in a curl of hair on my chest. "Go on."

I smiled at the ceiling. Dulcie was often bossy—in a thoroughly enchanting way. My smile faded as I returned to my tale. "I went down to the waterfront, seeking able seamen. I found what I thought I was looking for—five strong, eager men who knew their way around a drakkar."

"Drakkar," she repeated the old word for longship. "A beautiful, dangerous word…"

"I am so pleased you approve of it."

She nudged me playfully. "Keep going.…"

"I live but to obey your every command."

"Yeah, right. So keep talking."

I would much have preferred to continue our teasing banter. But that was not to be. "The five strong fellows I found gave what seemed to me to be solid references—references I never inquired about, I was so certain I could ascertain all I needed to know about a man by the look of him and his replies to my exceedingly short list of questions. I was quite full of myself, if you must know. Absolutely certain that, as I was Valbrand Thorson and everything always went the way I wished it, the hiring of five crewmen was a minor thing, easily accomplished."

"Well, now." I could hear in her tone that she was set on defending me. "I don't see what made you particularly full of yourself. It sounds to me like you did the logical thing. I mean, it wasn't brain surgery or anything that you were hiring them for."

"No. It wasn't. But I was the leader. The life of every

man on that ship was in my hands. And because of my..." I heard the building heat in my voice and stopped myself, inquiring curtly, "Dulcie, do you wish to hear the story or not?"

"Yes." She tipped her head up from the crook of my arm and gave me her angel's smile. "I do wish. Continue."

I took a moment to scowl at the light fixture and then, reluctantly, I went on, "We set out. The voyage at first was uneventful. We sailed from island to island—that's how the ancient Vikings did it. The ships, as you saw at the museum, had little space for living. But there are islands all over the North Atlantic. We would make land almost daily and we'd cook over an open fire—one of the five men I hired at the last minute had taken over cook's duties—and sleep the night on solid ground.

"Perhaps three days journey from Iceland, we reached a tiny island uninhabited save for gulls and the occasional shy seal. That was where everything went wrong. The cook fed all but his mates a sleeping powder in the stew. While we slept, they went about slitting throats."

Dulcie pressed closer to me and made a sound of distress.

"Shall I stop?" I longed for her to say yes.

"No," she whispered. "Please. Tell me the rest...."

I sucked in a breath through clenched teeth and let it out with great care. "They killed all but four of my men while they slept. Four of my men and me. When we survivors woke, we found ourselves bound upright to oars pounded into the ground. We woke naked—they had stripped off our clothes. And they had shaved our heads. They taunted us for a while, calling us bald babies, not men at all. Eventually the physical torture began. They cut off the male parts of my men and laughed at their screams of agony. My parts, as you well know, were spared. I think they intended to get to them later. They began cutting away other parts of the men—fingers and toes, then hands and feet. There was blood everywhere and the screaming went on and on. By the end, I was begging them to just kill us and be done with it. Finally they did kill what was left of those four.

"Then they went to work on me. They taunted me for a pretty boy and said they'd make it so I was only half the pretty boy I'd been. They did it with hot tar, which burned, I can tell you, pretty badly when they spread it on, a perfect black mask on the left side of my face. It hurt even more when they set it on fire. I remember...I was screaming and those bastard sons of fitzes were laughing...."

I didn't realize I'd stopped talking until Dulcie asked, carefully, "Valbrand?"

I swallowed, as if I could gulp down the memory—the smell of tar and my own burning flesh and worst of all, the coppery blood smell from my fallen men, the reek of bowels voided in agony and fear. I asked, "Shall I stop?"

She hesitated, but then she said, "No. Finish. Do it."

So I stumbled on. "The rest is...unclear to me. I see it in flashes. There was a rolling ball of blackness in my mind. It rolled and it grew and I remember the moment I broke free of their bindings, the hot spurt of joy within me, that I would take some of them with me as I died. I screamed again, but no longer in anguish. Now, it was a battle cry. Like the berserkers of old, I would hack my way through my enemies to the glory of my death. My shame was never-ending. Yet Valhalla would be mine."

All at once I found it difficult to breathe. I couldn't lie there, among the blankets and pillows, couldn't bear the touch of her clean, warm flesh to mine. I dragged my arm out from under her, threw back the covers and swung my feet to the floor. Head hung, I sucked in hurtful, wheezing breaths through a windpipe that felt like a stepped-on straw.

The bed shifted as she sat up behind me. She had the grace not to touch me—or to speak. She simply waited until my throat relaxed and I learned how to breathe again.

Finally I muttered, "I killed all five. There was the rolling blackness and there was my revenge. It's all...a blur to me now. But I do remember, in the end, hacking at their dead bodies with their own knives, cutting them into pieces so small that no one would ever guess they had once been men. Through it all, there was a ringing in my ears and the blackness, rolling...."

I paused, breathed in and out and in again. Then I said the rest. "I took all the bodies and all the parts of bodies and I loaded them onto the *Mooncutter,* using the ship's one rowboat. It took a number of trips.

"When I had them all on board, I cut the ship loose from her anchor and we floated—thirty dead men and me—out to sea. The rain started almost immediately, a cold curtain between me and the land. I imagined it diluting the river of blood I'd left behind, so that it would soak, at last, into the hungry ground, all signs of the carnage melting away, leaving the innocent land clean again, the only stain of guilt the one in my own mind.

"Once the island of death dropped below the horizon, I set the *Mooncutter* ablaze and I dived overboard. I thought to die, to be swallowed forever by the mother sea."

She whispered, "But you didn't die..."

"No. I washed up, useless flotsam, but still breathing, on yet another island."

"You are not flotsam, Valbrand," she said. "And you're not useless, either. I swear you're not. Do you realize I'd be dead now, if not for you?"

I turned and looked at her. She was crying, silently. As she had cried the night that I met her. With limitless dignity. No sobbing or sniffling. Just brimming eyes, a red nose and tears sliding slowly over her soft cheeks, leaving a glistening trail, dripping finally to the white sheet where she clutched it to her full breasts.

I reached out, brushed my thumb beneath her eye, capturing one fat tear. And I did what I'd longed to do that first night. Brought the tear to my mouth and licked it up with my tongue, tasting it, swallowing it.

She let me do that. She did not recoil or even blink, only went on looking at me steadily, finally murmuring, "Tell me the rest."

I shrugged. "I was quite mad by then, you see. I found a cave in the cliffs near the shore and I...claimed it. I lived there, in that cave, a mad animal, for an endless string of empty months. I knew how to hunt and fish—to set traps and fashion a crude spear. I could build a fire by rubbing sticks. Eric and I, as boys, spent much time in the Vildelund where all such basic skills are taught to the young. The people of that island, fishermen mostly, left me alone. But, of course, they did speak of me—in whispers, in pity and dread. The story spread off-island, of the wild man who lived in the cave on the island's eastern shore."

"And Eric, who was hunting for you by then, heard the stories?"

I nodded. "After months of searching, he found me—or what was left of me. Slowly, as one would coax a wild dog from his den, he plied me with food. Later, when I'd come out quickly at the sight of him, hoping for a treat, he offered blankets and basic tools. It took him weeks to get a word out of me. And more weeks to convince me to return to Gullandria..."

She held out her hand. I took it. We sat like that for a while, not speaking, looking into each other's eyes. I watched her tears dry.

In time, she asked, "What about the families of your men? What did you tell them?"

"The truth. That the men died at sea."

"That's all? No...specifics?"

"No specifics."

"But don't they have a right to know the whole truth?"

"Perhaps."

"Will you ever tell them the details?"

We planned that the truth *would* be told—after we had rooted out the traitors among us and justice had been served. "Perhaps, in time."

"But those men were husbands. Fathers. Sons. The people who love them have a right to hear exactly how they died, no matter how ugly the truth is."

I pulled my hand from hers. "The families of my slain men have been provided for. As to what they know of what happened on that island, it is not your decision, Dulcie—who is told what, when."

"I know, but there should be an investigation, shouldn't there? I mean, you ought to be trying to find out who those men were and why they tried to kill you."

She was beginning to irritate me. "Of course there's an investigation. It's ongoing. And it doesn't concern you."

"Yes it does. Anything about you—or Brit—concerns me."

I gave her the coldest look I could manage. "Will you make me regret, then, what I have told you?"

She sat very still. "So you're telling me I'm getting too close to all the undercover crap that goes on around here, right?"

I maintained my attitude of icy displeasure. "You have what you wanted, the truth of what happened on my Viking Voyage. Be satisfied."

She looked at me, narrow-eyed. "I know there's a bunch you're not telling me. Come on, all the weird stuff that's been happening lately...it's all gotta be related. Those kidnappers Monday night, the way Brit is always switching subjects on me. And now what happened to you, those evil sailors with their sleeping powders and their knives and hot tar." She pointed her chin at me, glaring. "Look me in the eye, Valbrand. Look me straight in the eye and tell me you're certain there's nothing—or no one—behind all the scary shit that keeps happening around here."

"You go too far."

Tears brimmed in her wide eyes again. "I'm sorry. But I hate this. I hate what's happened to you. I hate how you blame yourself. And I hate all these lies and half truths everyone keeps laying on me. As if I'm some idiot child, too young and naive to be let in on all the awful secrets. And now I see that you and Brit and Eric and His Majesty—and whoever else you include in your exalted inner circle—are treating the families of those men who died the same way that you're treating me. As if we don't have the right—or the capacity—to face what's really happened."

"The truth is," I informed her flatly, "that *you* don't

have the right. You are a guest here, for a finite period of time. You know little of our ways and you have no claim on our state secrets. It is not for you to tell the rulers here how to run this country.''

''I'm not trying to—''

''Enough.'' I chopped the air with my hand. ''We will not speak of this again.'' I rose from the bed and began swiftly to gather my clothing.

''Valbrand—''

''No more,'' I commanded. I was furious with myself. The woman was too intelligent by half. I should have kept my long, sad story of foolishness, misadventure and murder to myself, should have known she wasn't one to shed a tear or two over the horror of the tale and leave it at that.

She sat on the bed, adorable and angry—and uncharacteristically silent—as I dressed. I wanted to fling my clothes away and go back to her, to grab her and lay her down and bury myself again to the hilt within her.

At the same time, I despised myself more fully than ever. What was I, some mewling boy, to go whining to a woman with the sordid story of my failure as a man and a potential king?

I had to get out of that room. And she seemed to know it. She never said another word as I pulled on the rest of my clothing and made for the door.

Chapter 16

As you can probably imagine, I didn't sleep very well after Valbrand stalked out.

I kept replaying the awful story he'd told me. It was like something from a horror novel, the stuff of nightmares come to grisly, horrendous life. It astonished me that he'd survived.

I so admired him. On top of loving him.

I was also pissed off at him for walking out on me—at the same time as I could completely understand why he'd done it. Given the hush-hush routine I'd gotten from Brit and all the questions I'd asked that nobody would answer, I could figure out that he probably shouldn't have said so much to me. I knew that it was a proof of his trust in me that he had.

Yeah, maybe I should have just listened and held his hand and kept my opinions to myself. Been supportive instead of argumentative. Maybe I had blown it, preaching to him when the last thing he needed was someone telling him what he ought to do.

And whatever I *should* have done, I was absolutely sure that he meant that parting shot. We weren't going to be talking about his Viking Voyage—or the ramifications thereof—again. Damn it.

I finally dropped off around seven. I got up about one in the afternoon, showered and dressed and ordered up a big breakfast. I spent the rest of the day in the library.

Medwyn joined me. I looked up and there he was, as if he'd sensed I was hoping he might appear.

We discussed Viking wedding rituals and the various feast days of the winter months. And then we moved on to Gullandrian government.

Thursday, December 12

Grand Assembly: both a gold-domed building in the capital of Lysgard and a governing body. Freemen (meaning they are not jarl) are elected to the Assembly and are called assemblymen. Both assemblymen and representatives chosen from among the jarl meet at the Grand Assembly to argue law and decide on matters of importance to the public at large. Medwyn tells me the Grand Assembly is a little like the British parliament. But in Gullandria, unlike Great Britain, the king still retains most of the power.

Medwyn shared with me some Gullandrian expressions.

"Freyja guide your sword arm, Fulla guard your hearth." (Freyja being the Norse goddess of love and war and Fulla the servant of Frigg, the goddess of home and family.)

"Don't bicker over blame while the house burns." (Love it. Good advice!)

"He who fights shadows only squanders his strength." (Oh, yeah. Gotta keep that in mind.)

That night, the activities program announced another buffet and a different movie. There were to be back-to-back balls on Friday and Saturday, so I guess the entertainment committee had decided a couple of buffets in a row wouldn't hurt anyone. I dressed with great care and took a lot of time with my makeup and wore my hair down, the way Valbrand liked it.

The knock came at eight on the nose. I ran to the door and flung it back, a wide smile of greeting on my face.

But the man on the other side was a stranger—yet another prince assigned the duty of partnering Princess Brit's American friend. We exchanged stiff greetings and then went down together. It turned out he was old Prince Sigurd's grandson and namesake. The old prince spotted us when we entered the main solarium. He signaled us over with a wave of his tweedy sleeve.

So I sat with the two Sigurds and tried to enjoy the meal and the conversation and not to think too much about Valbrand. It was no surprise, I kept telling myself, that he would retreat from me, after all he'd told me—and the way I'd gotten into it with him afterward.

I fluctuated between beating myself up for being too hard on him and feeling self-righteous for saying what cried out to be said.

Old Sigurd had a few too many goblets of wine. He told me, leaning close, smelling sourly of alcohol, hair oil and mothballs, that Sigurd the younger just might someday be king. Anything was possible now, after all, what with poor Prince Valbrand so much altered from the man he had been.

"Word is," old Sigurd whispered woozily, "tha' the king's son no longer hash the slightes' inerest in laying claim to 'is father's throne."

About then, Sigurd the younger hissed at his grandfather, "Guard your tongue, old man."

"Sorry, so sorry," muttered Sigurd the elder. With a long, deep belch, he reached again for his wine.

I didn't stick around for the movie. I was tired and more than a little discouraged and I'd seen it before.

What I didn't see was Valbrand. Not that night or Friday night at the first of the two weekend balls, where I danced with my escort—yet another handsome prince—and chatted with Brit and her sisters and talked about the architecture of the ballroom with Medwyn and tried not to feel brokenhearted and forlorn.

What was he *thinking*? We only had a limited amount of time together. And that time was rapidly ticking away.

Though I didn't say a word to Brit about her brother, she must have picked up on my misery. She casually mentioned that Valbrand was away for a few days, "Taking care of a number of official visits he felt he had to make…"

The information didn't cheer me up much. He was gone and he hadn't even bothered to tell me he was going.

Hey. Maybe he'd avoid me right up to the wedding. I'd go home to America the day after—and that would be it. We'd never have another night together, let alone a little time just to talk, to get past the bad feelings from our one argument.

After Brit told me that Valbrand was gone, I gave up

on the ball and went up to my room. I felt dejected. Hurt. So very sad…

At first.

By dawn I was mad again. And by the time I'd had my breakfast and dressed to take the tour van into Lysgard, I was determined that, no matter what, before I left for home, I would track Valbrand down and we'd have a long talk, probably including some shouting on my part.

There were several others in the van with me: a pair of English ladies, distant relatives of Eric and Medwyn's, I learned. And a French couple related to the Thorsons, as well as various students whose fathers were princes. We all banded together to visit the Norse museum, which I was only too happy to get a chance to see again. We had lunch at a cozy little restaurant with a huge mural of Lysgard harbor on one wall. After lunch, we visited the Grand Assembly, the van driver doubling as a tour guide, taking us through the ornate main assembly room where Gullandrian law was made. Next, we visited a church built at the time of the reformation and said to have been dedicated to God's glory and His work on earth by Martin Luther himself.

By then it was a little after two and most of the group was eager to return to the palace, to have a few hours to rest and prepare for the evening's festivities. I wasn't ready to go back yet. The sun was shining, the day milder than usual. I wanted to stroll the cobbled streets for a while, duck into a shop or two, maybe find a café and order some tea and soak up the atmosphere.

And do my very best not to think about Valbrand and what he might be doing now.

The driver told me the right place to wait if I wanted to catch the later van at six. He also marked a route on

a map for me, so that I could shop and then take a stroll
to a small park that overlooked the harbor. "It's full dark
by four-thirty, though, miss," he warned me. "And it'll
be much colder once the sun sets…"

I thanked him and waved goodbye to my fellow tour-
ists.

I found a gift shop full of tacky souvenirs and bought
a bunch—for my mom and my sisters-in-law and my
horde of adorable nieces and nephews. Then I wandered
back outside, and up one narrow street and down another, following the map the van driver had provided as
the sun set over the rooftops of the brightly painted,
steep-roofed buildings.

Eventually I reached the little park on a point over-
looking the harbor. I sat on a stone bench that faced a
path—kind of a promenade, I suppose you could say.
Beyond the path was a white fence and beyond the
fence, a sheer cliff that dropped off toward the harbor
below.

I wrapped my coat a little closer around me and
looked out over the twinkle of harbor lights at the gently
bobbing boats, picking out the distinct shape of the occasional moored longship, the single sails and central
masts nowhere in sight. I assumed the owners must have
removed them while they were at anchor. On a closer
look, I didn't see the famous dragon- or serpent-shaped
prow ornaments, either. But Valbrand had told me those
were removable, too, that a Viking chieftain often ordered the ornament removed while at sea where it might
be lost in a gale—or while moored in safe harbors where
it could be stolen by thieves. To replace the prow ornament was expensive and the loss could bring bad luck.

I looked at my watch: almost five. The sun was long
gone and the light from the Victorian-style street lamps

standing at intervals on the path glowed golden in the darkness. I wasn't alone. People hurried past me on the path—probably headed for home, for a warm fire and the evening meal. Time for me to head back, as well—to the center of town, what they called Old Town—where I could meet the late van.

I gathered up my bags of souvenirs and started walking along the promenade, on my way to the street. I got about ten steps when I heard the sound of hooves drumming behind me.

A horse on the promenade? Yep. Coming on fast, too. Trotting or galloping or…well. Whichever's faster.

And where had everybody gone? All of a sudden, I was alone on the path—I mean, except for whoever was bearing down on me from behind.

I did the logical thing, stepped off the promenade to let the rider go by, turning back to look.

I recognized him immediately, of course. All that black—not to mention the mask. I adjusted my warm wool hat with a gloved hand, gripped my shopping bags a little tighter and waited for him to rein in beside me.

But he kept coming, faster if anything, the heavy hooves of that black horse clattering hard on the cobbles. I got nervous enough to back off some more.

He readjusted his direction so he was headed right at me. That did it. Maybe, I thought, that isn't Valbrand. Maybe the man's an imposter, some fake Dark Raider out to grab me—or run me down.

I dropped my bags of souvenirs and bolted for the copse of shadowy live oaks at the center of the park.

I didn't get far. He was on me in seconds. He reached down and scooped me up, dragging me in front of him, somehow managing to deposit me so I was sitting, legs to the side, between his thighs, in the circle of his strong arm. It was very impressive. After all, I'm no light-weight.

The minute he touched me—as he was hauling me off the ground, as a matter of fact—I recognized him as Valbrand and knew I was safe.

Safe—but not happy. "What the hell was that about?" I demanded. "You've scared ten years off my life. Put me down this minute. I mean it. This instant. I'm not kidding you, I am so completely serious...."

He held me with one arm and the reins with his free hand. The horse pranced twice in a circle, then headed—at a sedate walk now—for the dark trees.

"Valbrand," I whispered through clenched teeth. "Those are my souvenirs back there. I'm not just leaving them for someone to walk off with."

He chuckled then. I wanted to smack him—or maybe just turn and give him a good shove so he fell right off that horse. But I had a feeling that if anyone fell off, it wouldn't be him.

"Fear not, my darling, your trinkets shall be safe."

"Oh, I'm your darling now, am I?"

"You are, most assuredly, my darling one." He laid the bridle gently against the horse's ebony neck and the animal turned back toward the scattered shopping bags.

"Sweet talk will get you nowhere." It wasn't true—but I wasn't letting *him* know that. Yet.

"Here we are." He helped me to slide back down off the horse. I collected my bags. He held a black-gloved hand down to me.

"Not a chance."

He waited a count of three, his dark eyes gleaming behind the mask, before he whispered, "Please?"

I muttered a couple of bad words and extended my hand. He took it firmly and hauled me up.

Once he had me seated—this time with one leg to either side—in front of him, he whispered in my ear, "My dulcet one, you should not be out alone after dark."

"Dulcet. Hah. Very cute."

"I live to amuse you."

"Humph. And what are you doing here?"

"Only looking for you..."

We reached the trees and rode into them. In no time we came out the other side.

"Where are we going?"

"Back to the palace. It will take a while, as it's unwise for the Dark Raider to ride through the center of the city. Make yourself comfortable." He tightened his arm around me, briefly, pulling me back more firmly into the warmth of his body.

A lovely shiver went through me, one that had nothing at all to do with the cold. He brushed my breast—as if by accident. Beneath my coat and heavy sweater and bra, my nipple drew tight.

I elbowed him in the ribs—lightly. "Stop that."

He chuckled again. "As you wish, my radiant one."

Actually, the horse's gait was smooth and slow. And I wasn't all that uncomfortable. And it was nice to be leaning against him, to feel his strong body, warm and reassuring, at my back. Still, I couldn't resist remarking, "You know, you could have just come to get me in a car. The stallion is impressive, but really not necessary."

His lips hovered near my ear. "Starkavin is a gelding."

"Oh. Well, sorry. Forgot to look."

"He was gelded before I claimed him. A pity. I would have put him to stud. And yet a gelding is always the better horse for a rider. A stallion is ever at the mercy of his drive to mate. They are skittish and too quick to bolt.''

"When did you…uh, claim him?"

"In the Vildelund, several months ago. I took him off a pair of young miscreants…ones we call renegades. Wild boys who rob and rape for their entertainment.''

The horse's long mane had been groomed into a row of braids that lay along one side of its smooth neck. I patted the other side. It didn't seem to mind.

We left the park and took a series of narrow streets, Starkavin's hooves clopping at a leisurely pace against the cobbles, passing in and out of the pools of light the street lamps provided.

I dared, after several minutes had passed, to ask, "Where've you been since Thursday morning?"

A pause, and then he answered, "Away."

"Oh," I said softly, and pressed my lips tightly together. I was not going to start in on him, grilling him about what he'd been up to since he walked out on me. We weren't married or anything. We weren't even what you'd call a serious relationship—well, we were to me, but not in the wider scheme of things.

We were…a few joyous days and shining nights; days that passed too quickly, nights that were gone in a flash. I had to accept that. I had to take what we had and be happy with it, as I'd promised I'd do at the first.

He whispered in my ear again, "It came to me that I had been remiss in my duties. The families of my lost men deserved a visit from me."

Happiness spread through me—like sunlight spilling into a shadowed room. "You told them what really happened?"

"Not in the detail I told you, but yes. They know the men were murdered. And that I killed the murderers.''

I relaxed more fully against him with a sigh that came out as a cloud of mist on the icy air. "I'm so glad. You did the right thing."

"On reflection, I found you made a valid point." He said that only slightly grudgingly. And then he added, "However, the fact remains that I spoke much too freely to you. And I don't wish to discuss the subject again."

Should I have left it at that? Probably. But somehow I just couldn't. "Valbrand, you can never speak *too* freely to me. There's nothing you can't tell me. Nothing I can't take. No secret I won't keep if that's what you need from me."

"That may be," he replied. "But my decision stands. We won't speak of this again."

Sunday, Monday, Tuesday…

Those days rushed by in a blur of joy and pleasure. Valbrand spent each evening at my side and the nights in my bed.

And there were gifts, lavish ones that I tried—okay, okay. Not very hard—to refuse. Two new ballgowns: one of a wonderful bronze-colored velvet and the other of opalescent turquoise silk. He took me down into Lysgard on Monday to buy them and coaxed the dressmaker into completing the alterations that day. While we waited for the dresses, we drove out into the rolling farm country east of the palace, a place of open, now-fallow fields and fenced pastures where white Gullandrian horses and karavik—fat-tailed Gullandrian sheep—nipped the flattened grasses between patches of melting snow.

When we returned for the gowns, Valbrand insisted I must have shoes and the right evening bags. And then, well, what's an evening gown and the right shoes without some fabulous jewelry? The red-haired bodyguard accompanied us inside while we visited His Highness's favorite jeweler. We chose a necklace and earrings for each dress: topaz and diamonds; sapphire and diamonds. Valbrand also eyed an emerald bracelet—not to go with either of the gowns, he said, but because it matched the green in my eyes.

Tactfully, I pointed out to him that my eyes were hazel. He cupped my face in his hands and stared into the eyes in question and declared that of course they were hazel—hazel with striations of emerald-green. He turned to the fawning jeweler. "She'll have the bracelet, too."

About then, I finally got a backbone and told him that two necklaces with earrings to match were more than enough. No emerald bracelet—as gorgeous as the thing was—thank you very much.

Tuesday, he showed up when I was in the library with Medwyn. He sat down with us and we spoke quietly together of the ancient verbal art of flyting and an interesting aspect of Gullandrian divorce law.

Tuesday evening, December 17

Feast tonight in the large dining room. All ready to go in my bronze velvet and topaz and diamonds. Waiting for Valbrand's knock at the door…

flyting: a dispute or exchange of personal abuse in verse form.

a woman's place: in Gullandria, women are the protectors of house and home, daughters of Freyja, goddess of love, fertility and war and of Frigg, the goddess of marriage and hearth. Women cannot rule the land, but they can own property and divorce a husband at any time, while men can't divorce once there are children of the union. Women, after all, are considered wiser in matters of family and unlikely to end a marriage for any frivolous reason.

By Wednesday, a certain sadness was creeping in, fraying the edges of my joy. The time when I would leave was approaching too fast. I tried not to think of it, to stay firmly focused on right now.

The palace buzzed with excitement. Friday was the wedding—if possible, Gullandrians always married on Friday, which was Frigg's day.

This time, all rituals and festivities would be held indoors, though from the reading Medwyn had assigned me for my ongoing study of all things Gullandrian, I had learned that Gullandrians, like the Vikings of old, traditionally held the vow-saying part of the festivities outside, closer to nature and the deities of fertility and marriage. And this was a royal wedding, a union of the two most powerful families in the land. As a rule, for such an event, the bride would ride in state through the center of Lysgard and up the winding road to the palace.

Not this time. Once again, the possibility of bad weather was cited as the reason to stay inside. The exchange of vows would be held in the Chamber of the Skalds, the grand feast afterward in the main dining room. Then, in the Grand Ballroom, there would be dancing until dawn.

Thursday—all day and through the night—Brit was sequestered with her mother and her sisters and a wise woman, or *gydhja,* who, with the assistance of Brit's married kinswomen, instructed her on the importance and meaning of being a wife.

I wished I could have been there for that. Brit intended to be the first woman in Gullandrian history to take a

major part in the running of the country. She truly
wanted to be married to Eric. But the practice of wifely
virtues? Fine, if it didn't interfere with those other, more
important activities. Fortunately, Eric seemed more than
willing to accept Brit as she was.

While Brit was still receiving her wifely instruction,
the rest of us enjoyed a feast in the Chamber of the
Skalds, with music and recitations and the usual endless
round of toasting. Valbrand and I went upstairs at a little
after midnight.

We were kissing madly the second we got in the door.
We left a trail of fabulous clothing leading straight to
the bed.

By then, between us, we'd grown highly skilled at the
quick application of a condom. Our two sets of hands
worked as if ordered by one mind. I yanked open the
drawer, he took out the box, I grabbed the condom, tore
off the wrapper and slid it down over him.

And then he was inside me and I was beneath him,
awash in glory and heat and the rightness of *us*. He
braced up on his fists and he looked down at me, moving
within me in a slow, wet, wonderful slide.

He whispered, ''Dulcie, we'll make it last....''

I nodded, eager, yearning, wishing we could do just
that. Make our love last.

And last.

Beyond the day after tomorrow. Beyond forever. For
always.

At least.

He pushed in and I met him and slowly he pulled
back. And then again. And again. I reached down and
grabbed his hard buttocks and pulled him tight into me
so I could feel every inch of him, pressing so deep.

We didn't move. Not for the longest time. And inside, I could feel my body rising. Readying.

I came in a hard slam of stillness, contracting around him, my internal muscles milking him as the pleasure took me down.

He threw his head back, whispered hoarsely, "Ah. Yes. Like that…" And I felt him spurting, the little kicking twitch along the length of him inside me as he found his own release.

With a long sigh, he collapsed against me. I gathered him in, stroked his hair back from his scarred cheek, rubbed my hands in long, light caresses along the smooth skin of his back, tracing the power in the sharply defined muscles beneath.

He nuzzled my tangled hair, curled his head down to lick the sweat from my skin as it trickled along the side of my neck. And then, with a sigh, he slid sideways, guiding me with him, so he was still inside of me, but we faced each other, on our sides, my leg slung over him. Idly, he stroked my breasts, rubbing the nipples so they ached with delight.

We must have slept.

When I woke, he was moving again inside me, a wavelike, liquid glide. My eyes half-open, my head drooped back, I moaned and moved with him in a rhythm slow and sweet and lazy. That time my climax was gradual and spun-out, like a random current that somehow forms itself into something more purposeful, a whirlpool of sensation, spinning faster and faster— pausing—and then, miraculously, like a liquid flower opening, blooms wide.

He pushed in, hard. And then we both held absolutely still. Again, I felt his climax taking form from mine.

He kissed my hair and stroked my shoulders and we lay there as the pleasure faded down to a warm glow.

"Stay where you are...." He pressed his lips to my forehead and gently pulled away, leaving the bed long enough to get rid of the condom.

Within seconds, he was back and gathering me into his arms. I closed my eyes and slept some more.

When I woke again, he was standing at the window. He'd pulled back the heavy curtain and he stood with his naked back to me, looking out at the dark sky where the stars shone intermittently and dark clouds scudded across the half moon.

I sat up.

He must have heard the bed shift, because he turned and looked at me. By the shadowed moonlight, I could clearly see his eyes, see that he was thinking what I'd been trying not to think every day since the first time he'd come to my room.

If I could only stay...

I held out my hand. After a moment, he came to me and sat beside me, his warm fingers closing over mine.

"We have to talk about it," I whispered, as if what I said was something forbidden, something no one else must be allowed to hear.

And maybe it was.

He brought my fingers to his lips, brushed his mouth against them. "There is nothing new to say."

"There is. There's...a question I have."

He scraped his teeth, lightly, along the backs of my fingers, then pressed kisses where his teeth had been. "All right then. Ask."

"Will you be a candidate in the next kingmaking?"

He let go of my hand and turned away, dark head drooping. "Never," he said.

I dared to touch his shoulder and he twisted around again to meet my eyes. "You would make a great king," I said. "Don't you know that? I think you learned, *grew*, from the awful things that happened to you."

He looked at me steadily. "Do you hear yourself? The things that *happened to me*. As if I had no part in them at all."

"But it wasn't your—"

He was shaking his head. "It *was* my fault. I showed myself lacking. In wisdom. In foresight. And most of all, in patience. Thus, what kind of a king I would make matters not. It will never be."

"But I don't understand."

"It is so simple, really. There was…a road I was traveling. I turned from that road, until I lost it utterly. And now I have no right—and no desire—to seek that road again."

"Is it like…a penance, is that it?"

"No. Though penance is certainly called for."

I couldn't hold back a snort of exasperation. "You know, I've gotta say, I think watching while your men were tortured and murdered, having half your face burned off and going insane is probably penance enough."

He shook his head. "There is not enough penance, there never could be."

I made fuming sounds. I really wanted to smack him when he talked like that. But I stuck to the point. "So okay, if it's not about punishing yourself, then why?"

He was very calm right then. "I have been mad," he said. "I have been something not quite human. Slowly I find I am coming back from that. But I'm…not the same. The things I wanted then hold no appeal for me now."

"Like the throne?"

"Yes. Like the throne."

So I hit him with the big question. "Then, well, would it really be so awful if you married a commoner?"

A ghost of a smile haunted the smooth side of his mouth. "Was that a proposal?"

I wished. "No. You can relax. For the moment, anyway. I'm just trying to get the big picture."

"Ah, yes. The big picture…"

"When you're through being amused, maybe you can answer my question."

"Fair enough. No. My marrying a commoner would not be awful in the least—to me."

"But it would to your father, right?"

"Yes, it would."

"Because His Majesty won't accept the idea that you're not going to be king when he dies—and that means he can't accept you marrying a commoner, because that would mean you *couldn't* be king."

"That's it, exactly."

"But sooner or later, he's going to have to realize that the choices you make for your life are your own."

That phantom smile was still there. "Dulcie, my darling one. You don't know my father."

"But he's got no right to—"

He touched my face, light as a breath, to silence me. "You are thinking like an American again."

I caught his hand, pressed my lips to the heart of his palm and then dared to whisper, "So. If I don't go on Saturday, what will he do?"

Gently, this time, he pulled his hand from mine. "But you *will* go on Saturday. And I beg your forgiveness for having been so self-indulgent as to discuss this with you."

Heat rushed to my cheeks. "There's nothing to forgive, damn it. And we *have* to talk about it. We have to—"

"No. We don't. We agreed on what would happen from the first."

He was right. But I wasn't letting that stop me. "Things change—and there are always other options. If you think it's unsafe for me to stay here, why don't you come with me, to America? Just, you know, for a visit? Just to see if maybe you like it there?"

His eyes were so sad. "You know I can't do that."

Well, yeah. I did know—even though he had never said it in so many words. "Oh," I said bitterly. "That's right. Traitors to track down and punish. The necessity for a gruesome revenge…"

He said nothing—but why should he? I'd already put in words exactly what he planned to do.

I guess I should have left it. I *had* known what the deal was from the first. And he'd already apologized for so much as hinting that there might be a future for us. But the hopeless romantic in me was thoroughly roused and holding on for dear life. "So root out the traitors. Bring them to justice. And then take a nice, long vacation in L.A."

"No," he said, his voice so steady and sure it made me want to scream. "Best to cut it clean."

Chapter 17

Best to cut it clean, he had said.

I kept thinking about those words. Fuming about them. Turning them over and over in my outraged mind and finding them hideous.

Unfair.

Cruel.

Yes, in the back of my brain some wiser voice did try to remind me that the way things were turning out shouldn't be any kind of surprise. That I had accepted— even flung myself—into loving a man who had told me repeatedly that nothing long-term would be happening with us. I knew I had no right to be angry just because it was ending exactly as we had agreed it would end.

But that didn't stop me. I was mad and getting madder.

At two in the afternoon on Friday, ready for the most formal of formal occasions in my turquoise gown and aquamarines and diamonds, I received the summons to Brit's rooms. As her best friend, I'd been invited to join her and her sisters and her mother for the final wedding preparations, the all-important hair and makeup.

The summons, bizarrely enough, came by way of Lady Kaarin. I answered the knock and there she was, in strapless gold satin with a three-foot train, more beautiful than ever—if such a thing was possible.

"Miss Samples," she announced, smiling sweetly. "I have the honor to escort you to Her Highness's rooms."

I returned her smile, though mine was a little too wide and a little too stiff. "Great. Just let me grab my bag." I rushed back into the room, snatched up the fabulous beaded orchestra bag Valbrand had bought me, whirled again toward the door—and Lady Kaarin was standing right there, not three feet away. I let out a squeak of surprise and jumped back, almost tripping on the coffee table behind me.

She gave me another one of those oh-so-sweet smiles. "Forgive me. I didn't mean to frighten you." The hard gleam in her eyes said otherwise.

I forced a reasonably cool shrug. "No problem. Let's go."

She didn't move. "I have heard you will be leaving us. Tomorrow, is that right?"

I so did not want to answer her. Which was ridiculous. "Yes," I said. "Tomorrow. I've had a wonderful time here in Gullandria. I'll be sad to say goodbye."

Her mouth still smiled. Her eyes didn't. "I'd imagine so."

"So let's go," I suggested. Again. "Or was there something specific you wanted to say to me?"

"Lovely gown."

"Thank you."

"But then Valbrand always did have exquisite taste." Meaning I didn't. She added the real zinger. "At least in clothing…"

I clutched my Judith Leiber bag a little tighter. "You know, I think I can find my way to Brit's rooms without any help from you."

"Ah, but Dulcie—may I call you Dulcie?" It wasn't really a question. She went right on. "You see, I can't let you do that. Here at Isenhalla we have…protocols. Even rude Americans must learn that things are done a certain way."

I longed with all my heart to bitch-slap that woman. Which was very strange. I was, as a rule, not the violent type. "What is this?" I asked, with what I hoped was limitless dignity. "What's the *point* of this? You just said it yourself. I'm leaving tomorrow. You could be a little…graceful. You could stay out of my face until I'm gone."

She'd given up the pretense of smiling. Her perfect nostrils quivered and her elegant mouth curved in a sneer. "You are second choice. You know that, don't you? You're…the *other* redhead, that's what you are. Did you think he would marry you? Even hideous as he is now, with half his face melted off, he would never marry someone like you."

That about did it. "Get out."

She just stood there, glaring. I glared right back, the blood spurting through my veins so hard, I heard drums in my head. It was a Jerry Springer moment. I *knew* there was going to be violence. Ripping silk. Torn-out hair. I saw the two of us, rolling on the antique rug in our beautiful gowns, screeching obscenities and slapping each other silly.

And then…

It was over.

She spun on her designer heel and stomped out.

I dropped to the sofa and waited for my heart to slow down and my blood to stop boiling. It took a while.

Once my pulse stopped pounding and my hands quit shaking, I locked up my room and set out to find Brit's suite on my own. It wasn't that difficult.

The two stone-face soldiers guarded the door, as usual. Like two well-oiled parts of the same machine, they stepped sideways toward each other, each grasping a door handle and then stepping apart to pull the doors wide.

I went through. A maid greeted me and took me back to Brit's dressing room.

Brit was there alone, sprawled in a pink chair with a heart-shaped back. She wore an ivory satin bra, panties to match and a look of pure impatience. She also had her hair up in curlers the size of Coke cans.

She jumped up when she saw me. "Dulce. At last. I need you to do something with my... God. You look great."

I smiled my thanks. "Where'd everybody go?"

"They had to get ready, too. Well, except for the *gydhja*. She left when she'd finished imparting to me everything she thought I needed to know—which was, I am telling you, more than I *wanted* to know."

"Like?"

She waved a hand. "Well, all the stuff about *deferring* to my husband. It's just not going to be happening. But Eric already knows that." She heaved a sigh. "And the sauna was nice. For purification, you know. That was just me and mom and the wise woman—since Elli and Liv are pregnant, they decided to take a pass. I sat and sweated while the wise woman lectured. Mom, in the meantime, sweated a lot herself and nodded at all the right places and tried to keep from grinning at the whole idea of her troublesome youngest daughter learning to be a most excellent wife and helpmeet.''

''So now you are purified and ready to wed?''

''Yeah. Good to go—well, except for my hair. That's your job.'' She grabbed my hand and dragged me into the closet, which was fragrant with cedar paneling and as big as the living room of my East Hollywood apartment. ''The dress,'' she announced, holding it up to herself.

I fingered the ivory silk. ''Kind of medieval.'' The long, corsetlike waist came to a point at crotch level and the full, flowing sleeves had puffs midway between shoulder and elbow. It was embroidered in gold and trimmed with seed pearls. I grinned at her. ''You are going to look so beautiful in this.''

She scowled. ''Well, it goes with my bridal crown.'' She led me back to the dressing room where the crown waited on a wig head in a corner. It was gold-plated, the finish worn away in spots to reveal some other metal beneath, with high points ending alternately in crosses and clover leaves, set with hunks of rock crystal and woven with red and green silk cords.

''Wow,'' I said. ''It's…intricate.'' It looked very old—and very tacky.

''Been in the family for generations,'' she. told me with a shrug. Then she dropped into the chair in front of the wide mirror. ''Now,'' she said. ''Hair.''

''Yes, Your Highness.''

''I like your attitude.''

I stuck my tongue out at her in the mirror and went to work.

Her hair barely brushed her shoulders, which didn't

really fit with the flowing, romantic style of her gown. But I did my best: a few braids at the crown, pinned up in back.

"I love it," she said when I was done.

"You always do."

"I'm not kidding, Dulce, if you ever decide to give up writing, there's a major career waiting for you in hair design."

"Jose Eber, eat your heart out." I was gathering up the extra pins to put them back in the little plastic case. I glanced up and saw she was watching me.

"You okay?"

I bit my lip and shrugged. And then we just stared at each other in the mirror for ten seconds or so.

Finally she sighed. "All good things must come to an end, right?"

I gulped and made myself give her a nod.

"Damn it, Dulce..." She swiveled the chair around and stood. We grabbed for each other, hugging tight, my yards of turquoise silk enveloping her in her bra and panties.

I don't know how I did it, but I managed not to burst into tears. I was even the one who pulled back, taking her by her bare shoulders and holding her away. "Better get dressed, huh?"

She nodded. "You know, if it's any consolation— since you and my brother hooked up, he actually looks *happy* a lot of the time. That's a first in the months I've known him."

I brushed at the one stubborn tear that threatened to escape my lower lid. "Yeah, well. I'm glad for that— but I could have done without the last-minute visit from the dragon lady."

She gave me a puzzled frown. "The dragon lady?"

"Kaarin Karlsmon. The one you sent to show me the way here."

She let a low groan. "I swear. It wasn't me. Kaarin does a lot of walking people here and there. I turn in a list to the keeper of the keys—you know, like the head housekeeper? The list has things like who, of my personal guests, will need an escort for any given event— and who is officially coming to my rooms at any given time. The keeper of the keys decides who'll escort whom. I didn't even imagine that—"

"Hey. It's okay."

"Did she *do* something?"

"No. It was what she said."

"Which was...?"

"She made it extremely clear that she is not my friend, that's all."

Brit blew out a loud breath. "I don't get it. I mean, you know, I told you that she and Valbrand had a thing way back when. But since he came back, there's been nothing between them. I think they've spoken a total of maybe ten words to each other since we came in from the Vildelund in September."

"So she just hates me on principle?"

"Maybe she's jealous, now she sees him happy again. I don't know. How would I know? I told you, I never liked her much. She always seemed like a fake to me. Shifty, you know? And I promise, I'll see to it that she's seriously reprimanded for giving you a hard time today."

"Please don't."

"But—"

"Look. I'm out of here tomorrow. Just leave it alone. And don't tell Valbrand. He doesn't need to hear it. I only mentioned it to you because I thought you had sent her to my room."

"No way."

"Well, okay. Let's get back to the important stuff." With a flourish, I gestured toward the dressing room and her waiting wedding gown.

An hour and a half later, my best friend married her Viking prince. It was a twofold ceremony: the Norse half, culminating in the exchange of wedding swords and then of rings on the ends of the swords. And then the Lutheran minister took over to lead them through traditional Christian vows.

I was relieved to note that no innocent animals had to die; I'd read that in Viking weddings of old, the ceremony always started with a sacrifice of a goat, a sow, a horse or a boar, as those were the animals associated with the various gods of fertility. Fir branches would then be dipped in the blood of the sacrificed animal and flicked over the bride and groom and the assembled guests during the remainder of the ceremony. The meat would be served at the wedding feast.

But I digress.

Once the vows were said, we moved on to the dining room—raced, actually. Eric managed somehow to get there first and, as tradition decreed, barred the doors with his sword until Brit arrived, breathless and laughing, and he could lead her across the threshold, making sure she didn't stumble—stumbling being a bad omen for the success of the marriage.

There was the test of the groom's strength. Eric plunged a sword into a section of tree trunk—I figured that had to be physically impossible, that there had to be some trick to it. But trick or not, it was impressive.

Next, the bride and groom shared their first loving cup of ale, followed by the ceremony of Thor's hammer, which Eric placed in Brit's lap to promote fertility. I had to grin at that one. Brit had nothing against babies. But she only wanted two at the most—and not for a few years. Maybe that's why she looked down at that hammer in her lap as if she wasn't sure how it had gotten there and she hoped someone would remove it soon.

Once the basic rituals were accomplished, we all settled into an evening of toasting and feasting and enjoying the recitations of a number of talented skalds. Through it all—the vow-saying and the feasting—Valbrand stayed with me. We were...cordial, with each other, I guess you could say. Cordial and careful—and tender, too.

I wasn't mad at him anymore. As the day had progressed, my fury had kind of blown itself out. I was just trying to make it marginally easier on my poor heart. Trying to pull away a little at a time. Learning to accept that tomorrow I was going to let go.

As the hours passed, it only got harder. To smile and raise my goblet at the next toast, to laugh at the clever and good-natured flytings of the skalds. More than once, I looked up to find Kaarin Karlsmon watching me. She'd instantly glance away and start talking with great animation to Prince Onund on her left side, or a red-haired prince I didn't recognize on her right. I shouldn't have let her sly stares get to me. But they did. They kind of wore me down.

I had been chosen, with nine other single women— *not* including Kaarin Karlsmon, I was pleased to see— for the honor of readying the bride for her groom. At midnight, we led Brit upstairs. I removed her bridal crown and put it back on the wig head in the dressing room. I unbraided and combed her hair and we helped her out of her ivory wedding dress and into a white satin nightgown. Since I wouldn't be seeing her in the morning before I left, I got a last goodbye hug from her before she settled into bed.

The men burst in with Eric. We all fell on him—to "help" him undress. He put up with twenty pair of hands grabbing at him for about thirty seconds.

Then he shouted, "That's enough!" and ordered us out.

Laughing, chattering, heavy on the hormones and sexual innuendo, we all headed for the ballroom. Valbrand and I were swept along with the rest.

Once there, he took me in his arms. We danced.

"You are pensive tonight," he whispered.

"Um," I said. He could take that however he liked. I nuzzled my head against his shoulder and moved with him to the rhythm of the music and hoped I was going to make it through the night without crying or begging him to let me stay.

It was after two when we went to my room. We stood in the sitting area, before the fire, facing each other, both my hands in his.

He asked, "Would you like me to go?"

I squeezed his fingers and shook my head. He gave a tug—and I was in his arms. I pressed close, nestling against him, sighing.

Wishing...

No. It was no time for wishing. All that was left for us was that night.

We undressed slowly, careful of our finery—and, really, of each other. In the bed, we cuddled up close and then simply lay there, arms around each other, legs entwined.

He brushed my hair away from my cheek and I stroked the ruined terrain of his scarred temple, the welts and puckers at his mouth and his eyelid.

We slept.

Some time later, we woke and made love with slow tenderness. I let go and cried at the end, a steady stream of fat tears. At least I did it silently. He licked the tears from my cheeks and held me tighter as he came, pressing so hard into me.

All I wanted was never, ever, to have to let him go. It's the very worst thing about being a romantic. Life refuses to stack up to your dreams. There's altogether too much of saying goodbye. And forever?

Well, everybody knows there's really no such thing.

Before we slept again, he whispered, "In the morning—"

I silenced him with two fingers to his lips. "Just let me go, okay? Let tonight be our goodbye."

"If that's how you wish it."

It wasn't. What I wished was so much more than he was willing to give.

When I woke to daylight, he was gone. He'd left a velvet jeweler's case on his empty pillow. Inside was the emerald bracelet that he'd tried to buy for me the Monday before. I hardly let myself look it at. The sight of it only brought on a fresh flood of tears.

As I showered and dressed I considered leaving the gowns and the shoes and the glittering bags, the necklaces, bracelet and earrings behind. But that was only because some part of me wanted to hurt him, to shame him by throwing his beautiful gifts in his face. No. I would take them. I would be the only waitress at Magdalena's on Pico with forty thousand dollars worth of jewelry and two Judith Leiber evening bags—well, if I still had my job when I got back, that is.

As I was packing, the maid came in with an extra suitcase. She said she'd been told I would probably need it. I did. I never would have managed to fit those two gowns in the suitcases I'd brought with me. The maid asked me what time I'd be ready to go.

"Eleven," I said.

"A man will be up to see to your bags and the car will be waiting downstairs." She bowed herself out.

It was snowing when I left—very lightly, the flakes sparse and small, like flecks of laundry detergent whipping around in the icy wind. I emerged from between the massive main entry doors and saw Medwyn waiting beside the idling black car, his wispy beard blowing in the wind, snowflakes catching on his grizzled eyebrows.

With a cry, I ran to him.

As the driver loaded my suitcases into the trunk, Medwyn gave me a hug. I couldn't believe that I was actually wrapped in his long, skinny arms for a moment. It was kind of like hugging warm sticks. I felt his heartbeat, slow and steady. He smelled kind of smoky and sweet—incense, maybe.

He broke the embrace and took me by the shoulders and pinned me with a long, deep look. "Did you think to escape without granting an old man a word of farewell?"

The tears were brimming. I dashed them away, sniffling. "I'm so glad you didn't let me."

"Take this." He handed me a handkerchief—silk, monogrammed with the runic symbols that stood for his name.

"Thanks." I wiped at my nose and dabbed at my eyes. "Sheesh. I'm a regular waterworks lately...."

"Dulcinea." All of a sudden, he was sounding very stern. "You must hear me. Hear me well."

I gulped and blotted my eyes one more time. "Sure..."

He remained scarily solemn. "I need your strictest attention."

His strange tone had my heart beating faster and my throat going tight. I coughed into my fist to clear it. "Really. I'm listening."

He narrowed his eyes and peered at me intently, as if checking inside my head to make sure I really was paying attention. Finally he nodded. "A great challenge awaits you. Be strong. Do not surrender to your fear or to despair."

I gulped again. "Okay." I was thinking he was laying it on a little thick. Yeah, I was going to be miserable and lovesick for a while. And I figured Magdalena's was history. So there was job hunting coming up. And getting used to living in L.A. without Brit to tell all my secrets to.

But fear and despair weren't going to get me. I would put one foot in front of the other, take it a day at a time. And things would get better eventually.

If it got too bad, I'd go home to Bakersfield for a while and tell my *mom* all my secrets. She'd listen and she'd hold my hand and insist that everything was going to be all right. She'd give me the homework speech, the one that ended in, "So you see, honey, that no matter how awful things get, you are always doing your homework. The tough times are teaching you, making you stronger, more loving, more ready for the next wonderful and fulfilling phase of your life...."

What can I tell you? That's my mom. God, I missed her.

Medwyn's bony fingers dug into my shoulders. He still had that strange, piercing look in his eyes. "Be strong," he said again.

"I said, I will."

"You *can* triumph. It *is* possible."

"I know."

The eerie look softened. He stopped digging his fingers into me. "Yes," he said. He looked suddenly radiant. I know that's not a word anyone associates with a wrinkled old man. But he did. He seemed to glow. "I believe that you do."

The driver was back behind the wheel. Medwyn opened the backseat door and I slid in. I set my purse and my AlphaSmart case on the other side of the seat, then turned back to say goodbye.

"Thank you," I said. "For the days in the library, for all you taught me. For advising me on which books to read to get to know your beautiful country a little better."

He smiled then. A glowing, beatific smile. "Necessity, Fate and Being," he said. "May the three Norns of destiny show you the way." He pushed the door firmly closed and stepped back from the car.

I hooked my seatbelt and then turned to watch him through the rear window, a tall, painfully thin figure, arm raised in salute, snow whirling around him in a thickening cloud as we drove away.

Once he was out of sight, I realized I still had his handkerchief clutched in my hand. I stuck it into the pocket of my car coat, and got my Alphie from its carrying case.

Saturday, December 21. 11:20 a.m. Leaving Isenhalla. Gunmetal sky. Light snow blowing in whirling patterns across the winding downhill road.

Another big party tonight—they'll still be cele-
brating yesterday's wedding. And it's also the winter solstice, which is almost as big as Christmas
around here. As I left, they were decking all the
banisters and rails and mantels with spruce boughs,
bringing in tall firs that smelled of snow and ever-
green and putting them up in all the main rooms.

By tonight, those trees will be glittering bright
with thousands of lights and decorations. Quantities
of sweet ale will be consumed. There will be one-
on-one combat in the Grand Ballroom. Hauk will
fight. Hate to miss it.

But I'm on my way home.

God. I don't want to go. Want to tell the silent
driver, "Stop. Turn around. I'm going back...."

But I say nothing. The car rolls on down the
twisting road. I wouldn't be welcome if I went
back. Everyone—including V.—wants me gone.

And there are benefits. No matter how deep the
pile of manure, there's a horse in there somewhere,
right?

At least now, safely out of the palace, certain at
last that no one will read this without my knowing
it, I can write about him.

I can put it all down, the

My damn eyes were brimming again. I dug out Medwyn's handkerchief and dried my tears and blew my
nose.

We wound on, down the high, wide hill on which
Isenhalla stood, the only car on the road. *I am going to*

be okay, I thought. *I am going to face my fear and conquer my despair. Medwyn has said I can do it. And I will.*

I left my AlphaSmart waiting in my lap, and I stared out at the swirling snow as we reached the base of the hill and the land leveled out. From there, it was a gently curving road, lined with tall trees halfway to the airport. Soon, the trees would thin out. There would be open fields, sloping hillsides with tall, thin windmills here and there, metal blades spinning in the strong wind. I watched the trees file toward us and stream away behind, looking forward to the cheerful sight of the spinning windmills.

We were maybe a third of the way to our destination, still surrounded by trees on both sides, when I heard an odd, cracking sound—like a tree branch breaking or somebody clapping their hands once, hard.

I turned from my side window to ask the driver what it was.

The words died in my throat. He wasn't going to answer. He was slumped over the wheel, unconscious— probably dead. In fact, judging by the bright spray of blood across the dashboard and spattered on the window, he was *definitely* dead.

I only just had time to register all this—I was having a real problem accepting what was happening—when the car, driving itself now, zipped across the center line and launched itself into the deep ditch on the far side of the road.

We hit the opposite bank with a bone-crushing lurch. The front airbags inflated with a scary *whoosh*. My AlphaSmart hit the seat in front of me and then bounced back to bop me on the forehead, dropping, in the end, neatly to my lap where it had started. Metal screamed as the front of the car struck and crumpled. The engine roared in mechanical fury, the flattened nose crumpling some more, making awful cracking, snapping sounds punctuated with ear-flaying squealing noises as the car tried to drive itself into the half-frozen ground.

I screamed. Not that it did a bit of good.

The engine kept roaring, but we were going nowhere. It roared louder. And louder. And then, suddenly, revved to a fever pitch, it cut out.

I sat there, safe in my seat belt, staring at the dead driver—slumped now, toward the console between the seats—at the fan of dripping crimson on the windshield above the now half-deflated airbags. The blood was spotted here and there with chunks of stuff that had to be the poor man's brains.

My stomach rose toward my throat. I was going to chuck my cookies, just vomit all over myself—probably hurl right over the seat to spray the dead man.

"No!" I got out on a strangled groan. I was not going to do that. The man was dead and he deserved to be treated with a little dignity.

And wait a minute. Maybe he wasn't dead. As soon as I was through vomiting, I would have to see about that, and then get help.

I shoved the Alphie off my lap, fumbled with my seat belt, clapping my hand over my mouth as the gagging reflex struck again.

The latch gave. I leaned on my door, which had struck nothing and wasn't crumpled at all. It opened. I had to shove hard, as my side of the car was uppermost, and I was opening the door as much up as out. I swung my jean-clad legs into cold empty air and then slid out of the car, dropping into the ditch. The door, with the aid of gravity, slammed behind me.

Not that I noticed. I crouched in the crusty snow in the bottom of the ditch and vomited.

When the retching stopped, I stuffed a handful of what I hoped was clean snow in my mouth to rinse it. Breathing hard through my nose, I sat back on my heels.

That was when I noticed the man standing in the ditch with me. He wasn't tall—five-seven tops—and he looked military. Blue eyes like lasers. Wide shoulders. Powerful-looking thighs encased in camouflage khakis and lace-up black soldier boots. He wore a watch cap over his bullet-shaped head.

I blinked, wondering if maybe I was seeing things. I did, after all, have a bump on my forehead from where my Alphie had hit me.

But no. He was still there. And now he was striding toward me.

I gaped at him, bewildered. He came and stood above me and—I thought—reached down his hand. A split second too late I saw the syringe. By then he'd already plunged the needle into the side of my neck.

Unconsciousness came at me, surrounding me, swallowing me down. I sighed as the snowy ground came up to meet me.

Chapter 18

That afternoon, I crouched in the dirt of the training yard by the soldier's barracks not far from the palace. Nude to the waist and dripping sweat in spite of the winter temperature, I was practicing my skills at hand-to-hand with a hapless berserker who'd had the poor judgment to volunteer when I came looking for an opponent.

We were using daggers. Both of us were bloodied. Three times we'd come together, rolling, striking. I suppose I could have taken him, flicked my blade at a vital spot just deep enough to bring a drop of blood and the victory would have been mine.

But I didn't want it to end. I wanted something to occupy my mind—something other than emerald-flecked hazel eyes and lemon-scented red hair and the royal jet that was no doubt already winging its way to America. The berserker and his dagger were doing the job as well as anything else might.

We circled each other as the ring of men around us called out rough encouragements and placed bets on the outcome. Only Hauk would have dared to break through the shouting ring of spectators and call a halt.

And that's exactly what he did.

My sister's huge husband elbowed the circle of soldiers aside and stepped between me and my opponent. "Your Highness. I beg your indulgence."

I armed sweat and dirt from my brow. "I trust this is important, Hauk."

"Please. But a moment. Alone."

"Your Highness," my opponent announced between ragged, panting breaths, "I willingly concede victory to you."

I shook my head. "On the contrary. I surrender. Victory is yours."

He bowed. "As you wish, so shall it ever be."

Hauk called for a towel and one came flying. "Disperse," he commanded. The men wandered off as I toweled away blood-pink sweat and grime.

"Now," I said. "What?"

Hauk leaned close so that I alone would hear. "The young American's car has been discovered in a ditch on the road that leads to the airport. The driver is dead, shot through the head."

The smell of sweat and blood and dirt receded. There was emptiness—no scent, no sight, no sound. Around me. Within me. A hollow space where once, for a few brief and beautiful days, there had been warmth and a certain woman's smile.

Cursed, I thought. I am cursed. An evilness that walks the world. And where I go, the good and the innocent perish in flames.

I made myself ask it. "And Dulcie?"

Hauk shook his golden head. "Vanished," he said.

Hauk and I went together to the site. A pair of Lysgard police detectives, called in after someone notified the city authorities, had arrived on the scene first. There was some small difficulty convincing the pair to turn over the investigation of this particular crime to the king's men. In the end, though, Hauk reminded them that Gullandria is a monarchy. And the king's word is law.

"And it is never wise," I added, "to enter into a dispute with one's king."

The detectives apparently saw the sense in that, as they departed a minute or two later—leaving their crime scene techs at our disposal. Hauk gave me a pair of latex gloves and showed me where to walk in order not to disturb evidence. There were footprints on one side of the vehicle and a pool of what I guessed was vomit.

The evidence people said it appeared that the driver had been shot through the driver's door window, from the cover of the trees on the side of the road, perhaps two kilometers back, while the car was in motion. The car had veered across the road and into the ditch. Dulcie had climbed from the car, been sick—and then, judging by the pattern of footprints, been picked up and carried from the scene. In the back seat, they'd found a miniature computer and a purse with Dulcie's American driver's license in it.

I looked into the car, at the dead man in the front seat—at the emptiness behind.

"Excuse me, Your Highness," said one of the techs, trying to get by me to do his work.

I knew I was only in the way. I retreated to the bank and watched the professionals work. The light snow of the morning had stopped. The winter sun shone down on me, weak and lacking in warmth.

I watched Hauk take a sealed plastic bag with a square of white cloth in it and Dulcie's toylike computer from one of the techs. They spoke briefly and then Hauk climbed the bank to my side.

He held up the plastic bag. "They found this under the seat just now," he said. "Are those not the runes that stand for M and G?"

I nodded. "Mannaz and Gebo." I guessed, "Medwyn?"

"I was thinking of him...."

"He has been..." What should I call their relationship? I settled on, "Friendly. He's been friendly to her. She's shown a great interest in our land and our ways. Medwyn took it upon himself to be her tutor on all subjects Gullandrian."

Hauk said, "We should speak with him immediately." I was already turning for the car we'd driven down from the palace. But Hauk stopped me. "There's more." He showed me the tiny screen of the computer. "The technician just turned it on. This is what came up."

Prince Valbrand Thorson. Skuldaric Tower. Tonight. Midnight. Come alone, or the American dies.

Chapter 19

My father, furious, paced the space behind his desk. "Skuldaric Tower? That old ruin at the foot of the Black Mountains? The instructions are that my son shall go there—alone?"

I turned from the window before Hauk, standing to attention on the far side of the empty desk and looking exceedingly grim, could answer. "Your Majesty, I am right here. No need to speak of me as if I'm not in the room."

My father made blustery noises. "Ah. Well. Ahem. Whatever these ridiculous instructions found on some electronic toy, you, of a certainty, will not go. It's far too likely that the turncoat Jorund Sorenson and the traitor prince we seek are behind this plot. One man, no matter how skilled, could not stand alone against them. Hauk, send your best men immediately to surround the tower and rescue the unfortunate young woman."

"No," I said, before Hauk could reply.

My father halted in his angry pacing and demanded, "What? You dare to countermand the orders of your king?"

"I beg you," I said in a tone barely above a whisper, "do not do this."

Something in my words or my demeanor must have reached him. He waved a hand. "All right, Hauk. Not yet."

I realized I was holding my breath and slowly allowed it to escape. "It is for my sake that she was taken and that her life is at risk. I intend to follow the instructions of her kidnappers. I will be there, *alone,* at Skuldaric Tower tonight when the clock strikes twelve."

My father stood very still. I took it as a good sign that he was not already shouting.

Had the choice been mine, we would not be speaking to him of Ducie's kidnapping—not until I'd brought her back safe or died in the attempt. But Hauk, as the king's warrior, was oath-bound to report what he knew to his liege. So we'd come to do it together, calling Eric, Brit and Medwyn into the private audience chamber, as well. Eric and Brit sat silent in the chairs facing the king's desk. Medwyn stood back, behind my father and out of his path as he paced.

Osrik said, "This is madness. You will only be walking blind into a trap."

"I have no choice."

"But of course you have a choice. You can let Hauk's men go in your place. They are trained to deal with abductors and assassins."

"You read the instructions. Should I fail to appear—alone—they will murder her."

My father looked infinitely sad. "My son, don't you realize it's likely they already have?"

I showed him my back. If I'd remained facing him, I would have struck him. "I will not believe that."

"Valbrand's right." It was Brit, speaking up for the first time since we'd entered the room. I turned around again.

His Majesty was not pleased. "This discussion does not concern you, daughter."

"Of course it concerns me." Brit surged to her feet and stood, head high, fisted hands to her sides. "Dulcie Samples is my dearest friend. She's in danger. And I'm with Valbrand. I refuse even to consider that it's too late to save her. There's only one way to handle this and that's for Valbrand to go alone to deal with the problem. Eric, Hauk and I and a few trusted men will provide backup..." She must have seen the hot look I sent her, because she added, "At a safe distance. We'll be ready to move in at Valbrand's signal and not before. I, personally, have seen what my brother can do in a tough situation. If anyone can bring Dulcie back safe, he's the one. You have to let him go. Honor demands it."

It was beautifully said.

And our father knew it. "Honor," he muttered, as if he hated the word.

"Yes. Honor," Brit proudly repeated.

My father swore, a rank oath in the old language, and then he conceded wearily, "Very well. I suppose you have me. The choice is not ours to make."

It occurred to me that he had known as much all along. Brit took her chair again as I bowed to the king. "Thank you, Your Majesty."

Now he was the one turning away, in order to hide, I suspected, the power of his emotions. When he faced us again, he was composed. "The matter, then, is settled." He looked at Hauk and then at me. "What else? Ah.

The murdered driver. Compensation must be made to his family. And he shall have a hero's burial. I personally shall attend the services.'' He looked at Medwyn. ''See that it is done.''

The grand counselor bowed. ''So I shall, my liege.''

Hauk and I exchanged glances. We'd agreed on how we would handle the subject of the handkerchief found in the car. It was time to do that now.

Hauk said, ''Sire, in the waylaid car we found the missing American's small computer, already mentioned. We also found her handbag *and* a white silk handkerchief embroidered with the runic symbols Mannaz and Gebo.''

''That was mine,'' Medwyn announced without the slightest hesitation. ''I gave it to Dulcinea this morning, as she was leaving.''

My father swung on him. ''You saw the girl this morning?''

Medwyn seemed completely unconcerned. ''I did. I bid her farewell. The handkerchief was for the purpose of drying her tears. She was sad to go—and I was sad to see her leave. I am, my lord, quite fond of Dulcinea. I find in her a quick and hungry mind and a steady heart. I admire her greatly.''

''Enough,'' said the king. ''A testimonial is hardly called for.''

''Your pardon, my lord. Yet she is a lovely girl.''

''You have arcane knowledge concerning her, is that it? You have seen something in the future that shows this woman to be of special import to us?''

''My lord, I only ever see but dimly. Shadows across a darkened plain…''

''You evade my question.''

"Your Majesty, what is to be, is to be. My wavering visions will neither guide destiny nor change it."

"How helpful you are in this," my father sneered. "Your visions do not guide—and your words do not satisfy."

"And for that I have only limitless regret."

The two lifelong friends faced each other squarely. I thought of old lions, stiff in the joints and scarred from years of battle, yet ready to fight tooth and claw if necessity demanded.

My father accused, "I know, Medwyn, of the hours you have spent with the missing girl. Your two heads together—grizzled gray, untamed red—in my own library. It has been remarked upon."

"Sire, she wished to learn about our land. I was only too pleased to help her toward that end."

My father grunted. "My daughter. My bloodbound lifelong friend. And my son. Does this American enchant everyone she meets?"

The question was rhetorical but it occurred to me that there might be a line of inquiry here. "It's a thought worth pursuing. We've been assuming that Dulcie is a pawn and no more, that she's been kidnapped only as a way to draw me out. But what if there is some animosity toward Dulcie herself? Is there anyone at the palace who might have reason to wish her ill?"

"Maybe." We all turned to stare at Brit again. "Dulcie did say yesterday that she had some kind of run-in with Kaarin Karlsmon. Kaarin showed up at her room supposedly to escort her to my suite. Dulcie wouldn't tell me what was said, only that Kaarin made it way clear she was not Dulcie's friend. I offered to reprimand Kaarin. Dulcie said she didn't want that." Brit met my eyes. "She also asked me not to mention it to you."

"Whyever not?" I was stung that she had not seen fit to confide in me.

"I guess she…didn't want to bother you."

Osrik said, "Let's clear this up now. Order the Lady Kaarin to attend us here immediately."

Hauk went to fetch her. We waited, each minute an eternity. A full half hour later, Hauk returned to report that the Lady Kaarin was nowhere to be found. Since her belongings were still in her rooms, it was reasonable to assume she had not formally left the palace.

My father said, "Shall we, then, call the Karlsmon estate and discover if she is there—or on her way there?"

"No," I said. "If Kaarin is somehow involved in Dulcie's disappearance, we don't want her warned that we're looking for her."

"The keeper of the keys, then," Osrik suggested. "Let's find out what she has to say about sending Lady Kaarin to the young American's rooms in the first place."

The housekeeper was shown in ten minutes later. Though she kept her back straight and her chin up, she appeared more than a little distressed to be called before the king. She told us that Lady Kaarin had inquired about the American, asking if Dulcie would need a lady to accompany her at any time. Kaarin had said she admired Dulcie and would like the opportunity to meet her. The keeper of the keys had then granted Kaarin the duty of escorting Dulcie to Brit's suite on the day of the wedding.

As the housekeeper spoke, I stood by the window and looked out at the darkening winter sky and thought of the fury in Kaarin's eyes when she saw me looking at

Dulcie that night in the alcove. Immediately after that, I'd rejected Kaarin's offer to resume our relationship.

And Kaarin never had taken rejection well. I supposed I'd been a fool to imagine that she'd consider a sting on the cheek sufficient punishment for my having dared to say no to her.

Once the keeper of the keys was dismissed, I shared my thoughts with the others. "Kaarin has always wanted, above all, to be queen. I'd wager she would cast her lot with whomever she believed might carry her through to her goal."

"Onund," Brit said. "She's been seeing Onund." She shook her head, incredulous. "He's such a slimy little weasel. Could he really be the mastermind here, the one behind what happened to Valbrand and my plane going down and all the rest? I gotta tell you, it's a stretch for me to buy that one."

Osrik said, "Onund may not be fearsome of himself. But never forget that his father lost the throne to me and has hated me ever since. Gunther Havelock is a man of strong will and great determination. He keeps himself well away from me in order, I've always suspected, that I not be able to look in his face and know what an enemy I have in him."

Eric, quiet for so long, spoke then. "Perhaps," he said to Hauk, "you should assign a man or two to shadow Onund."

"Yes," said Brit. "And send some others to find out what Prince Gunther is up to—and Lady Kaarin, let's not forget her. As soon as she resurfaces, she'll need watching."

Eric continued, "It could be useful to know how, where and with whom all three of them spend their time. Also, if we have them under surveillance and we decide we wish to question them, we can nab them before they have any chance to slip away.''

"An excellent suggestion," declared the king. "Hauk, put men on the Havelocks—father and son—and on Lady Kaarin the moment she is found.''

"Your Majesty, it shall be done.''

"Good enough. Now. What else?''

My heart beat time to an anxious rhythm. Inside my mind there was one word and it was Dulcie's name. "I believe, for now, we are finished here. And it's a hundred and twenty kilometers to the Black Mountains and Skuldaric Tower. I must be on my way.''

Chapter 20

When I came to, I heard a man talking. "Night falls," he said. "You'd be wise to go."

A woman laughed, wickedly. "Jorund, darling. I wouldn't miss this for the world." I knew that voice. Lady Kaarin.

"Your absence at the palace could be noted."

"Impossible. No one suspects me."

A groan rose in my throat. Somehow I managed to stifle it. Next, I had to cough. I swallowed madly, and that passed, too. *Quiet,* I told myself. *Don't move....*

Even with my head pounding and my brain foggy and slow, I knew that the longer it took them to realize I was awake, the more they might say to help me understand what was happening here. Also, judging by the way I'd been treated so far—drugged into a stupor, carried off to God knew where—I had to figure that things would only get worse once they saw I'd regained consciousness.

Worse how, you're wondering?

Let's not go there.

This place that they'd taken me, what did I know about it?

Without sitting up and looking around—later for that, when I felt braver—my perception of my surroundings was severely limited. I was on my knees, crumpled into a ball, my hands and ankles tied, my head and left shoulder sagging against a curving, cold stone wall. A faint smell of rotting wood and mildew rose up from the floor.

I dared to open my eyes—just to slits. I saw a rough wooden floor with straw scattered on it. Everything was shadowed. Getting dark, as the man—Jorund?—had said.

So I was guessing they'd brought me to some old shell of a building, a place that had no electricity. And if it was near dark, that would make it some time around four in the afternoon, wouldn't it?

Wherever we were, it was drafty. I could hear the wind whistling around us, the icy fingers of it finding their way up inside my coat.

My bound arms and ankles ached. Bad. So did my head. And my stomach was definitely queasy. I had the unpleasant feeling that whatever was left in there might decide to come up any minute now. But I didn't move. I stayed in a ball, head and shoulder to the wall, eyes shut, trying not to shiver with the bone-chilling cold as Lady Kaarin and Jorund kept talking.

"It's too risky for you to remain here," Jorund said. "Don't be a fool."

"I am no fool and you know it. And it is my right as the architect of this plan to be here. Look at me." There was a breath-held kind of silence. And then she commanded, "Kiss me...."

Silence again—well, except for a number of low, teasing moans and some unmistakable slurping sounds. If I hadn't been so miserable and terrified, I might have smiled.

So. Lady Kaarin, who'd once been Valbrand's lover, was now doing some guy named Jorund. And almost engaged to Prince Onund. I wondered if she was sleeping with Onund, too. My guess? Affirmative. Judging by the quality of her moans and all that slurping, Lady Kaarin liked sex. And she was just the type to use sex to get men to do what she wanted them to do.

I could almost feel sorry for Onund. But then, who could say? Maybe he knew about Lady Kaarin and Jorund. Maybe he didn't care in the least. It wasn't as if I had any real clue as to what was driving these people. They were, in the truest sense, a mystery to me.

Eventually the moaning stopped and Jorund said, "You seem so certain this will bring him. Let's hope you have it right."

"Oh, I have it right. Exactly right. I've seen the way he looks at her." The lady was sneering. "He loves her."

They had to mean Valbrand—that Valbrand loved me. In spite of everything, my heart lightened. And then plummeted as I realized why I was here. I was the bait to lead Valbrand into a trap.

Jorund was chuckling. "My lady, is that the green monster I see there in those sapphire eyes?"

"Don't goad me. You will regret it."

"But did you not claim you would seduce him, gain his confidence, break down his defenses, make him dance like a puppet as you worked his strings? How could you do that if he loves this one here?"

"Don't," she said again in a deadly tone. "I warn you."

Into the uneasy quiet that followed, she muttered, "Yet it *is* incredible that he would choose her over me. Look at her...." I felt their eyes on me like lasers, burning. I held my breath. Did they know I was awake? I couldn't tell. Lady Kaarin continued, in the same disgusted tone as before, "A nobody. A fat muffin of a girl, ordinary as cheap soap."

I kept my eyes shut and my body bowed down and I gritted my teeth at opportunities missed. I should have jumped her yesterday in my room. Knocked out a few teeth, plowed bloody scratches down her pink cheeks, snatched out several fistfuls of that sleek, perfect hair...

"He'll be here," she said with absolute certainty. "At midnight. Alone as we have bade him. He'll stop at nothing to try to save her. And that means we have him. He'll walk into our trap and your men will take him."

"Don't underestimate him."

"I don't. But you have twenty men out there, killers all. No single man can stand against twenty. Tonight will prove the end of him and bring us an important step closer to putting Onund on the throne."

"You might have just let the good prince have her," Jorund suggested. "If he married a commoner—"

She didn't let him finish. "You say that merely to taunt me. He will never wed her and you know it. Had he not sent her away? No. We need him dead."

Jorund chuckled. "You *want* him dead."

"That, too. And he shall be."

"He's a crafty one, with more lives than the blackest of cats. And surprisingly resourceful, as well. He has escaped us before."

"And was that my fault?" Kaarin scoffed. "We both

know where the blame for that failure lies. Squarely on the narrow shoulders of my ineffectual groom-to-be and his father, Prince Gunther.''

Omigod. I could hardly believe what I was hearing—the answer to the question I was certain Valbrand had been tormenting himself with for months now—and Brit, too, I'd have bet. If only I managed to survive long enough to tell them what I knew...

Lady Kaarin was still on her rant and showing no sign of winding down. ''Really, when it comes to eliminating Thorsons, you men are constantly making a mess of things. It's your great good fortune that I've finally seen fit to join your cause and show you the way to get the deed done.''

''My lady,'' said Jorund dryly, ''your beauty is only equaled by your self-assurance—and don't turn on that light.''

''But it's getting so dark.''

''You want to give him a beacon to guide him right to us?''

''Well,'' she said grudgingly, ''all right. I suppose not.'' She made a delicate grunting sound. ''And why shouldn't I be confident? *I* know what I'm doing. Whereas you and Onund...'' She heaved a huge, fake sigh. ''Let us not forget the sabotaging of that bitch, Brit's, plane a few months ago. Surprise, surprise. Her Royal Highness walked out of that alive. And then there was the ambush of Brit and Eric Greyfell in the Helmouth Pass. I believe that was *your* brilliant plan, wasn't it, Jorund?''

Jorund did some more chuckling. It was not an especially pleasant sound. ''Yes. The fault there was all mine.''

''You *failed*. Say it.''

"My lady, I failed."

"In fact, you were captured, weren't you? Leaving old Prince Gunther to pay through the nose to see that you escaped before they went to work on you and you spilled your traitor's guts?"

"My lady, you have me. Hard by the balls."

"And I'm not even finished yet. Let us not forget the recent attempt to kidnap Her Royal Highness. Onund thought he was so clever to hire one unidentifiable thug to hire two more to go in through the secret passageways. Clever, clever... Except it didn't work. Just like all your other schemes. Failed. Utterly. So this time, we do it my way—and this time, I guarantee you, we will not fail."

"If you say so, my lady."

"You are an insolent cur."

"I fear you know me much too well."

"Come here. Now."

I heard boots on the floorboards. "Yes, my lady?"

I heard more kissing sounds. Lady Kaarin moaned, quietly at first. And then louder. By the end, she sounded like Meg Ryan faking orgasm in *When Harry Met Sally*—only with more commands: "Yes! No! There! That! Do it like that. Oh, yes!"

Once that was over with, they talked some more. But nothing as enlightening as what I'd heard before all the groaning. Again, he tried to get her to leave and she refused. I heard their footsteps, pacing. They would come close—probably looking down at me, checking to see that I was still out cold. And then, after a moment, the footsteps would move away.

I don't know how long I lasted, awake, aching with cold, keeping myself still through sheer effort of will. The muscles in my shoulders cramped and my legs twitched and my hands felt scarily numb below the wrists.

Bait, I kept thinking. *I'm bait to catch Valbrand.*

Dead bait, I was certain—dead as that poor fellow who had the misfortune to get the job of driving me to the airport. Jorund and Kaarin certainly wouldn't have said so much in front of me—even out cold as I was supposed to be—if they planned to let me out of here alive.

I tried to come up with some sort of plan. To put together a strategy, some way to get myself—and Valbrand, when he came—out of this mess.

But I was no Brit Thorson. I was an average girl from Bakersfield. I had a lot of discipline when it came to my writing, but I'd never made the time I should for regular visits to the gym, never gotten around to taking that Self-defense for Women class I'd always meant to look into.

The bleak truth was, I wouldn't be saving anyone. Most likely, because of me, Valbrand would die....

It was so pitiful. The best I could hope for was that, maybe, he wouldn't come. That we wouldn't *both* have to die.

I hoped for that—that he wouldn't show. I *prayed* for that.

But in my heart I knew my prayer wouldn't be answered.

He would be there. He couldn't be Valbrand and behave any other way.

I don't know how much time passed—hours, I'm almost certain. And then I heard boots coming toward me again. The boots stopped maybe a foot from me. "I know you're awake," said Jorund. "I've watched you twitching for some time now. Roll over and stretch out your legs and give the cramping a chance to pass."

"Oh, leave her alone," taunted Kaarin from across the floor. "Let her cower and shiver and twitch. It's what the likes of her was made for."

Jorund ignored her. "Come now," he said to me. "Roll over."

Since they both knew I had regained consciousness, I saw no benefit in continuing to pretend I hadn't. With a groan—it really hurt, by then, just to move—I rolled so my back was to the wall and managed, with great effort, to straighten my legs. They were bizarrely numb, so to get them in front of me, I had swivel onto one hip and kind of fling them out. They hit the floor like twin slabs of frozen meat.

I looked up at the guy named Jorund. "Hey, there," I croaked. My throat felt like I'd swallowed a bucketful of sand. "The guy in the ditch with the needle. How're you doin'?"

Kaarin stood maybe fifteen feet away, stunning as usual in lavender skiwear with a ruff of lavender fur around the hood. In the silvery darkness, she seemed to give off a kind of glow. Her skin shone like alabaster. If her lipstick was smudged, it didn't show in the dim light. Hard to believe that had been her moaning and making specific sexual demands not too long ago. She commanded, "Strike her. Hard. For her insolence."

I turned my head away from the expected blow. It never came. Jorund knelt beside me. "Drink." He took the back of my head and stuck an insulated canteen to my dry lips. I didn't argue. I latched on and gulped. He didn't let me have much. "Easy. Slow." He pulled the mouth of the canteen away.

About then, the circulation started prickling back into my legs. Like a million biting ants. I moaned and beat my heels against the straw and let out little whimpering sounds and despised myself. I really hated that they were watching me while I squirmed.

Kaarin smiled at the sight. Jorund simply waited until the worst of the agony had passed. Then he offered me the canteen again. He let me drink longer that time.

When I'd had enough, I slumped back to the cold wall with a sigh and, for the first time, really saw where I was.

The floor was strewn with half-rotted hay and rubble. To my right, a shadowed arch led, I assumed, out of there. There was a tiny dark window, maybe two feet tall and one foot wide, to my left, high up so I couldn't see out through it, or even tell if there was glass in it.

The starry night outside was visible, though—through the half-collapsed roof and through a ragged hole across from me, where the stone had come loose and fallen away. The hole was as big as a picture window. Beyond it, I could see the night-black shapes of the tops of trees and, beyond them, tall snow-covered mountains. Above the mountains, clouds streamed across the swath of starry sky like dark ghosts blown by the north wind.

The tops of trees, I thought. *A tower, then. I'm in a tower....*

Kaarin had turned toward the open place. Hugging herself in her warm jacket, she stared out at the night. If only I could be standing behind her. One good shove...

I imagined her screaming as she fell.

My, my, I was becoming downright bloodthirsty. But I figured that was better than cringing against my cold wall and whimpering in misery at my fate.

Jorund started untying my ankles. I stared at the top of his watch cap and hoped he'd untie my hands, as well.

You never know. I might get in a lick or two, after all, before they killed me.

He looked up and met my eyes. "At the crucial moment, you'll need to be able to walk."

"Why?"

He didn't answer, just finished at my ankles and then called Kaarin over and handed her the pistol from the holster beneath his arm. "Hold this on her while I finish."

Finish. I didn't much care for the sound of that. But as it turned out, it wasn't anything final. He just cut the ropes at my wrists—yeah, that was fun. More biting ants all up and down my arms—and tied my hands in front as I bit my lip and moaned and tried not to show how much it hurt from my shoulder blades to the tips of my fingers as the feeling came back. He said, pleasantly, "Just in case we want to put you on a lead—and no, that's not likely. But it's better if you're ready to do exactly as we require you to do."

Once my hands were tied in front, he wrapped more rope around my torso, pinning my arms to my sides. Then he gave me one more drink and dug a roll of duct tape out of a stack of stuff on the floor.

"We will need silence from you," he said, smiling much too cheerfully as he gagged me with the tape.

Through it all Kaarin held the gun on me. I looked back and forth from the hole in the barrel to the cold gleam in her china-blue eyes. One sudden move, and she would have shot me—and very much enjoyed doing it.

I didn't give her the satisfaction.

"And now," announced Jorund, rising from his work, "you're all ready to do your part."

"It won't be difficult," Kaarin said. "You'll be standing over there with Jorund behind you." She pointed to a spot opposite the entrance. ''Notice this lovely big pistol.'' She waved the gun for emphasis. ''It will be aimed at your head. They'll lead Valbrand in. We'll allow him to beg for your life. We'll make him crawl, I think. And he shall kiss my feet and bow down to the floor in front of me. Then, once he's thoroughly debased himself, Jorund will pull the trigger. Valbrand will watch you die— He's never been quite right, now has he, since he returned from what should have been his death at sea? Do you think he'll go utterly over the edge, when he sees your blood and brains go flying? Oh, I hope so. I would enjoy watching that—for a little while, anyway.'' She smiled down at me, eyes twinkling, a delicate flush on her smooth pale cheeks. ''Of course, once his drooling and sobbing becomes tedious, Jorund will kill him, too.''

Chapter 21

More hours passed. Jorund wore one of those radio headsets. Periodically, he would speak into it, checking with his men. Each time, he'd learn that all was quiet below.

I shivered and sat propped against the wall and waited, occasionally shutting my eyes and trying to imagine myself far away from there.

I thought of warm things....

Clean clothes fresh from the dryer. I would bury my face in them....

Or the ancient wall heater in my East Hollywood apartment. I'd turn it on high and stand with my back against it, until I could smell my shirt starting to scorch....

Or that big bed I'd left behind in my room at Isenhalla. The blankets pulled up close and Valbrand's strong arms around me, enveloping me in his body heat....

Snow began to fall.

It drifted down through the half-collapsed roof and formed glittering frozen patterns on the floor. Whenever the moon would peek through the clouds and spill its silver light, the flakes would glimmer, frosty and jewel-like at once. I thought how beautiful those snowflakes were. I set myself on admiring them, on appreciating the feel of the icy air as I sucked it in through my numb nose.

Strangely, by then, I wasn't really even scared. I'd been lulled, I guess you could say. By all the hours of just sitting, waiting...

For my own death—and the death of the man I loved. Still...

Well, I can't say my death was exactly real to me. Deep in my heart, I kept on believing that there had to be some way both Valbrand and I would get out of this.

I just didn't know how. So I admired the snowflakes drifting down and watched my captors while they waited, as I did, for Valbrand to come.

Since he'd retied me, Jorund was quiet. He stood near the wall or paced calmly back and forth across the center of the floor. He had a rifle. He carried it as he paced, looking as if he knew how to use it, stopping now and then to check with his men.

Kaarin wasn't as good at waiting as her lover. She paced on her own little section of floor. But she didn't do it patiently. She stomped her feet and muttered that it was too cold, that she would go insane if she had to stay in this hideous tumbledown tower room a single moment longer.

Then Jorund would tell her that she should go.

She'd reply that this was *her* trap they were springing

and she was not going anywhere until she saw Valbrand Thorson dead.

After virtually that same exchange had occurred five times, Kaarin suddenly announced, "Very well, Jorund. You win. I cannot bear this. Call a couple of your men to escort me out of here."

Jorund gave her one of his scarily good-natured smiles. "My lady, a thousand apologies, but I fear you *cannot* go now. It's too late, too likely you might encounter Prince Valbrand—or a gun battle involving him. You could be injured. Or worse. We don't want that." The gleam in his eyes said more than his words.

"Your insolence," Kaarin declared, "knows no bounds. When I am queen—"

He made a low, impatient sound. "But you're not queen yet. Are you?"

They glared at each other. She was the one who blinked.

After that, she turned on me. "Ugly cow," she said. "Perhaps I was wrong. Perhaps he won't come, after all. I could have completely misjudged him. Perhaps he's got more sense than to surrender his life for the sake of a fat little frizz-haired karavik like you."

There were a hundred spiteful and clever responses racing through my brain. Too bad the only sounds I could make were along the order of, *"Mnmph, ugh, unph…"*

She laughed at me. "What was that, Miss Samples? I didn't make that out."

"Enough," said Jorund.

She whirled on him. "How dare—"

He didn't let her finish. He looked at her as if he was on the verge of aiming his rifle straight at her shriveled little heart and said, "Enough," a second time.

She spun away and stared out the hole in the wall for a while.

The snow stopped.

Kaarin pushed back her sleeve and looked at her watch. Then she turned from the vista of mountains and dark sky to announce, "It's midnight. By the ravens of Odin, where is he?"

Jorund said nothing—and I *couldn't* say anything.

She faced the broken wall and stared out over the treetops some more. I watched her, imagining again how easy it would be, if I was only standing behind her, to push her over. It was while I stared daggers into that slim, lavender-clad back that the magic started happening in the sky.

It began with a few random ripples that slowly thickened and intensified into a semitransparent curtain of light: a rainbow of colors waving, ghostlike, above the white mountaintops.

"The borealis," Kaarin said, her voice uncharacteristically reverent. "Bringing battle," she whispered. "And certain death." She laughed, low. It was not a pretty sound. "Valbrand's death…"

About then, I began to hear the strangest crackling, static-like sound. A sort of hissing that started low and built, swelling until it filled the air. Was it the northern lights that made it? It seemed so to me. Neither Kaarin nor Jorund commented on the sound. I wondered if they even heard it. They gave no sign that they did.

I watched the spilling, weaving light, the colors waving and folding into each other. Neon blue to shimmering green, hot pink spiraling into crimson, deepest indigo spinning out into rippling purple, all to the accompaniment of that ecstatic electric hiss. I swear, at one point, the colors formed a long, green snake that whipped its way across the sky.

Kaarin made a sound low in her throat—"Acch"— and turned away from the sky. She began pacing again, as Jorund continued to do.

Slowly the snake melted into blue and from there to purple again, after which it faded back into the moving curtain of colors. I watched, enchanted, almost believing that this show in the sky was happening just for me. After all, such beauty and magic made it easier to forget, at least for a little while, that this was the night I was going to die.

It seemed, now and then, within the hissing crackle, that I could hear Medwyn's voice whispering to me: *Be strong. Do not surrender to your fear or to despair.... You* can *triumph. It* is *possible....*

I guess I should have known from the first that his warning wasn't about how to get over my broken heart, that it was something a lot more practical: it was what was happening right now.

Could I triumph?

I didn't see how.

But Medwyn had said it was possible. And I would hold on to that, hold on so tight...

The lights dimmed, diminishing to echoes. The hissing sound faded, too, vanishing at some undefined point, so I couldn't hear it anymore.

As the aurora slowly disappeared and darkness claimed the sky again, my doubts rose up, chattering louder than ever inside my head.

So many hours had passed. Maybe he really wasn't coming. Maybe he didn't even know he was *supposed* to come. However they'd sent word to him, the message must have gone astray.

Or maybe he just wasn't the man I had imagined him to be.

No.

I didn't believe that.

I *wouldn't* believe that.

If he didn't come, it was because he never got their message. And that was good, I reminded myself. It was excellent. There was absolutely no reason that both of us had to die. I could go to my grave knowing that he was safe.

It meant a lot, that he was safe.

It made it bearable that I would die.

Or so I tried to tell myself, though to be brutally truthful, nothing—not even knowing that Valbrand would live—was going to make having my brains blown out acceptable. I just wasn't all that noble. I felt the beating of my heart, the spurt of my blood through my veins, my lungs expanding with each icy breath I took…

I didn't want to give that up, you know? There were too many good books left unread, too many books I someday hoped to *write*. There was the devilish sound of my dad's laughter, the smell of *J'adore*, my mom's favorite perfume. There were my irritating nieces and nephews who looked so cute when they were sleeping.

And what about the quality of the light over the Los Angeles basin when you come down from the Grapevine? How could the light of the sun shining through deadly smog be so damn beautiful?

I just wasn't ready. I didn't want to go.

I watched the last pale flickers of the northern lights and lulled myself with thoughts of how my soon-to-be murderers were going to get theirs. Someday, Valbrand and Brit would figure all this out. I would smile down from heaven as I watched Kaarin and the rest of them pay for the crimes they'd committed, as I saw them suffer the most terrible tortures for all the innocent people they had killed.

"What's that?" Kaarin cried, jerking me from my vengeful reveries. "Down there…" She let out a screech and stumbled back as the lights in the sky flared bright again, accompanied by a burst of crackles and pops. "Freyja's eyes, it can't be…"

Jorund went to her, his rifle ready, as the lights danced over the mountains and the hissing and crackling seemed to rise in ripples all around.

She grabbed him, forcing him to turn his rifle aside. "Look. Down there." She had him at the gap in the wall and she flung out a hand toward whatever was below.

He peered over the edge, then let out a heavy breath that emerged as a white cloud in the icy air. "There's nothing. Bare snowy ground, the trees farther on…" The hissing sound was fading. The lights once more were growing paler. Kaarin dared to look below a second time, as Jorund pried her hands off him and stepped back, taking his rifle in both fists again. "See?" he said. "Nothing."

"B…but I swear to you. On the blood of my father. A rider. I saw a rider, all in black with a black mask, on a black horse. He was there." She pointed again. "By the edge of the trees."

All in black, I thought. *All in black with a black mask…*

Of course.

I should have known.

Jorund was backing away from Lady Kaarin. "I told you. There's no one there."

"But there *was.*"

"There couldn't have been. My men would have spotted him."

"He was…like the Dark Raider." Kaarin was wild-eyed. "You remember the Dark Raider?"

Jorund hawked and spat on the floor. "Phah. A tale told to children."

"But Jorund. Surely you recall? You said your men claimed they saw him, saw the Dark Raider. Remember, you said it was in the Vildelund, when you followed Brit there?"

"A tale, Kaarin. Bed talk, to amuse you."

"Not real?" She stared at him, disbelieving.

"Not real," he said. "Just a story."

"But you *said*—"

"No." He looked at her steadily. "It was only talk."

"Talk…" She seemed doubtful and hopeful at once.

"Yes. Talk." He looked at her piercingly, as if by the sheer force of his gaze he could convince her she hadn't seen what she thought she had.

"Ah. Well…" She shook her head as if to clear it. After a weighted pause, she frowned and insisted, "Yet I swear I saw *something* down there."

He suggested, almost hopefully, "Perhaps a deer."

"No. Not a deer. I'm certain. Not a deer…"

His expression changed, went from that piercing look to exasperation—and something else. Maybe the beginnings of disgust?

And yeah, I gotta admit. I was loving this: Lady Kaarin losing it. And Jorund beginning to wonder what the hell he was going to do about her if things got tight.

He started talking into the tiny microphone connected to his headset, checking in with his men.

Two of them didn't answer. This was becoming more interesting by the minute.

"Gunderkite," Jorund barked. "Check on Dartveith and Bertil." For that he got silence.

He hailed other men. And when the other men answered, he said, "Hold your position. It's likely the target is in your quadrant. Prepare for attack."

By then Kaarin was pacing again, furiously. "Never," she muttered. "I never should have come. I can't be caught here. That simply will not do...."

Jorund pointedly ignored her. I tried my best to do the same.

It was quiet for a little while, except for Kaarin's occasional mutterings and the steady tread of Jorund's boots on the old boards of the floor. The lights in the sky and the sounds that went with them seemed to have faded to nothing for good this time.

The air was still. Silence lay over us like a spell.

And then, with a suddenness that made Kaarin cry out, the wind came up. It blew in through the gap in the wall and down from the hole in the roof, swirling around us, making an eerie keening sound. The snow-sparkled debris on the floor rose, spun and dropped.

The wind died as suddenly as it had risen.

And out of the silence, from below, there came a man's wordless shout. The shout died to a hideous gargling sound.

And then there was silence again.

"Oh, no," muttered Kaarin. "Oh, no, no, no..."

"Down." Jorund shoved Kaarin to the floor. She fell with a sharp cry. "Oh! How dare you?"

"Silence, woman."

And Kaarin actually shut up.

Jorund crawled to the gap in the wall. He looked out, then sank back into the room and started trying to raise his men on his radio.

He got responses from four of them. I think, from the things they said, that they were all inside, with us, on the lower floors. Jorund told them to fall back to the ground floor of the tower and stand guard at the entrance; we were coming down.

"Come on," he said to Kaarin, "We can't stay in this room. There's only one way out."

"But nobody's even *seen* him—or them…and really, there can't be many of them, can there? If there were, surely one of your men would have—"

"Kaarin. We're going. Bring the lantern."

"But why, if we can't use it?"

"Bring it."

"But—"

"Bring it." The two words were deadly.

Kaarin picked up the large flashlight-style lantern. Jorund hooked his rifle strap over his shoulder and came for me, grabbing my coat by the collar and hauling me up.

"Down the stairs." He yanked me around so he was behind me. I felt something hard and round poke me in the back. "Go."

I went.

Beneath the arch, the darkness was total. I hesitated once I moved into the blackness. I was picturing myself pitching forward into nothingness.

"The lantern," Jorund said. "Now."

A golden light spilled from behind me and I could see my way down the twisting stone stairway.

There were five flights, each one ending in a landing and an arch that led, I assumed, to that floor's single room. The lantern light bounced off the gray walls and my shadow stretched thin below me and I hoped, with my hands tied to my sides, that I wouldn't lose my balance and go tumbling to the next landing down.

I did stumble—twice—but both times I caught myself by leaning my weight toward the outer wall and using it to stop my downward momentum. Both times it happened, I half expected Jorund to shoot me in the back. But he didn't.

And really, that would have been pretty stupid of him. Things were not going as he and Kaarin had planned. Most of their men were dead—or otherwise out of commission. Even I, with zero experience in situations like this one, could see that this new set of circumstances meant my value had increased. I was no longer merely bait. Now I might be useful as a hostage.

This was good. So why couldn't I quit shaking with fear?

We reached the entry vestibule on the bottom floor. It was strewn, as the room at the top had been, with sticks and stones and smelly straw. There were two arches, one that led out to a moonlit courtyard and one that led into blackness: the bottom-floor room.

I didn't see a sign of the men that Jorund had ordered to be waiting there for us. And what were those red streaks across the floor?

Before I got a chance to look at them a little closer, Jorund commanded in a hissing whisper, "The light. Turn it off." Everything went dark. "Not a sound," Jorund whispered. We waited, not speaking, as ordered. I could hear Kaarin's ragged breathing. Slowly, my eyes adjusted to the gloom.

By the silvery light from outside, Jorund was signaling at me, a finger to his lips, for silence—as if I could have made much noise anyway, with my mouth taped shut. He took his pistol from his belt and braced his rifle against the wall. Then he pointed at the lantern. Kaarin gave it to him and backed out of the way. Through the darkness, her eyes gleamed wildly—but at least she was showing the good sense to keep her mouth shut. I did notice, even quivering with terror as I was, that this time Jorund didn't hand her a gun to hold on me.

I considered that a very wise move on his part. Kaarin had the strangest look. With a gun in her hands, she might start shooting. I had no doubt at all that the first thing she'd shoot would be me, but after that, who knew what her next target might be?

Jorund signaled me against the wall where he could keep me in range and then he edged up on the black shadow of the arch that led to the inner room, keeping the lantern to the side until the last minute—when he pointed it into the room and flicked it on, aiming his gun that way at the same time.

In the sudden blinding spill of light, I saw what the red marks on the floor were: blood streaks. Someone had dragged something bloody through here. And in the room? Men. I could see two from my vantage point. Lying still on the floor in puddles of blood, boots pointing up. Were there more? Were there, maybe, four? From the one glance I got at Jorund's face, my guess would have been yes.

All that happened in an instant. Jorund doused the light as Kaarin let out a sharp cry. I blinked and pressed my back to the wall, shaking harder than ever, absorbing the reality of what I had seen. Those men on the floor had been dressed like Jorund: in military boots and camouflage gear.

Things were, at least from the point of view of my captors, getting seriously out of hand.

Kaarin started whimpering and muttering to herself. "Oh. Oh, my. Oh, no. Oh, no..."

As my eyes adjusted to the dark again, I saw the vague shadow that was Jorund set the lantern down. He switched the gun to his left hand and approached the whimpering Kaarin. I thought he meant to try to calm her.

And I was right. In a move so lightning-quick, I hardly saw it happening until it was over, he punched her square in the jaw. Her head flew back and made a breaking-watermelon sound against the wall behind her. She slid, boneless to the floor. Blood, black in the moonlight shining through the courtyard arch, flowed out, gleaming, from under her hair. Her eyes gleamed, too, as they stared blindly up toward the ceiling joists above.

I knew she was dead.

You'd think I might have been glad. But I wasn't, not really. I didn't feel anything beyond a fresh urge to hurl.

Jorund grabbed for me, whipping me around so I was pressed with my back against the front of him. He used his left arm as a vise at my neck. I felt the cold kiss of the pistol at my temple. "Don't make me shoot you any sooner than I have to," he whispered tenderly into my ear. "Quiet. Understand? Very quiet. No sudden moves."

I gulped and gave him a tight nod. Then I held still, awaiting my murderer's next command.

"Toward the door to the courtyard," he whispered. "Let's go."

Slowly, keeping close to the curve of the wall, we edged up on the outer door. When we got there, he paused to press the gun a little harder at my temple and to whisper, "I am deadly serious. One wrong move and I will put a bullet in your brain."

I sighed hard through my nose and gave him another quick nod, my eyes pressed tightly shut—because I gotta tell you, whatever happened next, I didn't really care to see it.

We stepped into the open archway. I dared to peek. I saw more stone walls, some of them half-collapsed. There was a man—correction: a man's *body*. It was propped against the wall to the right, a headset like Jorund's askew on his head.

Jorund said, out loud and very clearly, "Show yourself. Now. Or the woman is dead."

Maybe two seconds ticked by—the longest two seconds of my soon-to-be-terminated life.

Then the Dark Raider materialized out of a wall near the dead man. I blinked in surprise at the sight of him. He held a pistol, same as Jorund. It was pointed our way.

"Let her go," the Dark Raider said.

Jorund pressed his pistol all the harder to my temple. "Not until you set your gun down." He dug that pistol barrel into the side of my head. I shut my eyes, expecting the end.

There was…a moment. An awful, endless moment where nothing happened. I opened my eyes and made myself shake my head frantically. *Don't do it,* I told Valbrand inside my head. *Shoot him. Shoot him now….*

But Valbrand didn't follow my silent commands. Very carefully, he crouched and set his pistol on the ground. I whimpered then, shaking my head some more.

"Be still," Jorund commanded, pressing the gun harder than ever to my head. "Kick the gun away," he told Valbrand.

Valbrand kicked. The gun went spinning across the courtyard.

I moaned in my throat.

We were finished now. It was over. We were both going to die....

"Release her," said Valbrand.

Jorund chuckled then. "I think not. Unmask. I want to see your face and I want to see it now."

I saw then that Valbrand was looking at me, not at Jorund. From behind the black mask, he was seeking my eyes. I met his gaze.

And as we stared at each other, I found I felt...calmer. My love for him welled up inside me. It was warm and it was strong and it was...telling me what to do.

It came into my mind that I might have one chance to be of use here. *Whimper,* said a voice inside my head. *Quiver a little. Don't let him think that you're calmer. Give him no hint that you might be planning something....*

So I whimpered and shook, just like before. Behind the Dark Raider's mask, Valbrand's black eyes were talking to me. I knew what to do.

"Unmask," Jorund commanded again.

Valbrand lifted his hand toward his face. And I did it. I let my knees buckle.

After that...

Well, I don't remember too well. There were shots. And shooting sparks as bullets ricocheted off the stone walls of the courtyard. Blood got all over me, shiny black in the dim light.

I remember thinking, *God. Please. Let none of this blood be Valbrand's.*

I was on the icy ground, looking up, the Dark Raider above me. He tore off the mask and tossed it aside. I think I whispered, "Valbrand..."

He dropped down beside me. I heard him calling me.

And then everything turned white. Just this lovely, hazy, blinding white.

When I was little, my mom went on this kick about the sheets. She said she loved the smell of them when they were dried naturally, in the open air. She had my father string a clothesline in the backyard, so she could hang our sheets in the sunshine to dry.

I would ride my plastic tricycle under those sheets as they were blowing in the summer wind and look up at them, laughing to be blinded by all that white.

The whiteness that night was like that. Bright as clean sheets in the summer sun. I stared into it.

And then the whiteness vanished. I saw nothing. I felt nothing. It was all so peaceful.

Yet even the peacefulness faded. Until there was nothing. A blankness.

The world, the whiteness, the sense of a final peace…

All of it.

Gone.

Chapter 22

I woke up in a white bed in a green room and my mom was there. She looked at me—kind of shocked. And then she smiled. I think I smiled back. A woman in a white jacket came in.

By then, my eyelids were too heavy to keep open. I let them droop shut.

The next time I swam up from the dark through the layers of white, Valbrand was there. He took my hand. I looked into his shattered face and I think I said, "Yeah. Good…"

And I slept again. I woke to find my mom and Brit there at the same time. And another time, I saw Medwyn.

I asked, "Do the northern lights make crackling sounds?"

"They do, Dulcinea. But not everyone hears them."

"I saw Valbrand—in the courtyard below the tower. And here, by my bed. He's okay, isn't he?"

"Yes. He is well."

The next time, my dad was there. "My little motor-mouth," he said, and he kissed my forehead. I smelled his aftershave. And coffee on his breath. I think I cried a little.

Later, my dad sat on one side and my mom on the other and they each held one of my hands while the doctor told me I'd been in a coma. Fluid on the brain from being shot in the head.

But they'd put in a shunt and the fluid had drained. And it looked like I was going to be just fine.

No hair, though. I had just a faint, fuzzy red halo when they took off the bandages. They'd had to shave me to put in the shunt. But it would grow back, they promised. "Oh, no kidding," I said and I laughed. I mean, like I'd been thinking it *wouldn't* grow back?

I guess they treat you like that when you've had a life-threatening head injury. Like really obvious things won't be clear to you when you come back from near-death.

Or maybe it was just that they couldn't quite believe I *had* come back. And yeah, maybe, in a way, I didn't believe it, either. I didn't feel completely a part of the world after I woke up. I had a great awareness of my own fragility as a human being. And a sensation of distance, of being far away.

I'd missed Christmas and New Years. And I'd lost the whole month of January. Pfft. Gone. Never to be recovered.

My dad came in to say goodbye on the first Sunday in February. He'd taken seven weeks of family leave and he had to get back to work. Mom would stay on with me for a few more days. They figured by then I'd be ready to travel. I'd already been out of bed, several times that day and the day before. I would walk up and down the hall by my room.

Tomorrow, they were checking me out of there. I'd stay at Isenhalla for a short time, a guest of the royal family. And I'd be back in East Hollywood pounding the pavement in search of my next subsistence job within a week or two.

When my dad left, I lay with my face turned toward the room's narrow window. Outside, the snow sparkled, painfully bright, beneath a sun that was already sinking toward the horizon in the middle of the day.

I heard the door open and turned to see Valbrand standing there. He had my AlphaSmart in his hands. "I thought perhaps you'd be requiring this soon."

"Oh," I said. "Hi…"

He stood there smiling his beautiful grotesque smile.

I reached out. He came to me, set the AlphaSmart on the bed stand and wrapped his warm fingers around mine. I shut my eyes in pleasure and turned my head toward the window again as I felt his lips brushing the back of my hand.

"They say you will recover completely."

I don't know why it was so difficult, suddenly, to face him. I made myself do it and whispered, "Sit down. Please." He let go of my hand to pull up a chair. Once he was seated, I said, "I have about a thousand questions."

"Don't you always?"

"Lady Kaarin?"

He shook his head. "Dead."

I squinted, as if the light was too bright. "I knew it. Jorund?"

"I killed him."

I nodded, and had to swallow. "I, uh, I'm guessing,

since no one's been asking me any questions, that you know it was Prince Onund Havelock and his father who tried to have you assassinated at sea, that the Havelocks and Jorund were behind the plot against your family." I swallowed again. "And Lady Kaarin was in on it, too—though from a few things she said I kind of gathered she'd only recently gotten involved."

He was looking at the fuzz on my head. "Like a baby chick," he said. "A red one."

I wrinkled my nose at him. "Go ahead. Feel it."

He reached out and rubbed his palm over the frizz. I caught his hand, kissed it as he had kissed mine. "It'll grow back," I said.

He laughed. "Did you think I believed it wouldn't?"

"No. No, I..." And then I laughed, too.

The laughter faded and we were left just looking at each other, at the miracle of our both being here, breathing. Touching. Laughing.

"You're too thin." He traced the bruised places beneath my eyes and the new hollows in my cheeks. "But the doctors say you'll be round and lovely again in no time."

Round and lovely. Oh, I did like the sound of that. I sighed. And then I remembered that my questions had yet to be answered. "What about Prince Onund and Prince Gunther?"

"Locked securely away," Valbrand said. "Onund, in hopes of saving his coward's skin, told all. It's a huge scandal, that father and son of one the most revered and admired families in the land are bloodthirsty assassins who would stop at nothing to reclaim the throne they lost."

"Yes, but this means that the longtime assault on your family is over, right?"

"That is exactly what it means."

We sat silently for a while, pondering the wonder of that.

And then, at last, he started to talk to me, to tell me, without my having to prod him, what had happened in the six weeks that I'd been unconscious.

"Your mother and my mother are now the best of friends...."

I wasn't surprised. "I always thought they'd like each other, if they ever got the chance to meet."

"There has been something of an upset between my father and his grand counselor. Medwyn spent three days in Tarngalla."

Had I heard that right? "The tower prison?"

"My father threw him in there when he dared to declare that he did not believe I would ever be king."

"Oh, God. But he's out now, right? I saw him. He came to visit me...."

"Yes. My mother got him out. I don't know what she said to my father, but she closeted herself with him for hours. When she emerged, Osrik sent the order that Medwyn should be released."

"And then?"

"My father called me to him. He asked me if I was certain that I no longer desired to try for the throne."

And?"

"For the first time, he listened when I told him that I would never be king."

"So," I said. "This is good, huh?"

"It is. In fact, Eric and I have been talking in depth. It has occurred to me that we might...reverse our roles. That Eric would try for the throne."

"And you would be his grand counselor?"

"Yes. It's a job I believe I might do well."

"Oh, Valbrand. I think so, too...."

"In the spring, Eric leaves for his Viking Voyage." He chuckled. "Brit swears she will go with him, though such a thing is never done, for a man to take his woman a-Viking."

I didn't say anything. There was no need. We both knew Brit. She would be heading out with Eric in the spring.

"And so," said Valbrand, "should fortune turn her kinder face this way, my father's brave daughter will be queen, and his grandson may someday rule the land."

"It's perfect," I said, as if I had engineered it all myself. In a way, I've gotta tell you, I felt that I had. "And your mother and father? Are they reunited, then?"

"She has already left for America." His eyes gleamed. "However, I'll wager she shall return."

"But why leave, if she loves him...?"

"Dulcie. We all must come to love in our own way."

"Yeah," I said, my throat clutching and my eyes swimming. I gulped. "Yeah..."

He leaned close. The way he looked at me, you never would have guessed I was fuzzy-headed bald with no makeup and ugly black circles under my eyes. He whispered, "I thought I had lost you."

"But look. Here I am."

"Ah, Dulcie. I love you so."

I sniffed and dashed at my eyes. "I know it."

And then we were quiet again—well, except for my sniffling and then, once I reached for a Kleenex, the honking sounds I made when I blew my nose.

"Did you also know," he asked when I had the tears more or less under control, "that you're something of a national heroine?"

I laughed at that one. "Because I ducked on cue?"

"No—though I'm very glad you did—but because, at dire threat to your life, you rooted out a nest of traitors and saved the royal family from destruction."

"Well, now. We both know my heroism wasn't exactly a conscious decision."

"Did you know that the grand counselor is free to marry whomever he chooses?"

I stared at him—well, *gaped* is more like it. "Are you leading where I think you're leading?"

"I am."

"But you always said—"

"That was long ago—or it seems so, to me."

"Oh, and everything's different now?"

"It is."

"Why?"

"Because at last, it's all put to rights. And more than that, because you *lived.* Your living changes everything."

I wasn't getting it. "Everything's different because I lived…."

"Yes." Those dark eyes were gleaming. "I can hardly begin to fathom the beauty…the goodness…the *hope* in that. In you. Lying here. Right now. Alive. It makes things…possible again. It means I can begin to see what life can be. It means I can ask you—"

I reached over the side of the bed and put a finger to his lips. "Shh," I said. "Not now…"

He didn't look happy with me. But he didn't argue. And we were quiet, holding hands, not saying much of anything, until the nurse came in to check on me and he left.

He came the next day, with my mom, to take me to the palace. They gave me my old room back. I said I wanted to be alone and I sat on the Louis XV sofa and I wrote for three hours.

Just impressions, you know. Mostly dreck. But that's usually how it goes. Especially after a long time away from the page.

The next day I received a summons for a private audience with the king. It went very well, I thought. His Majesty was way more cordial than he'd been before. He thanked me. Now, that was a good moment.

Valbrand was waiting to escort me back to my rooms. When we got there, he pulled me into his arms and he kissed me.

I kissed him back. Thoroughly.

"Marry me, Dulcie," he said.

"I'm considering it."

He asked me again the next day. "Dulcie, will you be my wife?"

I confessed, "I just can't. Not right now."

He said, "Woman, you will drive me mad."

We stared at each other.

And then we both burst out laughing. I mean, it wasn't as if he hadn't been there before.

"What do I have to do?" he demanded. He wasn't laughing by then. He scowled at me. "What do you want of me?"

"Nothing," I said. "Everything..." And then I admitted, "Well. I guess, a little time."

My mom returned to California without me.

I stayed on, in the room that I had begun to think of as mine. I watched the snow melt and the days grow longer. I met often with Medwyn in the library. I was continuing my study of Gullandria and its ways.

And I wrote. Every day. Mostly journaling, trying to…come back into myself fully again.

After that day I admitted I needed time, Valbrand was beautifully patient with me. I suppose there wasn't another man in the world who could better understand what I was going through. I'd seen death close up. I think maybe I'd surrendered to it. It took time to find my way back to my living self.

In June, Eric and Brit and their crew set off on their Viking Voyage. They came back six weeks later, safe and tan and so proud of themselves.

Valbrand, at last fully returned from his own death, made frequent trips to France for a series of peels and skin grafts that would, to an extent, repair the damage to his face. I would go with him, sit in his hospital room with him, reading and writing.

Once, after a particularly grueling procedure, when they had brought him back to his room and he lay there, face covered in a special plastic mask the doctors said would speed healing, he whispered, "The Dark Raider's mask was so much simpler."

I leaned close. "And what about the Dark Raider now?"

"Gone," he said so low I almost couldn't hear it.

"Gone where?"

"Into legend, where he belongs…"

Autumn came: September, October, November.

It was in December, exactly one year after the ordeal in Skuldaric Tower, that Valbrand proposed to me again.

We stood together in the snow under the stars, revelers all around us, watching the bonfire His Majesty had ordered laid and lit in celebration of the winter solstice.

I looked at him, at his ever-changing face, and knew

that within he was steady and true—and the only man for me.

He said, so softly, "Marry me, Dulcie. Be my wife."

And by then, there was only one answer and it was, "Yes."

*   *   *   *   *

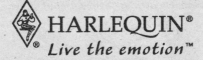

Coming in July 2004
from Silhouette Books

Sly McEwen's final assignment for top-secret government
agency Onyxx had gone awry, leaving only questions behind.
But Sly had a feeling Eva Creon had answers. Locked inside
Eva's suppressed memory was the key to finding the killer
on the loose. But her secrets may have the power to destroy
the one thing that could mean more than the truth…
their growing love for each other….

Available at your favorite retail outlet.

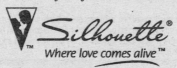

If you enjoyed what you just read,
then we've got an offer you can't resist!

Take 2 bestselling love stories FREE!

Plus get a FREE surprise gift!

Clip this page and mail it to Silhouette Reader Service™

IN U.S.A.
3010 Walden Ave.
P.O. Box 1867
Buffalo, N.Y. 14240-1867

IN CANADA
P.O. Box 609
Fort Erie, Ontario
L2A 5X3

YES! Please send me 2 free Silhouette Intimate Moments® novels and my free surprise gift. After receiving them, if I don't wish to receive anymore, I can return the shipping statement marked cancel. If I don't cancel, I will receive 6 brand-new novels every month, before they're available in stores! In the U.S.A., bill me at the bargain price of $3.99 plus 25¢ shipping and handling per book and applicable sales tax, if any*. In Canada, bill me at the bargain price of $4.74 plus 25¢ shipping and handling per book and applicable taxes**. That's the complete price and a savings of at least 10% off the cover prices—what a great deal! I understand that accepting the 2 free books and gift places me under no obligation ever to buy any books. I can always return a shipment and cancel at any time. Even if I never buy another book from Silhouette, the 2 free books and gift are mine to keep forever.

245 SDN DNUV
345 SDN DNUW

Name	(PLEASE PRINT)
Address	Apt.#
City	State/Prov.	Zip/Postal Code

* Terms and prices subject to change without notice. Sales tax applicable in N.Y.
** Canadian residents will be charged applicable provincial taxes and GST.
  All orders subject to approval. Offer limited to one per household and not valid to
  current Silhouette Intimate Moments® subscribers.
® are registered trademarks of Harlequin Books S.A., used under license.

INMOM02   ©1998 Harlequin Enterprises Limited